The Commission

The Commission

Michael Norman

Poisoned Pen Press

First U. S. Edition 2007

10 9 8 7 6 5 4 3 2 1

Library of Congress Catalog Card Number: 2006929248

ISBN: 978-1-59058-358-6 (1-59058-358-2) Hardcover

Poisoned Pen Press
6962 E. First Ave., Ste. 103
Scottsdale, AZ 85251
www.poisonedpenpress.com
info@poisonedpenpress.com

Printed in the United States of America

"Yet the way men live is so far removed from the way they ought to live that anyone who abandons what is for what should be pursues his downfall rather than his preservation; for a man who strives after goodness in all his acts is sure to come to ruin, since there are so many men who are not good."

—Niccolo Machiavelli,
The Prince

Prologue

He had been seeing the young prostitute for almost a year now. They had met at the Satin & Lace club in South Salt Lake City where she worked as a nude dancer. They'd hit it off right away. He found her youthful good looks, hard body, and sexual enthusiasm intoxicating from the very beginning. They got together as often as his professional schedule and family demands would allow.

He got up and began to dress. She stirred briefly, rolled over, and went back to sleep. It was almost 11 p.m. He wanted to get home soon in case his wife tried to call him from her parents' home in California where she was visiting. He deposited a crisp, new one-hundred-dollar bill on the night stand, kissed her gently on the back of the neck, and quietly left the room.

A six-foot-high cedar fence separated the motel parking lot from a McDonald's restaurant. The familiar smell of fast-food burgers and fries filled the still night air. He climbed into his new Lexus, turned north onto State Street, and headed home into the exclusive Avenues district. For a Saturday night, south State Street was relatively free of the usual transients and hookers who often plied their trade in this part of town. The amount of lust on south State Street would have made old Brigham Young turn over in his grave—clearly not what he intended when the streets of this dusty frontier town were neatly laid out one hundred and fifty years earlier.

Levi Vogue paused to reflect on what a charmed life he was leading. At forty-four, he'd recently been appointed by Governor Nelson Strand to a second five-year term as Chairman of the prestigious and highly visible Utah Board of Pardons and Parole. Having established a statewide reputation for being tough on crime and criminals, his political ambition extended far beyond the Board. He was a member of a prominent and wealthy Republican family. He had two grown sons attending college. And he had a supportive, if boring wife, who was the epitome of what former Vice-President Dan Quayle meant when he stumped around the country preaching family values.

◇◇◇

This growing obsession he had for the young prostitute—he knew he needed to end it and end it soon. His occasional stops at the Satin & Lace club were also a problem. It would be just his luck to run into some former prison inmate he had paroled who might remember him. Or worse, what if he ran into some prominent member of the community dallying in the den of iniquity? It was just the type of potential scandal that could jeopardize his position on the Board of Pardons, not to mention ending any hope of a future political career. Besides, she sporadically dated a possessive, jealous boyfriend who had a reputation for dealing violently with strip-club customers who tried to become overly familiar with her. Who knows what he might do if he became aware of their occasional trysts at the Starlite Motel.

He was living on the edge, and he knew it. But, he liked living on the edge.

He glanced quickly at his watch, noting that it was almost 11:30 as he entered the circular driveway that led to the stately, older Victorian home he and Margaret had purchased five years earlier. As he frequently did during the warm spring and summer months, he parked in the driveway near the garage. As he climbed out, he failed to notice the approaching figure who emerged from the shadows next to the house. When he glanced up, he thought the figure looked vaguely familiar, but wondered why anyone would be wearing a long trench coat on a warm spring night.

The advancing figure stopped less than twenty feet from him. For an instant, each looked at the other without speaking. Only when the sawed-off shotgun emerged from under the coat did he realize what was about to happen. He wanted to scream, "No," but before he could say anything, he saw a bright flash of light and heard an explosion as the shotgun discharged. The deafening blast caught him high in the chest and propelled him onto his back. He felt the warm dampness of his own blood as it puddled under him on the cobblestone drive. A strange numbness followed. He looked up at the stars in a hazy state of disbelief as the dark figure crouched over him. The last thing he felt was the cold touch of the shotgun barrel as it was placed under his chin. The second blast nearly decapitated him.

Chapter One

The telephone woke me from a restless sleep. I glanced at the clock across the room with its small red numbers and strained through bleary eyes to make out the time. I'd been telling myself for months to move the clock closer to the bed or buy another one with bigger numbers. Wearily, I picked up the phone.

"Yeah."

"Sam, this is Norm Sloan. Sorry about the hour, but we've got a major problem."

I became instantly alert. Rarely did I receive a telephone call in the middle of the night from the Executive Director of the Utah Department of Corrections. Calls like this always meant that something had gone seriously wrong somewhere, usually at the state prison. As the head of the Special Investigations Branch (SIB) of the Utah Department of Corrections, problems with inmates or prison employees usually ended up on my desk.

"What's happened?"

"I just received a call from the governor. Levi Vogue has been gunned down in the driveway of his home. The preliminary examination of the crime scene appears to suggest an execution-style hit."

"Oh, shit. Is he alive?"

"No. They pronounced him dead at the scene."

"What about his family?"

"Out of town from what I was told."

"Do you know if the governor is planning to involve the state attorney general's office in the investigation?" I asked.

"The governor didn't say anything about it. As far as I can tell, this one's strictly in the hands of Salt Lake City P.D. and the county prosecutor."

"Who's been assigned as lead investigator?"

"They've given it to that hot-shot female homicide detective—you know, the one who gets more publicity than the Pope."

"That would be Kate McConnell," I said. "They couldn't have made a better choice. She's as talented as they come."

"That's her," said Sloan. "Look, Sam, I'm assigning you as my personal liaison to Salt Lake P.D. Do everything you can to help them get it solved quickly. And Sam, don't delegate this to anyone else. Nobody knows our prison and parole populations better than you. Let's just hope the perp turns out to be some asshole not connected to our offender population.

"In a worst-case scenario, if the offender turns out to be one of ours, the politicians will do what they always do—look for scapegoats. It's probably occurred to you that in the assignment of blame, you will be perceived by some as culpable. It's your office that serves as the intelligence gathering unit for the department. There are those on the governor's staff, and in the state legislature, who will ask how an incident like this could have gone undetected. I'll expect you to provide daily briefings either to me or my administrative assistant, Brad Ford. Get on it, Sam, and good hunting."

Sloan was a survivor. He started at the Utah State Prison thirty-two years ago as a clinical social worker and clawed his way up the ranks to the top. The governor appointed him as executive director five years ago.

He and I have bumped heads more than once. My dislike of authority, chains of command, and political maneuvering have often gotten me into hot water. Fortunately, I'm very good at what I do, and that keeps me employed and him out of trouble.

Sloan had made no secret of his worry that the killer might be one of our ex-cons with a score to settle. Damage control would be at the top of his agenda. While I wanted to give Sloan the benefit of the doubt, the tenor of his message wasn't lost on me. If the killer of Levi Vogue turned out to be an ex-con, I would make a tempting sacrificial lamb for the political bureaucrats. I wondered if Sloan might become one of those bureaucrats.

I scratched a note on the kitchen chalkboard to Aunt June explaining that I'd been called out on a case and would phone her later in the morning. As the single parent of an eight-year-old, I don't know how Sara and I would have made it without her. After my divorce, she moved in to assist with my transition into single parenthood. That was almost two years ago. She has since become an indispensable part of our lives. I looked in on Sara, and then quickly left the house.

I live in the resort town of Park City, not far from the base of the ski mountain. It's not exactly convenient to working at the Utah State Prison, but a great place to live if you can tolerate the thirty-plus-mile commute.

As I crested Parley's Summit and began the descent into Salt Lake City, a scary thought occurred to me. Rather than an isolated attack, what if the murder of Levi Vogue was part of a broader conspiracy to kill all of the parole board members? The lives of the other board members could be in imminent danger. An unlikely scenario? Yes. Something I could afford to ignore? Definitely not.

I reached for my cell phone and dialed Salt Lake P.D. dispatch. I was connected to the dispatch duty sergeant.

"Sergeant Malone; how can I help you?"

"Sergeant Malone, this is Sam Kincaid from the Special Investigations Branch of the Utah Department of Corrections. I'm on my way to assist your homicide unit at the home of Levi Vogue and I need your help with something."

"What can I do for you?"

"We've got two parole board members who live in the city and two who reside in Salt Lake county. If I get you their names and addresses, could you have patrol officers contact them and make sure that everybody is okay?"

"Not a problem—be glad to do it. We'll contact the ones in our jurisdiction and I'll have the sheriff's office send deputies to the homes of the two who reside in the county. Anything else?"

"Yeah, there is one more thing. Do you think you could arrange special patrol coverage of their homes for the remainder of the night?"

"Not a problem."

Chapter Two

Death investigations were nothing new for me. My 17 years working inside the prison system for the Special Investigations Branch brought me into close contact with death and serious bodily injury all too frequently. Prisons were like that, and the Utah State Prison was no exception.

I was not surprised by the pandemonium when I arrived at Vogue's home. The red and blue emergency lights from police and fire units were visible from two blocks away. Neighbors and curious onlookers had gathered behind police barricades across the street from the victim's home. The area had been cordoned off with yellow tape reading "Crime Scene—Do Not Enter." Members of the press scurried about everywhere attempting to gather whatever information became available. A helicopter from one of the local news stations hovered overhead.

As I approached the crime scene, Fred Saunders, an experienced investigative reporter with the *Salt Lake Tribune*, spotted me. "Kincaid, is your presence here an indication that Mr. Vogue's murder was likely committed by a former inmate at the prison?"

"Hello, Fred. No, it isn't. It's much too early to speculate on anything like that. I'm here as a liaison from Corrections to assist Salt Lake P.D. in any way we can."

"Who asked you to assist Salt Lake P.D. in the investigation?"

"No comment," I replied as I pushed past him toward the entrance to the crime scene.

I showed my ID to a young patrol officer whose primary responsibility was to control access by logging people in and out. I was immediately escorted to Salt Lake P.D. Homicide Detective Lieutenant Kathryn McConnell. I'd known her casually for several years. Our paths had crossed on numerous occasions at meetings and professional training conferences.

Attractive in an athletic sort of way, McConnell was tall and slender with a body that was muscular and well defined. She had chestnut colored hair with large hazel eyes, a small nose, full lips, and the kind of fair complexion that probably couldn't tolerate much sun.

She was the kind of woman any healthy, red-blooded male would want to take a tumble with, yet she always seemed to display an aura that suggested you wouldn't make it to first base, much less hit a home run.

My cursory look around the crime scene told me that things were well under way. One lab technician was measuring, diagraming, and photographing the scene. Another was busy videotaping the entire area. A third, assisted by two uniforms, was conducting a grid search of the property.

As I approached, McConnell broke away from a conversation with a well-dressed young detective, probably her partner. She extended a long, slender hand and said, "Hi, Sam. Sorry about the circumstances, but it's nice to see you again."

"Thanks, Kate. Nice to see you, too. What have you got so far?"

"Not much. Two neighbors called it in almost simultaneously. The shots apparently rocked the whole neighborhood. The perp also burglarized the residence. We don't know if it was a planned, professional hit, or whether Vogue got home at the wrong time and blundered into an in-progress burglary.

"Two uniforms arrived at about the same time, took one look at the victim, and knew there was nothing they could do for him. They secured the area and called for help. Once backup arrived, they found the point of entry and conducted a room-by-room search of the house. By that time, the perp was long gone. Fortunately, nobody was home. A neighbor told us that Mrs. Vogue is away visiting her parents in California, and apparently, both sons attend college someplace out of state. As you'll see when we go in, the interior of the place was badly trashed. We'll have to wait until Mrs. Vogue returns to find out what, if anything, was stolen."

Although we hadn't had time to discuss how best I could assist, it didn't take a rocket scientist to figure out that McConnell would focus the investigation on anyone who might have wanted Levi Vogue dead. In reality, that might turn out to be a lot of people in our prison or parole populations.

Chapter Three

A member of the medical examiner's office was busy examining the body as McConnell and I moved in for a closer look. The faint odor of urine and feces was unmistakable. Vogue was lying on his back with his left leg twisted under his body. White chalk had been used to trace around the prone figure. His dull, vacant eyes were half-open and staring blankly into space. The expression on what was left of his face appeared to reflect surprise rather than terror or fear, I thought.

The force of the blast had blown away most of his jaw and mouth. One of his black penny loafers had come off and was lying next to the body. He was wearing an expensive Brooks Brothers gray suit. The white dress shirt was soaked in blood and covered a gaping wound in the upper chest area. A burgundy colored paisley tie had been stuffed into the suit coat pocket. A brown leather wallet was lying next to the body.

The medical examiner, Harold Voddel, approached McConnell. "You've got a fresh kill here, Lieutenant, that probably closely coincides with the calls from the neighbors who reported the incident. There are early signs of postmortem lividity in the lower back and legs. His body temperature is down three degrees. It's too soon for even early signs of rigor mortis. I'd estimate his time of death at about two hours ago. I'll be able to tell you more precisely after the autopsy."

"Jesus," I said. "Look at the size of these entry wounds."

"This work was done up close and personal," replied McConnell. "After the medical examiner gets him cleaned up, we'll have a better idea about the angle of the slugs and the approximate distance from the shooter. Although it's hard to tell with all this blood, there doesn't appear to be any discernable pellet pattern around either wound."

After donning latex gloves, we carefully examined Vogue's wallet and discovered that it contained several credit cards, but no cash.

McConnell turned to Voddell. "Bag each item of clothing separately and give us an inventory of all the items on his person. We'll hang on to the wallet."

"Sure," grumbled Voddell. Kate appeared to be lecturing the young assistant medical examiner, and his tone of voice suggested he resented it.

"Call me later this morning and let us know when you're going to perform the autopsy. I'll either attend personally or send somebody."

"Okay," replied Voddell.

"Did you search his car?" I asked.

"Not yet. We'll do that after the crime scene crew finishes processing it for trace evidence."

"Shall we take a look inside the house?"

"Yeah. Let's do that now. We'll have to navigate around the lab crew."

The Vogue home was a fashionable two-story Victorian affair built in the early 1900s.

The upscale Avenues section of the city had long since been declared an historic district. Aside from the homes, the Vogues had probably been attracted to the neighborhood by the eclectic mix of residents that included many of Salt Lake City's politicians and business leaders.

We walked around behind the house and entered the same way the killer had. One of the glass panels near the door handle had been broken. All the perp had to do was reach in and unlock the French doors. He would have been inside in a matter of seconds.

McConnell wasn't exaggerating when she said the place had been trashed. Books had been randomly pulled from shelves and scattered around. Almost all the decorations in the family room had been smashed, including some crystal pieces, and several expensive Lladros. Shards of broken glass and crystal lay everywhere.

"You know, Kate, this break-in has a real amateurish feel to it—not the kind of job a pro would do."

"I had the same thought. It looks like the kind of random property destruction we see when juveniles pull burglaries and destroy lots of property merely for the hell of it."

While McConnell headed upstairs to inspect the second floor, I wandered back into the study and sat down in front of the computer. I know just enough about computers to get myself into trouble. I didn't see any CD-ROMs; so I went straight to the hard drive. Nothing much out of the ordinary. There were several letters, mostly sent to family members; Vogue's resume, and a number of routine parole board e-mails sent by the victim to various members of his staff. When I hit the icon for Quicken I discovered that the Vogues tracked virtually all spending in that program. I would remind Kate to arrange for a police computer specialist to download all the family financial records for review.

I joined Kate in the upstairs master bedroom. The upstairs looked much the same as the main level—trashed. Mrs. Vogue had an expensive collection of fine jewelry. Some of it was stored in jewelry cases inside drawers that had been opened, with the contents left untouched. Several pieces were displayed in plain sight, on jewelry trees, located on top of one of the bedroom dressers.

"I don't get it. Why would a thief walk out of here and leave all the expensive jewelry behind?" said Kate.

"Maybe Vogue interrupted the burglary before the suspect had time to gather up the valuable stuff."

"Possible, I suppose, but my gut tells me that when this thing finally shakes out we'll discover that the burglary was a ruse designed to cover a planned hit—and quite possibly a hit carried out by one of your ex-cons."

One of my ex-cons!

"Getting a little ahead of yourself, don't you think, Lieutenant?"

"Maybe. So indulge me for a minute, Sam. Parole board members decide the length of the prison sentence for each inmate, correct?"

"That's right."

"I would think that would make some inmates angry enough to want to do bodily harm to the parole board member who dished out the lengthy prison sentence."

"Possible, yes, but not very likely. Listen, Kate, parole board members occasionally receive verbal threats from inmates. That comes with the job. But we've never had an incident where a threat resulted in an attack on a board member. That's never happened in Utah or anyplace else that I'm aware of. That said, there's a first time for everything."

"Do I get the feeling you want to turn this investigation away from the offender population in the Department of Corrections?" Her tone betrayed just a tinge of suspicion.

We're certainly getting off on the right foot, I thought.

How not to sound caustic, a weakness of mine? "I'm not trying to steer this investigation in any particular direction, Kate, but I think it's important to consider all the possibilities. Of course I hope the perp isn't someone under our jurisdiction. We'll have a serious public relations problem on our hands if the killer ends up being somebody recently paroled from the prison."

"Okay. Hypothetically then, tell me how this thing might have gone down if the perp was somebody from the prison population?"

As I spoke, I considered the possibility that the killer might well be someone directly or indirectly connected to our offender population. "If the killer was one of ours, it could be a former inmate acting solo, purely for revenge. Or it could be some nut case with big-time mental health problems. We certainly have enough of them floating around. It might even be gang related."

"The gang possibility intrigues me," said Kate. "Tell me more."

"If a prison gang was involved, it could have gone down in a couple of different ways. It might have been a called hit from a gang leader who is either in or out of prison. Or, one or more renegade gang members could have taken it upon themselves to exact revenge on a member of the Board of Pardons because they don't like the lengthy sentences currently being handed out to gang leaders. It might even be part of an initiation ritual in which a gang member wannabe was ordered to do the killing as a part of being 'jumped in' to a particular gang. Those would be the most likely scenarios."

"Thanks. That was enlightening," said McConnell.

I couldn't tell if she really meant it, or if she was patronizing me. I decided to give her the benefit of the doubt for now.

We had accomplished about all we could at the crime scene, so we agreed to meet at police headquarters for an early-morning strategy session.

Chapter Four

It took only a few minutes to drive from Vogue's home in the Avenues to police department headquarters in downtown Salt Lake City. It was just after four. I made a quick stop at an all-night convenience store where I purchased several cups of burned coffee and a bag of doughnuts. What's a meeting among cops without coffee and doughnuts?

Kate McConnell was meticulous and well organized. I saw that at the Vogue residence. This meeting was going to be about reviewing the case and assigning each of us specific leads to pursue. We met in a small conference room adjacent to a much larger open area that housed a number of detectives. At this time of the morning, the place was as quiet as a morgue on Christmas.

As I entered the conference room, McConnell and the nattily dressed young detective I'd seen at the Vogue residence were busy clarifying the rules of an office betting pool on the NBA playoffs. She introduced him to me. His name was Vince Turner.

"This is how it works," said Turner. "Everybody puts two bucks in the pot. Then each person guesses the game's final score—say I pick a score of 102 to 98. That means the winning number for me is 200 points. Whoever hits the number or comes closest wins."

Kate seemed to be thinking. "Sounds good, but how do we settle ties?"

"Besides total points, you also have to pick the winner."

"What if there's still a tie?"

"Then nobody wins and the entire pot moves to the next game."

Turner looked up at me and smiled. "There's still time, Sam. Care to join our office pool?"

"Sure. Here's my two bucks."

Turner had just transferred to Homicide from the robbery unit. He was built like one of those guys who doesn't have a job, but instead spends most of his waking hours at a Gold's Gym pumping iron and admiring himself in the mirrors. His handshake sent a jolt of pain up my arm. I'm sure I heard bones cracking in my right hand. I wasn't sure whether this was a greeting or the beginning of an arm-wrestling contest I would surely lose.

I downed a lukewarm cup of coffee and a semi-stale doughnut while McConnell quickly got us on track.

"Let's take a minute and talk about what we know and what we don't know. We know the vic was killed execution style in the driveway of his home with some type of shotgun. So far, we have no witnesses, no murder weapon, no suspect, and no physical evidence. We know the killing had a professional look about it, yet the burglary of the home appeared very amateurish.

Turner interrupted. "So, you're questioning whether the burglary was real, or simply a cover for a well-planned act of premeditated murder?"

"That's right. And we don't know whether the perp was working solo, or whether others were involved. We don't know how the perp got to and from the crime scene. And, perhaps most important, we don't whether the victim and the perp knew each other. If we're going to clear this one, we need to focus on who might have wanted to see Levi Vogue dead and who stood to gain from his death."

"Wouldn't it be wise to eliminate family members and friends before we look elsewhere?"asked Turner.

"Absolutely," replied Kate. "Things like life insurance policies, trusts, and inheritances, as well as the stability of the marriage in general. And what about his relationship with his sons? We can't overlook the possibility of a Menendez brothers scenario."

As much as I wanted to lay this whole ugly episode on the back of a disgruntled family member or friend, or perhaps a burglary gone awry, all of my cop instincts told me we wouldn't find an answer to this puzzle by following either of those trails. I listened quietly as McConnell and Turner discussed the relative merits of how to pursue the issue of possible involvement by family or friends. Kate then asked for my input.

"My recommendation is that you pursue three directions simultaneously. The first would be family member involvement. I'd run in-depth background investigations on all immediate family members as well as any friends or acquaintances.

"I'd also suggest that somebody go to work with your burglary detectives, as well as those at the Salt Lake County Sheriff's Office, and try to identify suspects who commit burglaries using a similar M.O. My sense is that this avenue is least likely to produce our killer.

"Finally, I'd focus my attention on the possibility that Vogue was killed as the result of his work on the Board of Pardons. That would entail following any investigative leads related to our prison and parole populations. We'd probably need to go back over every parole case Vogue handled since his appointment more than five years ago, looking for any inmate who might have threatened him. In fact, we'd want to include any prisoner who ever threatened any of the board members."

"That's a comprehensive approach and I like it," said Kate. "Let's give equal attention to the family/friends angle and the possibility that the murder was job related. How about if Vince and I pursue the burglary and family possibilities while you follow the employment trail."

"Sounds like a plan," I said.

McConnell and Turner were paged by the lab technicians at the Vogue residence. They left me in the conference room with nothing better to do than snoop through Vogue's wallet, which Kate had left on the conference room table. I put on the latex gloves and removed the wallet from its plastic evidence bag. It contained the usual Social Security card, Utah driver's license, a plethora of charge cards, and several pictures of Margaret Vogue and their two sons. Looking into one of those little nooks and crannies, where normally a person wouldn't place anything, I discovered a small yellow Post-it note with a faded telephone number penciled in. The phone number read 555-5484. I quickly jotted the number down and placed the Post-it back where I found it.

Turner returned to the conference room and announced our first break in the case. "The crime lab team just discovered two fresh cigarette butts lying near the side of Vogue's garage. Given where the killing took place, that would have been the logical place to wait."

"That's good news," I said. "If we get lucky, those butts might yield a latent print or maybe even a DNA sample."

"Sam," said Turner sheepishly, "I'm embarrassed to ask you this, but I've never worked a case with anyone from the Department of Corrections before, and I've never heard of the Special Investigations Branch. Could you fill me in on what it is you guys do?"

"Sure," I replied. "No need to feel embarrassed. In the SIB, we make it a practice to keep our heads down and maintain a low profile. We assist the Salt Lake County Sheriff's Office in the investigation of crimes committed at the state prison either by inmates or employees of the department. We also assist federal and local law enforcement agencies with fugitive apprehension, drug trafficking at the prison, as well as solving crimes committed in the community when the offender is on probation or parole. And sometimes we conduct internal investigations involving prison staff accused of violating department policy. We used to be responsible for handling pre-employment investigations, but last year we managed to dump that job on somebody else."

Moments later, Kate returned, and our planning session broke up. I was anxious to get busy. McConnell had informed us that Margaret Vogue had been notified of the murder, and was making arrangements for a prompt return to Salt Lake City. Right or wrong, I felt a sense of personal responsibility for the murder. Had the SIB failed to do its job properly? Could this murder have been prevented with better intelligence information? It was a moot point now, but I promised myself that this case would not go unsolved.

◇◇◇

It was a little past six when I left police headquarters. I called home. I had agreed to take Sara to school on my way to work this morning. I wondered if she would remember my promise. On the third ring, a sleepy voice near and dear to me answered, "Kincaid residence, Sara speaking."

"Hi, Pumpkin! How are you doing this morning? You're starting to sound so grown up when you answer the telephone."

"I know," she wearily replied. "Daddy, did you forget that you were supposed to take me to school today?"

"No, honey, I sure didn't. But something came up at work, and daddy had to leave in the middle of the night while you were still sleeping. But guess what? I'm on my way home right now to pick you up. How does that sound?"

"Yea, daddy. Can we stop at Daybreak Donuts on the way to school for some hot chocolate and a doughnut?"

"Sure. I think we can manage that. You hurry and get cleaned up, and I'll pick you up in about thirty minutes. And Sara, no arguing with Aunt June about what you wear to school today. You can't wear the pink dress with the white tights again this week. They're dirty, and besides, if you wear them again, people at school might think it's the only outfit you own. Okay?"

"Okay," she said, a note of disappointment in her voice.

"See you in a few minutes."

I knew the run home would be inconvenient. But I've also learned how important it is to Sara for me to keep my promises. It has been especially hard for her since the divorce.

The divorce was amicable as divorces go, but Sara and I both attended family counseling for several months after the split. Aside from the usual problems common to most marriages, how do you tell an eight-year-old that her mom had grown tired of the full-time mother role and simply wanted to get out of Utah and back to her career? Nicole was a flight attendant when we met and has returned to the airline. She's based in Atlanta, which puts her back in her Georgia roots, close to her parents, but a long way from Sara. She travels to Salt Lake City as often as her flight schedule allows. Because of Nicole's frequent travel, we decided on joint custody with me as the custodial parent.

Chapter Five

Sara was wiping chocolate from her mouth when I dropped her at school before returning to Salt Lake City. I stopped at the Salt Lake Roasting Company, where I ordered a large cup of French roast and perused the morning *Salt Lake Tribune* looking for news of the Vogue murder. There was only a small breakout piece, since it had occurred too late at night to receive full coverage. It would be the story of the day and probably the story for weeks to come.

After downing the coffee, I used my cell phone and called the number I'd found in Levi's wallet. On the third ring, a male voice answered, "Starlite Motel; how can I help you?"

"How much is your rate for a single for one night?"

"Forty plus tax," came the reply.

"Okay, and what's your address?"

"3640 South State Street."

"Okay. I'll call you back. Thanks."

I wondered what Levi Vogue was doing with the phone number to a motel on South State Street. While I didn't know anything about the Starlite Motel in particular, I knew the area well enough to recognize that it was located in a part of town devoid of upscale hotels, and that it was well known for its hookers, pimps, and drug dealers.

◇◇◇

It was still early as I headed for the Board of Pardons office in South Salt Lake, a few blocks from the headquarters of the Department of Corrections. The Utah Board of Pardons and Parole had five full-time members appointed by the governor, each serving staggered, renewable, five-year terms. As the result of Vogue's murder, the board had lost not only one of its members, but also its chairman.

My reasons for visiting the Parole Board office were twofold: I wanted to interview any available board members. I also wanted to search Vogue's office and seal it so that nothing could be removed without our knowledge. I wouldn't need a search warrant as long as I received permission from Lawrence Gallagher, the Board's administrative secretary. By the time I arrived, three board members were sequestered behind closed doors in executive session, while the secretarial support staff appeared noticeably subdued. I found Gallagher in his office sitting behind his computer, clustered behind two large stacks of parole files. Gallagher was a politically well-connected Democrat with a strong desire to be appointed to the Board of Pardons himself. Unfortunately, members of the Democratic Party in Utah were about as common as white tigers in North Dakota.

He glanced up from the e-mail message he was preparing and said, "Sam, I hope you're coming with good news. I've got a group of very nervous parole board members meeting in executive session right now trying to figure out who's going to run this place in the absence of the chairman, and wondering whether they might be next in line for a surprise visit when they go home tonight. I stopped fielding calls from the media more than an hour ago. They're hungry for information, any information, and they're driving us nuts."

"Sorry, Larry. My quota of good news ran out as of this morning, and don't tell the press squat."

"Then to what do we owe the pleasure of your visit—never mind, I know. You want to search Levi's office, right? And I'll bet you don't have a warrant?"

"Very good, Larry. You're right on both counts—I don't have a warrant, and I do want to search Levi's office."

"I locked it this morning as soon as I heard. The office looked undisturbed. As to your search, I don't see a problem as long as the rest of the board members approve."

I found myself pleading my case for the search before a stunned and visibly nervous group of parole board members. So far, there was little to tell them about the murder of their colleague and friend. In the end, they gave me permission to search his office and saved me the time and trouble of obtaining a warrant.

A cursory search of Levi's office turned up little of value. I rummaged through his four-drawer file cabinet and desk but found nothing out of the ordinary. A search of his computer hard drive and several discs provided no clues that might help us solve his murder. All of the computer files contained information pertinent only to his work on the Board of Pardons. The only thing of significance I found occurred when I examined his Rolodex. When I got to the letter "S," I found the initials SLM and the phone number to the Starlite Motel. The motel was going to be my next stop. On my way out of the office, I snatched a small desk photograph of Levi and Margaret that appeared to have been taken fairly recently.

Three board members had agreed to immediate interviews. The fourth was vacationing and not scheduled to return for two weeks.

I began with the board member with the least amount of seniority. Judith James-Hyde was serving her first term and had been on the job a mere nine months. She had been a career prosecutor, first with the Salt Lake County Attorney's Office, and most recently, a deputy attorney general with the Utah State Attorney General's Office.

"Judith, how are you holding up?"

"Like everybody else, I'm in a state of shock. It's hard for me to accept that Levi will never walk through that door again. He's gone for good."

I nodded. There seemed little to say.

"Tell me Judith, how well did you know Levi?"

"Reasonably well, considering that I've only worked here for a few months. I knew him slightly before because of my assignment in the Attorney General's Office, where I represented your department as well as the Board of Pardons. Other than an occasional business lunch, I never saw him socially outside the office. I did meet his wife, Margaret, at our office Christmas party last December."

"Do you have any idea about what kind of relationship Levi had with his wife and children?"

"Not really. I mean he seemed highly devoted to his family and the Mormon church. He talked nonstop about how proud he was of his two sons. I never heard him say anything that would lead me to think there were problems at home. I recently overheard him talking with another staff member about being active in a Boy Scout troop, and I also think he coached a youth soccer team. But that's about it."

"What about the days and weeks leading up to the murder? Did his behavior change, or did he seem upset about anything?"

"I've been in here this morning thinking about that. I didn't see any changes in his demeanor or mood. Nothing."

"Were you aware of anyone he might have been having problems with—anybody he might have been afraid of?"

"Well, there are always inmates. As you know, some of them can be downright scary. But if he was afraid of someone, he never mentioned it to me. And that's something I would've remembered."

I nodded. "I'm sure you would. Who did Levi socialize with outside the office? Anybody come to mind?"

"Not really. I imagine he had friends in the church. That wouldn't be unusual. Come to think of it though, since I joined the board, Levi seemed to be spending more and more time with Bill Allred. Almost like they'd become pals."

"You mean hanging out together away from work?"

"Well, both actually. We're all thrown together in the office, so that's a given. But, yes, I had the impression that Levi and Bill were spending time together away from work. Several times I heard them talking about working out at one of the local health clubs, although I don't know where or how often."

"When was the last time you saw Levi?"

"Late yesterday afternoon. I left for home at about five-thirty and Levi was still in his office."

"Thanks for your help, Judith. If you think of anything else, no matter how trivial it may seem, you know where to find me."

My next interview was with William Allred, a retired prison warden who had been employed by the Department of Corrections for twenty years prior to his appointment to the Board of Pardons. Allred was nearing the end of his second term. As I recalled, his appointment had been a controversial one. Many people believed that his selection had less to do with ability, and more to do with his reputation as a tough prison warden. He had always projected an attitude that said, on his watch, inmates would not be running the asylum. That attitude resonated well with Utah politicians and probably played a major role in his hiring.

Allred invited me into his office. I glanced around the room thinking that I'd never seen a dirtier, more cluttered space. Files were scattered everywhere and piled on everything. I moved a two-foot-high stack from an office chair to the floor so I'd have a place to sit.

Allred glanced up from a file and said, "Sorry about the mess. One of these days I'll get around to straightening it up. I hate to rush you, Sam, but we're going to have to keep this short. I've got a full docket of parole grant hearings scheduled for this afternoon, and I'm still not finished reading the files."

"Thanks for seeing me on such short notice. I'll try to keep it brief."

"I sure hope I can help. Levi's murder has shocked and devastated everybody in this office. How are Margaret and the children holding up? Has she returned from California?"

"I don't really know. I haven't had any contact with her. My guess is that she's on her way back to Utah."

"And how is the investigation proceeding?" he continued. "Did you find any physical evidence at the crime scene? Any suspects yet?"

I started to wonder who was interviewing who. Before I could answer, Allred apologized. "I'm sorry to be asking all these questions, Sam. It's just that the rest of us are feeling a little jumpy. I know everybody will feel a sense of relief once somebody's in custody."

I treated Allred's questions the same way I would had they come from the press. That means I used my standard line of evasive bullshit and didn't really answer any of them.

I asked Allred the same questions I'd previously posed to James-Hyde. And with one notable exception, I received almost the exact same responses.

"Away from the office, who were Levi's friends?"

The question seemed to momentarily catch him off-guard. For a split second, his facial expression registered surprise. "Well, I really haven't any idea about that. There was this guy from his church ward. Levi once told me that he and this guy, and, sorry, but I can't remember his name, sometimes attended Jazz games together. Other than that, my sense is that Levi spent most of his time with family."

"Did you and he socialize outside the office?"

"Once in a great while, but not very often."

"And when you did go out, what kinds of things did you do together?"

"When we did go out, and it wasn't often, we'd usually go to lunch. That's really about it."

"Seems like I heard from somebody that the two of you spent time together lifting weights. Is that true?"

"Well, yes, that's true. On rare occasions, Levi and I have lifted together. I maintain a membership at a Gold's Gym in Midvale and Levi attended a couple of times as my guest."

For whatever reasons, Allred wanted to distance himself from any personal relationship with Vogue. I wondered why. While he didn't outright deny the friendship, he certainly downplayed it.

The third member, Gloria Perez, was a former law school professor at the University of Utah. She was three months shy of finishing her second term. From what I'd heard, she badly wanted Governor Strand to appoint her a third time, and rumor had it, he wasn't going to do it.

Perez looked tired and drawn. Her mascara had run, and it was obvious that she'd been crying. As the board's senior member, I had hoped my interview with her might lead to some startling revelation that would shed light on Levi's murder. But it didn't. About the only interesting answer came when I asked if she could identify any of Levi's friends. She gave me three names. Bill Allred's was the first.

The picture of Vogue that emerged from his three colleagues was remarkably similar. They respected him as a highly capable parole board member and administrator. In his personal life, the picture they painted was of a man of high moral character, devoted to family, church, and community.

None of his colleagues recalled Vogue being upset or distracted by anything in the days preceding his murder. They were unable to identify anyone who disliked him or who might have wanted to see him dead.

As I left the Board of Pardons, I asked Gallagher to secure Vogue's office and not let anyone in without obtaining authorization from me or Kate McConnell. He agreed.

Chapter Six

My next stop was the Starlite Motel. Before I got there, my cell phone rang. It was Kate.

"I wondered if I might interest you in a front-row seat at Levi Vogue's autopsy? It's scheduled for one o'clock this afternoon."

"Thanks for the offer, but I'll pass."

"Chicken?"

"Absolutely." I had long since developed a strong aversion to attending autopsies. I've never gotten used to the smell of a ripe corpse. When I couldn't avoid them, I always attended smoking a strong cigar. And I don't even smoke.

I agreed to meet Kate later in the evening so we could review what we had learned that day.

◇◇◇

I arrived at the Starlite Motel and contacted the manager, Frank Arnold. The motel was not one I considered upscale, but it wasn't bad either, considering the surrounding neighborhood.

Arnold was an older man with a ruddy facial complexion that probably belied years of serious drinking. The one thing that stood out about him was a voluminous nose. It looked like it have been broken on more than one occasion, but nonetheless, would have made Karl Malden envious.

I introduced myself, showed him a picture of Levi Vogue, and asked if he recognized the photo.

"I wondered if you guys might be coming around. It sure as shit didn't take you long."

"So you do know him?"

"Well, not exactly, but I have seen him come in a few times. He usually doesn't stop here at the front desk. He typically drives in and goes straight back to one of our guest rooms."

"To meet someone, I presume? You wouldn't happen to know the name of the fair maiden?"

"You know," replied Arnold, "I ain't under any fuckin' obligation to talk to you, am I?"

"No, sir. You surely aren't."

"In that case, you come back later and talk to the lady who owns this place. She comes in around three in the afternoon. Her name is Lou Ann Barlow. She knows a helluva lot more about this than I do."

"And why is that?"

"Because the young lady you're referring to happens to be Lou Ann's daughter. I live with Lou, and I ain't gettin' involved. Christ, she'll toss my sorry ass out on the street if she thinks I've been talkin' outa school."

"Yeah, I can understand that, and I'll be happy to come back later. But, surely you can give me her name—not much harm in that."

"I suppose that's true. Her name is Sue Ann Winkler. She works as a dancer in a club called Satin & Lace."

"How did she meet Levi Vogue?"

"I don't know for sure, but they probably met at the club. That's how Sue Ann meets most of her male friends. And I don't have a clue whether an exchange of money was a regular part of the friendship, if that's your next question."

Unlike most of the Salt Lake strip clubs that served alcohol and required the dancers to wear pasties and a t-bar on the lower extremities, Satin & Lace didn't serve alcohol. It was a nude club. Strip joints like this are known as "pop shops" in the trade. The dancers perform on stage and are encouraged to sell customers table dances and private sessions in private rooms. The rooms are monitored with cameras to provide security for the dancer and to enforce the no hanky-panky rule. Of course, whatever arrangement a dancer makes with a customer outside the club usually goes unnoticed. That's not to say that the hanky-panky rule is always enforced by the club's management. Police vice squads know that the private rooms provide safe harbor for hand-jobs, oral sex, and even intercourse.

I recognized that Vogue's apparent involvement with a local stripper might be completely unrelated to his murder; however, I couldn't ignore it. Perhaps there was another side to Levi Vogue—a more insidious side that belied the public image of the successful, happily married, church-going family man.

Chapter Seven

It was late in the morning and I hadn't made an appearance at my office. Actually, I have two offices. The Department of Corrections requires that I maintain an office at central headquarters in Salt Lake City. My staff in the SIB, however, is housed in one of the administrative buildings at the state prison twenty-five minutes south of Salt Lake City. That's the location of my other office. In reality, much of what we do require our presence at the prison.

I knew I would return later in the afternoon to the Starlite Motel, so rather than driving south to the prison, I headed to department headquarters. I had a tentative plan, and I wanted to assign my most experienced investigator to do some of the legwork.

Terry Burnham had been a Salt Lake City police detective for twenty-four years until his retirement three years ago. Like a lot of cops, the adjustment to retirement did not come easily. In less than a year, he concluded that evening bridge groups and weekly golf outings with his fellow retirees left him empty and unfulfilled. So two years ago I offered him a job in the SIB. He was a good hire, and adapted quickly to the prison environment and the world of the inmate. He was the best investigator in the SIB.

Burnham hadn't been in my office for more than five minutes when we were interrupted by Norm Sloan's administrative assistant, Brad Ford. He wanted an immediate update on the investigation so he could run the information back to Sloan. As soon as Sloan told me he expected daily briefings on the investigation, I sensed that Ford might become a nagging pest. My instincts appeared to be correct.

Ford stood nervously in front of my desk, unsure of whether he should sit down in the empty chair across from Burnham or remain standing. I didn't invite him to sit. "Brad, what can I do for you?"

"Well, Sam, given the old man's insistence on regular briefings, I thought you and I should agree on a time each day, maybe late in the afternoon, when we can get together for updates on the investigation."

You've got to be kidding me!

"We can talk about that later, but now isn't a good time," I said. "You've caught me right in the middle of an important planning meeting."

"When would be a good time?"

"I'll do my best to get back to you first thing in the morning, how's that?"

"That's not good enough—what do you expect me to tell the director?" A sour note of irritation now showed in an otherwise unflappable demeanor.

Tell him any damn thing you want. Just get the hell out of my office!

"Tell him things are progressing smoothly and that I'll get back to him as soon as possible. Now, you'll have to excuse me."

Ford's face turned bright red. He started to speak, but instead, turned on his heel and marched out the door.

"I guess I don't have to tell you where he's going," Burnham said.

"I'll probably catch hell later, but it won't be the first time. Let's get back to work."

Officially, Ford was Sloan's media spokesperson, and unofficially, his self-appointed administrative assistant. People in the department perceived him to be a self-serving climber who lacked significant corrections experience and as someone who hadn't paid his dues in the field. Leaks to the press or divulging too much information might enhance his prestige and visibility while damaging our investigation. We couldn't afford that.

Burnham and I agreed to pursue leads from the angle that someone in our offender population was responsible for Vogue's murder. Several tasks required our immediate attention.

"Terry, why don't you start by searching our computer database for inmates, past or present, who have ever threatened members of the Board of Pardons. While you're at it, let's identify anybody who has threatened or assaulted any member of the prison staff."

"Okay. I'll get right on it. How far back do you want me to go?"

"Six years ought to do it. There's no point in going back prior to the time Vogue was hired as a parole board member."

"Okay. Anything else?"

"Yeah, one more thing. Contact Gallagher at the Board of Pardons and tell him that we're going to need a list of every parole case handled by Vogue from the time he was hired until his death. They won't let the files out of the office, so you'll have to review them there."

"I can do that. I'll also cross reference Vogue's parole cases against whatever turns up from our own database."

"Good idea. If you get lucky, you might just find a match."

I explained to Terry what I had learned at the Starlite Motel. I told him that I would discreetly attempt to determine whether Levi's murder was in any way connected to his trysts at the motel.

"You want me to begin putting feelers out among our inmate snitches?" asked Terry.

"Not yet. I'd like to hold off on that until I talk to the director. Keep me posted on anything you learn. The Old Man is going to be all over me on this one. I can just feel it."

◇◇◇

On my way back to the Starlite Motel, I detoured past the Gold's Gym in Midvale. I was greeted at the front desk by a perky-looking brunette with well-toned muscles and less body fat than Kate Moss. She identified herself as the gym manager. Her name was Brandy Alexander, leaving me to wonder exactly what it was that possessed parents to name children the way they do. When asked about Bill Allred's membership at the gym, she quickly produced his membership records.

"Mr. Allred joined the gym almost five years ago," she said, staring intently into the computer screen. "He visits regularly, three to four times a week, usually in the evenings."

"How about guests?" I said. "Is he allowed to bring guests?"

She paused while bringing up a different screen. "Yes, it looks like Mr. Allred brought another gentleman by the name of Levi Vogue with him, let's see, on nine different occasions over six months. Mr. Vogue came in often enough that we eventually got him to join."

"And when was that?"

"Three months ago. It's funny, though, my computer tells me that Mr. Vogue never came back after joining—not once in three months."

Alexander printed me a copy of the membership records and I left the gym wondering why Allred had chosen to downplay his friendship with our murder victim. It was clear from the records that Vogue visited the gym as Allred's guest more frequently than Allred cared to admit.

Chapter Eight

Lou Ann Barlow turned out to be a real piece of work. A former stripper turned motel owner, she had a mouth on her that would have made Larry Flynt blush. I was ushered into her small office behind the front desk. She was standing in front of a four-drawer file cabinet, with her back to me, busily filing.

She was a tall, statuesque peroxide blond, who, in her early fifties, still looked good enough to take center stage. Despite the cosmetic surgery, her face showed some age, but her body was long and lean with outstanding breasts.

She caught me gaping at her pronounced chest and said, "I'm up here, honey. How the fuck can I help you?"

I showed her my identification and muttered an embarrassed introduction.

"As Mr. Arnold probably told you, I'm investigating the murder of Levi Vogue. I understand that your daughter, Sue Ann, was involved in a relationship with him. Frank told me that they sometimes met here at the motel. What can you tell me about that?"

"Nothin' really. And Frank tends to get talkin' about shit that isn't any of his goddamn business. I'll have to speak with him about that."

"Look, I know you're trying to protect your daughter, but she might have information that would help us solve a murder. She's not in trouble, but it is imperative that I talk to her as soon as possible."

"Like I already told you Mr.—what's your name again?"

"Kincaid, Sam Kincaid."

"Oh, yeah. Well, Mr. Kincaid, like I already told ya, I don't really know anything. I will tell you this, though. My Sue Ann wouldn't have anything to do with no murder."

She was starting to piss me off. "Mrs. Barlow, let me put this to you another way. I'm in the middle of a murder investigation, and like it or not, your daughter is somehow involved. I don't know if she's a suspect or a material witness, but I'm going to have to talk with her. I need your cooperation. It would save us both a lot of trouble if you'd help me out."

"None of my fuckin' business, honey. Now if you'll excuse me, I've got some heavy-duty filing to do here."

Diplomacy had obviously failed, and I knew it was time for a small attitude adjustment. "Good idea. When the Fire Marshal and the people from the health department show up, they'll probably need to check those records. When's the last time you had a top-to-bottom inspection of this place?"

She didn't like that idea very well. Actually, I don't know a soul in either the health or fire departments, but what the hell, it worked. Her tone became noticeably more congenial.

"Okay, okay, honey. You made your point. I don't need that kind of problem. I'll tell you what I can, but it ain't gonna be much."

"I'd appreciate that very much, Mrs. Barlow."

"Sue Ann has been seeing this Vogue fella for nine or ten months now. She's nuts about the two-timin' bum. She knew he was married and had several kids. I tried to tell her that married guys like him aren't about to leave the wife, kids, and their cozy upscale lifestyle for a stripper—even a young, pretty one like my Sue Ann. But Sue Ann doesn't listen very well. I haven't been able to tell her anything in years, particularly as it relates to men."

"So, how often did they get together?"

"From what she said, I got the impression she was seein' him once or twice a week."

"Where would they meet?"

"Mostly here at the motel as far as I know. It bothered her that he didn't want to take her out in public. He was probably afraid of being seen by one of his rich, uptown friends. On occasion, he'd drop into Satin & Lace to watch her dance. I think he got off watching all that young pussy.

"One time he tried to talk Sue Ann into bringing another one of the dancers back to the motel with her. He said he wanted to try a threesome."

"And did Sue Ann comply with his request?"

"No, I think she told him that the other dancer wouldn't go for it."

"I'm sorry to ask you this, Mrs. Barlow, but do you know if Vogue was paying Sue Ann for their time together?"

"You know, she never said, and I didn't ask her. I do know that he was constantly buying her presents. Come to think of it, she did mention one time that he paid her rent."

"Could they have been spending time together in Sue Ann's apartment?"

"Yeah, I guess it's possible, but Sue Ann shares the apartment with another dancer. As paranoid as this ass-wipe was about his precious reputation, I doubt he'd want to spend time at her apartment with the roommate around. Besides, the girls have a rule about not bringing guys back to their place."

"Do you know when they were last together?"

"Frank was working the front desk last night and he said Vogue drove in about seven-thirty and left about eleven."

"Is Frank certain it was Vogue he saw last night?"

"Yeah. He drives a fancy new white Lexus. It's the only thing he drives. We don't get too many of them around here."

"Thanks for your assistance, Mrs. Barlow. Is there anything else you can tell me that might be helpful?"

"Just one thing, and you didn't hear it from me, okay. Sue Ann has this boyfriend, a real scary SOB if you know what I mean. His name is John Merchant. People call him Big Bad John. He's a real possessive, jealous guy with a God-awful temper. A first class jerk if you ask me."

"Why should I be interested in Sue Ann's boyfriend?"

"Because he almost beat a guy to death with a tire iron one night outside Satin & Lace. It seems this guy was paying a little too much attention to Sue Ann during a table dance—getting a little too handsy for his own good. John took exception to the attention the guy was givin' her and started a fight. According to Sue Ann, it wasn't the first time he came after a customer he thought was coming on to her. The club kicked both of them out, so John took a tire iron to the guy in the parking lot. Now the management won't even allow him in the club when Sue Ann is working."

"Did Merchant end up serving time for the assault?"

"Yeah, he ended up gettin' some kind of fancy deal that kept him out of prison. They threw his ass in the county jail for almost a year. He's been out a couple of months now and is back seein' Sue Ann. I told her to dump him like a hot rock, but, like I said, she ain't listening to me these days. That's the guy you need to be checkin' out."

"Was Mr. Merchant aware of the relationship between Vogue and your daughter?"

"I wouldn't know that. You'd have to ask Sue Ann. They seemed to spend enough time together that it wouldn't surprise me if he figured it out."

"One last question, Mrs. Barlow, and I'll let you get back to that filing. Do you happen to know if Merchant is a smoker?"

"Like a chimney—couple of packs a day, I'd guess."

After obtaining Sue Ann's address and pager number, I left the motel and ran into Frank in the parking lot. I didn't have the heart to tell him he was about to catch hell from Lou Ann and should probably expect to sleep on the couch for the next few nights.

Chapter Nine

It was late in the afternoon, and I hadn't heard anything from McConnell. I decided I'd better let her know that we now had a possible perp in our murder investigation. Certainly, John Merchant fit the bill. And I couldn't rule out involvement by Sue Ann Winkler, even though her mother had tried to convince me she was nuts about Vogue and wouldn't have had anything to do with killing him. With Merchant, we had motive, not so with Sue Ann, at least not yet.

Before calling McConnell, I grabbed my cell phone and dialed the office. My assistant, Patti Wheeler, answered on the first ring. "You've been a bad boy again, haven't you? I've been trying to reach you all afternoon."

"I know," I confessed. "I know I should keep my cell turned on. But you know how much I hate the damn thing. So, tell me what's going on."

"Two things. First, Brad Ford must have gone straight to Sloan and complained that you brushed him off when he asked you for information on the status of the investigation earlier today. Sloan wants to talk with you ASAP. From the tone of his voice, I think you should assume that you're going to get your butt chewed."

"Doesn't sound like much fun, but it won't be the first time. What else?"

"The Salt Lake mayor and chief of police are holding a news conference this evening at five to report on the investigation. Apparently, the press has been pestering everybody all day for some details on the case. They want you and Lt. McConnell to brief them on the investigation beforehand and then attend the news conference just in case something comes up. Sloan wants you there, too. You know how paranoid he is about press relations."

"Okay," I said. "Where are they holding the news conference?"

"The mayor's conference room at city hall."

"Have you heard from McConnell this afternoon?"

"Oh yeah, she called a little after one o'clock looking for you. She was at the Medical Examiner's Office for Vogue's autopsy."

"Well, good for her. It could be worse. It could have been me attending that autopsy. I bet she won't be going out tonight for spaghetti."

"Gross. Anybody ever tell you what a macabre sense of humor you have?"

"Only you, dear, only you.

"Patti, will you run Sue Ann Winkler and John Merchant through the Utah Bureau of Criminal Identification and the National Crime Information Center? I want past criminal history on both and any outstanding warrants. And run Merchant through our database and tell me whether he's currently on probation for assault.

"Call me back as soon as you have something."

"Sure. And Sam, keep your phone turned on, will ya?"

"Yeah, yeah."

I decided to call Norm Sloan to update him on the investigation and absorb whatever tongue-lashing he felt inclined to administer. On the second ring, Brad Ford picked up. It was obvious from his condescending tone of voice that he was delighted I had called.

I was transferred to Norm Sloan, who wasted no time on preliminaries. "Mr. Kincaid, so nice of you to favor me with a call.

I hope it wasn't too inconvenient for you. Brad reported earlier in the day that you were too busy to brief him on the status of the investigation. That made me very unhappy. Tell me, do you realize I have someone to whom I'm accountable?"

I'd heard this tone before. When Sloan wanted to chew somebody out, he rarely raised his voice or swore. Instead, he used an acrimonious, caustic tone that left no doubt in the mind of the recipient just how unhappy he was. Since I'm working to improve my tact and diplomacy, not usually two of my strengths, I responded in as contrite a manner as possible, hoping it didn't sound as phony as it felt. "Yes sir, I know you're accountable to a variety of different constituencies."

"Do you, Mr. Kincaid! Well, at least we're making a little progress. I'll just bet you've heard of Orrin Spencer Walker. You know the chap. Governor Walker. The same Governor Walker who wanted me to fire you a couple of years ago over that little disturbance at the prison. You can probably imagine how embarrassed I was this afternoon when he called, and I had to tell him my star investigator hadn't checked in all day, and I didn't know a thing about the investigation. It won't happen again, will it?"

"Absolutely not. You're right. I'm sorry for leaving you hanging out like that. It won't happen again."

"Good," he snapped. "It better not. Now bring me up to speed, and for God's sake, give me some good news. I've had calls today from two television stations, both daily newspapers, and half the radio stations in town."

I spent the next few minutes giving him the good news and the bad. I tried the good news first by explaining that we had identified a likely perp. The bad news outweighed the good news by a long shot—that our suspect might currently be on probation for aggravated assault. It didn't help his disposition any when I told him the suspect's girlfriend had been having a clandestine affair with Vogue for several months, and that this might be the motive for his murder. It really made his day when I explained that Sue Ann Barlow was a nude dancer in a club frequented by Vogue.

"Oh, that's just dandy, Kincaid. What you're telling me is that the Chairman of the Board of Pardons was a sexual pervert, hanging around nude bars with a stripper, and that the guy who killed him is in our offender population. It doesn't get much uglier than that."

"So far, none of this information has been corroborated. We haven't had time to interview Winkler or her boyfriend. We'll get that done as quickly as we can."

"What other kinds of leads are being pursued?"

"The usual focus—family and friends, the local B&E crowd. Terry and I are looking into the possibility that the murder was somehow connected to his employment on the board."

"What about physical evidence?"

"Can't say for sure. The lab crew was still processing the house as well as Vogue's car when we left. They did find a couple of fresh cigarette butts by the side of the garage, but they may or may not be connected to the murder. They'll be checked for latent prints or possibly a DNA sample."

"And the murder weapon?"

"No weapon, no shell casings.

"There is one avenue that I haven't pursued yet."

"Yes. And that would be?" snapped Sloan.

"We haven't put the word out among our inmate snitches. If Levi's murder is in any way connected to somebody in our prison population, inmate informants would probably hear about it."

"I don't want you to do that yet. Let's hold off, for say, twenty-four hours, and see if the investigation produces an arrest. If not, then you can have my blessing for using prison snitches. I know how useful they can be, but at the same time, the last thing we need right now is a prison disturbance on our hands. Only use prison snitches as a last resort."

To his credit, Sloan had learned to choose his battles carefully. He'd been savvy enough to successfully navigate the troubled waters of an angry public that wanted increasingly punitive measures against criminals; a state legislature eager, in the name of re-election, to placate that angry public; and a governor who wanted nothing more than to have his corrections department operate smoothly and quietly without creating political waves for his administration. So far, Sloan had been successful at doing just that.

Sloan concluded our telephone conversation with some words of caution: "You know, Sam, be damned careful with this information about Levi's extracurricular activities. Between Vogue's and Margaret's families, they swing a lot of political clout. If this gets out, the press will have a field day with it. And if the families conclude that we've turned this murder investigation into a character assassination of the dearly departed, they'll close ranks fast and turn up the political heat. In the meantime, let's hope the murder is unrelated to both his fooling around and our offender population, then maybe this will all go away quietly. If it doesn't, keep your head down because the fallout is likely to get real serious. And Sam, if it turns out that you're the guy who exposed the marital infidelity, things could get a lot more difficult for you."

An ugly case growing uglier by the minute, I thought.

Chapter Ten

I still hadn't caught up with McConnell when my cell phone rang. It was Patti calling to give me the low-down on Sue Ann Winkler and John Merchant.

"There are no outstanding warrants on either party at the present time. Winkler has two prior misdemeanor arrests: one for possession of a controlled substance, and the other being a minor in possession of alcohol. That's it for her. Merchant is quite another story. He has two priors for driving under the influence, two for possession of a controlled substance, one for resisting arrest, one for assault on a police officer, one for domestic violence, one for carrying a concealed weapon without a permit, and his most recent scrape with the law resulted in an arrest for attempted murder, plea bargained down to aggravated assault. He is currently on probation in Salt Lake County for three years on the agg assault conviction. His PO's name is Jenny Owens.

"Oh, and one more thing," said Wheeler. "I contacted the juvenile court, and they show a lengthy juvenile record on him starting at age eleven. Lots of drug and alcohol offenses, several property crimes, and two aggravated assaults. Nice guy, huh."

"Yeah, a real Boy Scout. Leave a copy of Merchant's probation file on my desk and take another directly to Sloan's office. And get me Jenny Owens' home telephone number. I need to talk to her before I have a little chat with Merchant."

◇◇◇

I met McConnell in the lobby of City Hall. We were five minutes late for our briefing with the mayor and chief of police, so there was little time to exchange information. On our way upstairs, I filled her in on the developments in the case from my end. We agreed that Winkler and Merchant deserved top billing on our list of suspects, particularly in light of the fact that at the moment, they happened to be our only suspects. We decided to run them down after the press conference.

The news conference was predictable and largely uneventful. The most interesting part of the show turned out to be an angry exchange between Mayor Porter Baldwin and Police Chief Ron Hansen moments before the press conference. The tension between the two was palpable.

The ensuing argument involved two separate but related issues: How much information about the case should be divulged to the assembled media, and who should conduct the news conference.

To no one in particular, Chief Hansen said, "Let's talk about what we should and shouldn't reveal to the press. We should refrain from discussing any leads currently under investigation as well as the possible physical evidence found at Vogue's home. Also, I think we should resist speculating about possible suspects or motives for the murder."

"Well, Chief, that about covers it all," replied the mayor caustically. "Since you'd like to prohibit us from discussing just about everything related to the case, why bother conducting a press conference at all?"

"I think, Mr. Mayor, that we need to conduct the press conference in a way that doesn't compromise our investigation. It's possible that our killer could be following the case through local news sources."

"That's well and good, Chief, but we also have an obligation to inform the press and the public about the steps we're taking to solve a brutal homicide committed against a prominent public official from our community," countered the mayor.

Fortunately, Kate intervened before this rancorous exchange escalated further, and offered a compromise that seemed acceptable to both the mayor and Chief Hansen. "Mayor Baldwin, may I suggest a middle ground position that should satisfy your needs without compromising our investigation."

"Please do," he replied curtly.

"I don't think we have a problem telling the press that physical evidence was found at the crime scene so long as we don't reveal the specifics of what we found. We can explain that crime lab personnel are examining the evidence but that we can't comment further until we receive their report. It's also okay to tell the press that the investigation has produced several leads so long as we avoid revealing the specifics. As for speculating about possible motives or suspects, I strongly concur with Chief Hansen that it would be premature to start down that path so early in the investigation."

Both nodded agreement.

That issue settled, Chief Hansen moved on. "I believe that it would be best if Lieutenant McConnell and I conducted the press conference."

"Sorry, Chief, but I disagree," said the mayor. "Given the nature of this crime and the potential political ramifications for the city, I think it only appropriate that I conduct the news conference, assisted by Lieutenant McConnell."

Not having a ready response, and realizing that the mayor sat higher on the food chain that he did, Hansen reluctantly acceded to the mayor's wishes.

The conference room was larger than I expected, and for this occasion, an elevated stage was placed in the center with a speaker's podium and attached microphone. The U.S. and Utah State flags decorated each end of the stage. All four local TV stations were present, as well as representatives from the city's two daily newspapers and a handful of radio stations.

McConnell and I followed Mayor Baldwin and Chief Hansen onto the stage and assumed a position off to one side. The mayor, with Chief Hansen at his side, read a short prepared statement and then opened the news conference to questions. The questions were standard fare. What evidence did we have? Had the investigation produced a suspect? Was there a motive for the murder? Were we close to making an arrest?

A reporter from the *Salt Lake Tribune* asked the question I'd hoped wouldn't be asked.

"Mayor Baldwin, did Levi Vogue's murder have anything to do with his work as the Chairman of the Utah Board of Pardons and Parole?"

"I can assure you that the police are looking at every possible motive for this horrific crime, but at the moment, it would be premature to comment any further."

At the end of the press conference, the various news teams broke away into different parts of the room and began live feeds directly to their respective evening news programs.

Kate and I attempted to make a hasty exit, hoping to avoid any chance encounters with inquisitive members of the press. Instead, we found ourselves in a second meeting with Chief Hansen and the mayor. I wasn't sure what this meeting was going to be about, but my nose told me it would have the same ripe odor as my unwashed gym socks. And guess what? I was right.

"I want to thank both of you for helping us with the news conference and for all your hard work in this dreadful murder investigation,"said Baldwin. "I want you to understand that I have the utmost confidence in you and in the ability of our police department to bring this case to a successful resolution. However, I feel compelled to share with you a conversation I had just prior to the news conference with the victim's father, Richard Vogue. Mr. Vogue made it very clear that the family expects this case to be solved rapidly, and he openly questioned whether sufficient personnel have been assigned to the investigation. I did my best to placate him, but I need to know how many detectives you have working on the case."

Before Chief Hansen could speak, Kate responded. "Mr. Mayor, as the lead investigator, I can assure you that we have more than adequate resources in place. The makeup of the present homicide team consists of four officers, two from our own department, and two, including Mr. Kincaid, from the Department of Corrections. We have additional personnel available as circumstances dictate."

The look on Mayor Baldwin's face was one of skepticism. He wasn't finished. "Mr. Vogue also wanted us to know that any interviews with members of the immediate family, including Margaret and her two sons, would need to occur in the presence of the family's corporate legal counsel and at a location acceptable to the family." Looking directly at Kate he said, "I hope that won't be too inconvenient."

I could tell this news caught her off-guard. She didn't look happy.

Mayor Baldwin concluded by stating the obvious. Richard Vogue II, as Chairman of the Board and CEO of Vogue Chemicals, an international specialty chemicals firm, was not a man to be trifled with. He was a billionaire with political connections that extended to the White House. What Mayor Baldwin didn't have to say was that under no circumstances would he risk alienating such a powerful ally, especially with the next mayoral campaign a mere nine months away.

Chapter Eleven

We dropped Kate's car off at police headquarters and headed straight for my office to collect the probation file on John Merchant.

"Tell me something, Kate. What was that nonsense about at the press conference between Mayor Baldwin and your boss? It almost sounded personal."

"I don't know for sure. I can tell you what the local rumor mill is saying, though. Chief Hansen has been an extremely popular chief, not only with the department, but with the public as well. I keep hearing that he intends to retire soon and has set his sights on the mayor's office. My guess is that Baldwin probably feels threatened and isn't about to risk playing second fiddle to Chief Hansen in any public arena. And you can't discount the political heat that this case is generating. If either the mayor or the chief got the chance to dis the other publicly on this thing, they'd probably do it."

"That makes sense. And it wouldn't be the first time a popular sheriff or police chief made the leap from public employee to political hack."

We reviewed the probation file and then used my office speaker phone and called Jenny Owens, Merchant's probation officer. Owens was experienced and very competent. I wanted whatever insights she could provide regarding Merchant. We needed to find him fast and eliminate him as a suspect, or somehow tie him to the Vogue murder.

She picked up on the fourth ring. "Owens. How can I help you."

"Jenny, Sam Kincaid. How are you?"

"I'm well, Sam. How about you?"

"I'm good, thanks."

I introduced Kate to Jenny over the speaker phone and explained that we wanted a probation status report and her professional take on John Merchant. I didn't tell her why, but she figured that out very quickly.

"Geez, sounds kind of serious, Sam. This wouldn't have anything to do with the murder of Levi Vogue, would it?"

"It could; and I'll have to ask you to keep it confidential."

"Sure thing. Your timing is rather interesting. He was in to see me the day before yesterday for his scheduled visit. If you looked at his probation agreement, you probably saw that his conditions include completion of both an anger management class and an outpatient alcohol treatment program. I recently called the clinical social workers who are running those treatment groups, and I basically got the same story from both. He's just going through the motions. He shows up, but makes absolutely no effort or contribution in either group. He knows we'll revoke his ass in a heartbeat if he misses any sessions. He reports to me when he's supposed to, makes his monthly victim restitution payment, and maintains sporadic employment, mostly in low paying labor jobs. And that's about it."

"And your personal impressions of him?" I asked.

"My take on him is that he's a very angry man. He reeks of hostility and resentment. I can't tell if it's because I'm a female officer or if it's a more generalized hostility toward any authority figure. I've been giving some thought to transferring him to the caseload of a male officer to see if his disposition improves. He gives me the creeps. And did you get a look at his size? The guy goes six-five and weighs about two-forty. And I'm not talking about a fat boy either. He's built like one of those steroid-using pro wrestlers you see on TV."

"Thanks for the insights, Jenny. It sounds like we'd do well to call out the troops tonight when we go looking for him."

"Absolutely," Owens replied. "Look, Sam, I don't want to pry into what you're doing, but, since he is a part of my caseload, I'd sure like to tag along."

"Fair enough," I replied. "You're welcome to join us. Given what you've just told us, having another agent along makes good sense anyway."

We called Burnham and arranged for him to meet Jenny and establish visual surveillance at Merchant's home. I instructed Burnham not to initiate contact until McConnell and I caught up. I wanted to talk with Sue Ann Winkler prior to confronting Merchant. Other than the killer, Winkler may have been the last person to see Levi Vogue alive.

McConnell and I drove to Sue Ann Winkler's apartment and found nobody home. We then headed over to her place of employment, the Satin & Lace Club.

"Kate, I'd be happy to go in and handle this if you'd rather wait here."

She faintly smiled and said, "Thanks for being so thoughtful, but this isn't my first trip to a strip joint."

"Cop pay is that bad," I quipped.

This time she frowned and said, "Smart ass."

A couple of stout-looking bouncers greeted us at the front door. They were busily checking customer identification and collecting a hefty twenty-dollar cover charge. We were directed toward a long mahogany-colored bar located at the back of the premises, where we met the club manager.

Customers sat singly or in small groups, with waitresses serving soft drinks, and the dancers moving from customer to customer soliciting table dances. The performers on stage appeared to be dancing two-song sets, then rotating to the next stage until they had danced on all three.

McConnell glanced over and caught me looking at a beautiful redhead performing on the stage nearest us. "Guilty as charged."

Feeling a little defensive, I said, "Look, I was only admiring her athleticism. If I were to end up in a position like that, it would take a crow-bar and a trip to the chiropractor to put Humpty-Dumpty back together again."

"Sure," she said with a slightly self-righteous smirk. "Pay attention, and let's get this over with so we can get out of here."

"I am paying attention," I protested weakly.

The club manager escorted Sue Ann Winkler, a.k.a. Jasmine, to our table. She didn't look at all surprised to see us, so I assumed her mother had warned her about our impending visit. Unlike her mother, Sue Ann was petite, five-one or five-two at most, slim, small breasted, with blond hair cut so short it would have looked masculine on just about anyone else. On her, however, it looked just right. All in all, a very cute young woman.

We were escorted to a small business office behind the bar, which offered privacy and a measure of insulation from the loud music.

The manager asked, "Would you like me to stay, Sue Ann?"

"Thanks, Jason, but I'll be just fine."

McConnell explained that we already knew about her relationship with Vogue, but needed her to corroborate some of our information. Kate began by asking, "Describe your relationship with Levi Vogue."

Sounding relaxed and composed, she responded, "I was his friend and his lover."

"How long had you been seeing him?"

"About eight or nine months, I guess."

"How frequently did you spend time together?"

"Once, sometimes twice a week. It always depended on his schedule, whenever he could get away from work or his family."

"Where would the two of you meet?"

"Usually at the motel, which, as you know, my mother owns."

"Is that the only place you got together?"

"Yeah, for the most part. Sometimes we'd go back to my apartment as long as my roommate wasn't around. We didn't do that very often though."

"So you're telling us that most of your contacts with Mr. Vogue occurred at the motel or your apartment. Is that correct?"

"That's what I'm telling you," replied Winkler.

Sue Ann Winkler was proving to be one cool customer. I couldn't tell if someone had coached her beforehand, but so far, she was good. However, her external facade was about to show some cracks as McConnell asked a plethora of increasingly uncomfortable questions.

"Did Mr. Vogue compensate you for your time and companionship?"

"At first he did, but after a while, I told him that I didn't want his money. By then, I was in love with him."

"So, after your initial involvement, he stopped paying you. Is that correct?"

Starting to look a little exasperated, she responded, "Look, he was always buying me little gifts, and on occasion, he paid a bill for me. Now, can't we get on to something a little more important? I don't see what this has to do with Levi's murder."

Kate ignored her protest. "What kind of 'little gifts' and bills are we talking about—cars, boats, jewelry, vacations?"

Winkler forced a smile. "Sorry, no cars, boats, or vacations. Sometimes he bought me jewelry or clothes, and, on occasion, he paid my credit card bills or picked up my rent."

Sensing that the interview was becoming contentious, I interrupted. "Sue Ann, if we're going to find Levi's killer, and I know you want that as badly as we do, we need as much information as possible about his associates and how he lived his life. Unfortunately, that often requires us to ask some seemingly irrelevant and highly personal questions. I know this isn't easy, but please try to bear with us."

That seemed to calm her down, but it didn't last long. "During the times you got together at the motel, was it just the two of you, or was anyone else ever present?" asked Kate.

Winkler hesitated long enough for us to realize that this question had caught her off-guard. She stammered a reply: "I don't think I understand the question. What do you mean?"

"I'm trying to be as delicate as I can, Ms. Winkler, but what we really need to know is whether Mr. Vogue was involved in any unusual sexual practices that might have some connection to his death. Things such as group sex, sadomasochistic sexual behaviors, anything of that sort?"

"Jesus, who the hell have you been talking to?" replied Winkler.

No response from either of us created an awkward period of silence. "Okay," she continued. "So Levi had some unusual sexual interests. I still don't see what this has to do with his murder, but I'll answer the question anyway. Several times, Levi asked if I would bring another dancer back to the motel. He said that he wanted to try a three-way—you know, two women and a guy."

"Did you comply with his request?" McConnell asked.

"Never. I always lied to him about it. I told him that the other dancer wasn't into that sort of thing. That seemed to satisfy him."

"So you never participated with him in any group sex, is that correct?"

"No. I didn't say that. I just wasn't interested in arranging a group scene with another dancer. I didn't want to share him with anybody else. Twice, Levi showed up at the motel with another guy. He introduced him only as Jerry, and that's about all I can tell you about him."

"Can you describe Jerry?" I asked.

"Yeah. He was a white guy, a little older than Levi, probably mid-to-late forties, about six feet to six-one, medium build, short, brown hair."

"Did he have any facial hair or any distinguishing body characteristics such as tattoos or body piercing?"

"Clean shaven. No piercing that I can recall, but he did have a tattoo on his upper arm. It was a small dragon. Red, I think."

"Which arm?"

She thought a moment and then said, "I can't remember."

"Did Levi ever explain to you who this guy was?" I asked.

"He acted funny about that. He seemed real guarded about it. Once, I think he said that he worked with the dude, but I can't be sure."

"So what did the three of you do when you were together?" McConnell asked.

"Well, Levi was kind of a watcher, a voyeur, I guess you'd call it. That's what attracted him to the club in the first place, I think. He liked to watch. He liked to watch me masturbate. With this Jerry, it was the same thing. Levi got off watching me do the guy. Once, I did them both at the same time, but mostly he liked to watch me get him off. I finally told him I didn't want to do it anymore so he stopped bringing the guy around. He didn't like it, but he never brought the dude back."

"So, you never saw this Jerry again, is that right?"

"Yeah, that's right."

"Just a few more questions, Ms. Winkler, and we'll be finished," said Kate. "When and where was the last time you saw Levi alive?"

"I saw Levi last night at the motel. I had the night off, and his wife was out of town, so we agreed to meet at six-thirty. He actually didn't get there until a little after seven. He'd stopped at a Mexican restaurant we like and brought some takeout dinner for us."

"Which Mexican restaurant?"

"Rosa's Cantina on Ft. Union Boulevard."

"Did he act nervous or upset about anything? Was he behaving in a normal way?"

"If he was upset about anything, I sure didn't notice it. I've thought about that a lot today, and last night seemed just like any other time we've been together. We talked, ate dinner, and then had great sex. We watched TV in bed together until I fell asleep. I woke up about midnight and Levi was gone. I didn't know anything had happened to him until one of my girlfriends called. She heard about it on the news this morning."

"Do you have any idea who might have killed him?" Kate asked.

"None whatsoever," replied Winkler.

"Tell us about your relationship with John Merchant. Is he still your boyfriend? Are you still seeing him?"

The look of surprise on her face told us that she wasn't expecting to be asked about John Merchant. "You must've been talking with Mommy Dearest. She never did like Johnny much. As to your questions, the answers are no and no. He's not my boyfriend any longer, and I quit going out with him three or four months ago."

"Was he aware of your ongoing relationship with the victim?" I asked.

"Look, if you're suggesting that Johnny had something to do with Levi's murder, I don't think so. It just isn't his style. Johnny's possessive and insecure, but he wouldn't kill anybody."

"Is that so, Ms. Winkler? Isn't it true that John Merchant has quite a temper? In fact, hasn't he hit you before? Isn't it also true that Merchant is on probation with the Corrections Department for almost beating a guy to death here at the club because he thought the guy was flirting with you?"

"Okay, so he's got a temper. That doesn't make him a killer. He never hit me. If Mommy Dearest told you that, she's a liar. Johnny is fucked up in a lot of ways, but I'm telling you, he's no killer. As to whether he knew about my relationship with Levi, how would I know? I sure didn't tell him. But sometimes I got the feeling he was following me, almost like he was stalking me. A couple of times he'd just show up unannounced at my apartment, or be waiting in the club parking lot when I got off work. I told him to stay away, but he just ignored me."

"Ok, Ms. Winkler, just one more question. Is John Merchant a smoker?"

"Yeah, probably a pack a day. Why?"

"Which brand does he smoke?"

"He'll smoke any damn brand he can get his hands on—whatever he can find on the cheap or bum from somebody."

I gave Winkler a business card and encouraged her to call if she thought of anything else.

We immediately headed back to meet Owens and Burnham, who were pulling surveillance duty at our suspect's home. It was time to roust John Merchant and really lean on him. This was a guy with motive, opportunity, and means. We felt that Winkler had told us the truth about most things, but not about her relationship with John Merchant. On a ten-point defensiveness scale, Winkler scored an eleven the moment Kate brought John Merchant's name into the discussion. She was still involved with him. We felt certain of that. As for us, we were about to find out just how bad Big Bad John really was.

Chapter Twelve

The Satin & Lace Club was located about ten minutes from John Merchant's home. I radioed Burnham and Owens to find out if anything was happening at the house. Burnham reported that everything appeared quiet with no sign of our suspect or his car.

As McConnell and I got close to Merchant's home, my radio cracked and Owens said, "The suspect has just arrived home and appears to be in a real hurry. He just jumped the curb and drove across the front lawn. What's your ETA?"

"We're just a couple of minutes away," I replied. "I'll bet somebody tipped him, and I've got a pretty good idea who. Let's get on him quickly. There's probably something in that house that he doesn't want us to see."

"Roger that," replied Owens. "We're gonna follow him right through the front door. There's an alley running north and south behind the house. You guys come in that way and cover the back. That okay?"

"Sounds good. We're about there. Be careful with this guy."

We turned into the alley and spit loose gravel as we accelerated between homes. Before I could bring the car to a full stop, McConnell bailed out and broke into a full sprint crossing into Merchant's back yard. I cursed, jumped out, and followed her. The only place of concealment was a large maple tree located about twenty-five yards from the back door. Doing what I thought was prudent, I sought cover behind the tree. I yelled at Kate to stop. She either didn't hear or chose to ignore me. She never broke stride. When she was perhaps fifteen feet from the back door, it suddenly opened, and Merchant launched himself off the porch, gun in hand. Neither person had any time to react. Merchant hit McConnell head on, lifting her three feet off the ground, and dumping her unceremoniously on her backside. She managed to roll away, but lost her weapon in the process. He stopped suddenly and made a half turn back toward her. At that moment, I emerged from cover in a low, combat position yelling for him to drop the weapon. He turned in one motion and raised the handgun. I fired once, striking him in the upper right shoulder. He dropped like a stone.

The next couple of hours were pandemonium. Salt Lake City P.D. responded with a shooting team, Internal Affairs officers, a crime scene unit, and a Department media spokesperson. The Department of Corrections sent the head of Field Operations and a deputy director. TV and print journalists descended on the place like locusts in a corn field. As for Kate, other than having the wind knocked out of her, sore ribs, and a badly bruised ego, she was fine.

◇◇◇

John Merchant was another story. He had lost a lot of blood by the time he was loaded aboard the life-flight helicopter and flown to the University of Utah Medical Center. I sent Terry with him in case he said anything about this incident or the murder of Levi Vogue. He didn't.

For us, the bad news didn't end there. The subsequent search of his home and car produced nothing that would connect him to the murder. Our best hope had been that the search would yield the murder weapon. What we did find was a refrigerator full of beer, more than a kilogram of marijuana, weighing scales, and plastic baggies—all the trappings of a small-time dope dealer. The weapon was a twenty-five caliber Beretta with the serial number filed off. Assuming he survived, Merchant was facing several new felony charges, including illegal possession of a firearm by a convicted felon, multiple drug counts, and assault on a police officer. He'd also made himself a great candidate for having his probation revoked. Jenny Owens was anxious to go to work on that.

As for me, I wasn't doing so well. I'd been in this business for seventeen years, and I'd never shot anyone before. After the initial rush of adrenaline, reality was setting in. The incident unfolded in a flash. I'd shot someone. That person was fighting for his life and might die. How would I feel if that happened?

It had been less than twenty-four hours since Levi Vogue had been killed. We had hoped John Merchant was the investigative lead that would break the case. Without evidence from the search linking him to the murder, I was less convinced that we had the right guy. We needed to determine his whereabouts at the time of the murder, and we needed to do it quickly.

Chapter Thirteen

Kate and I spent the next two hours undergoing tape-recorded interviews with the Salt Lake City P.D. shooting team. In addition, I had the dubious distinction of being interviewed for a second time by a high-ranking representative from the Executive Director's Office.

Sloan had dispatched his administrative law judge, Rachel Rivers-Blakely, to do the honors. Rivers-Blakely was a tough but fair-minded attorney who had carved out a reputation while working for the Utah State Attorney General's Office. She would recommend to Sloan whether my actions in the apprehension of John Merchant were consistent with the department's use-of-force policy.

Her primary responsibility in the Department of Corrections was to advise Sloan in matters relating to employee discipline and inmate grievances. In short, her job was to help keep Sloan's ass out of a sling by limiting his exposure to civil suits from either disgruntled employees or unhappy prison inmates—and the department had plenty of both.

At the conclusion of the interview, Rivers-Blakely informed me that I was being temporarily placed on administrative leave with pay, pending reviews by the Salt Lake County Attorney's Office and by Sloan.

Shooting incidents always result in two independent reviews: one by the department for policy violations, and another by the prosecuting attorney's office, to determine whether State criminal laws had been violated. The potential consequences are serious. If criminal charges were filed against me, it would probably be career-ending, even if I wasn't convicted.

As I left police headquarters, McConnell caught up with me. She wanted to talk. We agreed to meet at a bar located several blocks from the police station. I arrived a couple of minutes ahead of her. I ordered a cup of black coffee for Kate and a Bailey's Irish Cream and coffee for me.

Kate arrived, and after a couple minutes of awkward conversation, finally got around to telling me what was bothering her. In a word, it was guilt.

"Sam, I want to thank you and offer an apology."

"No apology necessary."

"I'm afraid I disagree. I do owe you an apology," she said. "You're in this mess because of something I did. If I hadn't taken off on you when we arrived at Merchant's home, the shooting episode probably wouldn't have happened. I should have taken cover, rather than putting myself in a place where you had to come to the rescue. And by the way, thanks for saving my tail. Once I hit the ground, I remember two things distinctly. The first was the sensation of feeling like I'd been hit by a train, and the second was seeing Merchant stop and point the gun at me. When you yelled and came out into the open, he turned to face you. That distraction may have saved my life."

"Look, Kate. The shooting probably would have happened whether you stayed with me or not. Nobody is responsible for what happened to John Merchant except John Merchant. There's no need to blame yourself. He had the gun. He had the dope. He decided to make a fight of it. And I think when the smoke finally clears, the shooting will be ruled lawful, and we'll both be back to work. Besides, I love the notion of having a beautiful woman feeling indebted to me."

I was talking with more confidence than I actually felt. I subscribe to the old saying that anything that can go wrong, probably will. Pessimism runs deep in my blood.

She smiled. "Yeah, well, don't make a habit out of it. It can be downright dangerous." Our conversation drifted away from work and into our personal lives. "Sorry to hear about your divorce. I'm sure the adjustment must be emotionally painful. How are you doing?"

"Where did you hear about my divorce?"

"Take a guess. The police rumor mill, where else?"

"I'm actually doing okay, all things considered. Mostly, I don't have time to sit around feeling sorry for myself, which is a good thing. I've got an eight-year-old daughter to raise. She really misses her mom, and I know she doesn't fully understand why it happened. Between this job and playing Mr. Mom, I don't have much time to sort through my own issues."

"I knew you had a child, but I had no idea you had custody. How did that happen?"

So I gave her the lowdown, trying carefully not to sound like a whining martyr or an angry, blameful ex-husband. I wondered, though, why it mattered. But somehow, I felt like it did.

The conversation had started to make me uncomfortable, so I attempted to change the subject. I discovered, however, that McConnell was not only attractive and engaging, but persistent as well. She wasn't having any of it.

"Have you been dating since the divorce?"

"Not really," I said. "Actually, friends have tried to set me up a couple of times, but it hasn't felt right, so I just don't do it. I figure when the time is right, I'll know it. Until then, I'm staying on the sidelines. Besides, I don't have a lot of leisure time. When I'm not working, I try to spend as much time with Sara as I can."

"Sounds to me like you've got your priorities straight."

"I hope so. Since you brought the subject up, I haven't heard anything about you in the police rumor mill."

"That's simple," she said. "I just refuse to date people in the police fraternity. Cops are the worst kind of gossips. You know that. Sleep with one and it's apt to be all over the department."

She was right about that. Somehow Kate had managed to keep her private life private—a nearly impossible feat.

"Since you refuse to date inside the police fraternity, how is it that I saw you at a Jazz game last spring with Tom Stoddard from the D.A.'s Office?"

She smiled and said, "You are the observant one. Tom has been my one and only exception to the rule. I've been seeing him on and off now for almost two years. We try to keep it very low-key. The truth is that I don't date much at all. The career has always come first. But I must admit to having moments lately where I wonder whether putting career over my personal life is such a good decision."

"Tom probably has some feelings about that."

"Tom would like us to be a lot more serious, but that's not going to happen, at least not now."

Even with the dose of caffeine, sheer exhaustion finally took over. We left the bar just ahead of closing. As we parted, Kate turned and said, "Hey, Sam, don't plan on an extended vacation sitting at home on your backside. It's not going to happen."

Chapter Fourteen

By the time I made it home, it was after two. I parked in the driveway so I didn't have to raise the garage door and risk waking Sara and Aunt June. I entered quietly through the front door and tip-toed into the kitchen.

The light above the stove was on, and I found a note from Aunt June reminding me that Sara's parent-teacher conference was scheduled for this morning at seven-thirty. She wanted to know if she needed to go in my place. Aside from the early morning hour, the time was actually good since I had just been placed on administrative leave.

Despite my attempt to be quiet, Aunt June appeared in the kitchen wondering if everything was okay. I briefly recounted the events of the past twenty-four hours, including the shooting of John Merchant and my subsequent suspension from duty. She had heard about the shooting on the ten o'clock news and hoped I wasn't involved. The press hadn't released any names.

"I'm real sorry you had to shoot that man. It must make you feel just awful," she said. "But I know one thing. If there had been any other way of handling the situation, you would have taken it. You just be patient. In the end, you'll be exonerated and back to work sooner than you think. I'll say a little prayer for you and the fellow you had to shoot."

At six a.m., I awoke with a start to find a pair of small, very cold feet pressed against my bare leg. Sara had slipped out of her room and into mine, something she does with some regularity.

"Wake up, Daddy, you're snoring again," she said, grinning.

"The only person who snores in this family is lying beside me right now," I replied with as much indignation as I could muster. "In fact, you snore so loud sometimes, you sound just like the Lion King."

"I do not," she said with a giggle.

After a few minutes of light bantering and plenty of tickles, we agreed to get dressed and go out to breakfast before her parent-teacher conference. Sara is a very social and very bright little girl. If it's true that much of who we are is a product of our genetic makeup, then Sara was lucky to get her mom's propensity for good grades, because she certainly didn't get it from me.

By the time we finished breakfast and made it to school, I was just in time for my appointment with her teacher. Her grades were among the best in the class. She had, however, received an unsatisfactory mark for citizenship, which reflected a growing tendency to be the class chatter-box. We would have to work on that.

I spent the remainder of the morning restlessly loafing around the house wondering how long it would be before my fate was decided. At twelve-thirty the phone rang. It was Burnham calling from the University of Utah Hospital. It seemed that John Merchant had come out of surgery and was much improved. After a few hours in intensive care, he was moved into a regular room with the added luxury of twenty-four-hour security at his door. And he was singing like Placido Domingo at the Boston Pops.

"Guess what, Sam? No sooner had this asswipe come out from under the anesthetic when he demanded to talk with Jenny Owens. She called me right away and I met her here. The tough guy is in there right now babbling like an idiot. You'd think Owens was his mother instead of his PO. He alternates between wanting to discuss the murder and demanding that we cut him a deal for his cooperation. I think he's scared shitless that he'll end up at the prison hooked up with some inmate, bigger and tougher than he is, shoving something up his candy ass every night."

"I'm not surprised that he wants to cut a deal. He's looking at several new felony charges and a certain probation revocation. That gives us some serious leverage. I hope she remembered to Mirandize him before she started asking questions," I said.

"No problem. She took care of that first thing," said Burnham.

"What did he have to say?"

"That's the bad news. Merchant denied any involvement in or knowledge of the murder. He claimed not to have even known about Vogue's relationship with Sue Ann. He maintained that Winkler makes just about as much money turning tricks for customers from the club as she does from dancing. And get this little tidbit. It seems that Sue Ann is in business with her mother. Most of the trick activity occurs at the motel with Mom getting a percentage of the action. The old broad even pulls a few tricks herself with selected clients," said Burnham.

"Does he have an alibi?"

"We're checking that out right now. He claims he spent the evening of the murder at the home of his brother in Midvale. He says they had dinner, drank a couple of beers, and shot pool all evening. We ran a check on the brother. He's clean. No prior record, gainfully employed, married with a couple of kids. We passed the alibi information along to McConnell, and she's got somebody from her team trying to contact the brother for verification."

It was now clear to me that if Merchant's alibi checked out, our investigation would be back at square one. A confirmed alibi would eliminate him as a suspect.

I hadn't been off the phone long when it rang again. Caller ID provided me with a number I instantly recognized. It was Sloan calling from the private line in his executive office suite.

"Hi, Sam. I've got good news and bad. Which would you like first?"

"Let's have the bad."

Sloan actually seemed to be enjoying this moment of quiet torment. "Well, the bad news isn't really all that bad," he said after a lengthy pause. "You have an appointment tomorrow morning at nine with Dr. Marilyn Hastings from the Employee Assistance Program. And don't waste your breath complaining, because it won't do you any good. Any employee involved in a shooting incident goes straight to counseling, no exceptions. And Kincaid, I know your tendency to disparage department policy and procedure, but don't trifle with me on this one. If the department shrink gives me any indication you're not being cooperative, I will suspend you from duty immediately. Am I making myself clear?"

"Absolutely. I assume this means I'm back on the job."

"That's the good news. I received a call from the Salt Lake County Attorney's Office late this morning advising me that they have concluded last night's shooting was justified, and that no criminal charges will be filed against you. Somebody from Salt Lake City P.D. must want you back on the case pretty bad. I don't think I've ever seen a deadly force case reviewed so quickly.

"Also, my executive management team, after consulting with the department's administrative law judge, has concluded that your actions did not violate department policy on the use of deadly force. I concurred with their conclusion.

"To answer your question, yes, you're reinstated and may return to work at once. Understand, however, that I'm bending the rules here a little. Technically, I shouldn't let you go back to work until the department shrink gives you clearance. I'll assume this is just a formality so long as you do your part."

We concluded our conversation with Sloan reminding me that while the apprehension of a probation violator was important, it brought us no closer to finding Levi Vogue's killer.

Chapter Fifteen

Late in the afternoon, I was summoned to a meeting at police headquarters for a status report on the investigation. McConnell had temporarily commandeered a small conference room near the office of the Captain of Detectives. The walls were adorned with flip-chart paper identifying investigative leads that had been assigned to each member of the team.

Besides McConnell and me, Burnham from my office and Vince Turner were there. By fate and circumstance, the four of us had become, at least informally, the Vogue homicide investigation team. Also in attendance, much to my chagrin, were Captain Hyrum Locke, head of the Detective Bureau, and Deputy Chief of Police Clarence Puffer.

Puffer was a fifty-something career bureaucrat with a largely unremarkable career that had spanned more than twenty-seven years. He was a likable man of modest abilities whose career had flourished by making few enemies, avoiding controversy, and dodging difficult decisions whenever possible. The best thing I could say about him was that while he wouldn't be much help, neither would he get in the way. I wish I could have said the same about Captain Hyrum Locke.

Locke wasn't particularly popular with his own subordinates in the Detective Bureau because of his tendency to seize the spotlight and assume credit for the accomplishments of others. Also, he'd spent several years commanding the Department's

Internal Affairs unit, not an assignment that endeared you to your fellow officers. I decided to keep one eye on the ball and the other on Locke.

"You should all know that Mayor Baldwin has received a second telephone call from Richard Vogue reiterating his demand for a rapid resolution to the investigation," said Locke. "The mayor is under extreme pressure from the Vogue family. It has also been suggested that I should assume direct command over the investigation. I've decided not to do that, at least for the time being. I do, however, intend to work more closely with Kate from here on out."

Translated, that meant Locke would remain far enough in the background to distance himself from blame if the case went unsolved, yet close enough to seize the spotlight from Kate in the event an arrest was made. The guy was smart and calculating, I had to give him that.

Kate's nonverbal demeanor suggested that she was irritated with Locke's interference, but had to be careful how she responded. "Hyrum, it's a little early to press the panic button. The investigation is still less than forty-eight hours old and we have a variety of solid leads."

As I guessed, Puffer appeared content to sit quietly absorbing as many details about the investigation as possible. He'd probably been asked to serve as a conduit of information directly to Chief Hansen and indirectly to Mayor Baldwin. Before Locke could respond, Puffer looked up from the legal pad he was scribbling notes on and asked, "So what's the status of our main subject, this John Merchant fellow?"

"Unfortunately, I personally checked his alibi and it looks solid. If the cigarette butts we found at the scene provide a DNA sample or latent prints, we'll compare it to Merchant's. In the meantime, he's not going anywhere. When he's well enough, he'll be transferred from the hospital to the Salt Lake County Jail. He's looking at several new felony charges and an impending probation revocation hearing. But right now, I'd have to say it doesn't look promising," said Kate.

"I should say not," said Puffer. "Any other persons of interest?"

"Nope, not at the moment."

"Vince, what have you got for us?" asked Locke.

"I got a warrant for Vogue's Lexus, which we had towed to the police impound lot. The lab guys found a variety of latent prints but most of them belonged to Vogue. Winkler's prints were also found, but that's no surprise. There were other unidentified prints lifted from both the exterior and interior of the vehicle. Some of them will probably belong to other members of the family. I did find a plastic bag containing a half dozen adult video tapes, all of them run-of-the-mill commercial hardcore except one. The amateur tape featured Winkler performing alone and then with our victim doing the horizontal mamba," said Turner.

That revelation raised a few eyebrows, including my own. "I wonder if anyone else has a copy of that tape. Sue Ann neglected to tell us about that little detail when we spoke with her. Maybe somebody was trying to blackmail him," I said.

"Worth looking into," said Locke.

Turner continued. "I'm also working with our burglary dicks to try to identify anyone from the local B&E crowd using the same modus operandi—so far, nothing."

"Thanks, Vince. Kate, what have you got for us?"

"The autopsy results confirmed that the time of death was between eleven and eleven-thirty p.m. The contents of his stomach included a partially digested Mexican dinner, which was consistent with the statement given to us by Sue Ann regarding their meal at the Starlite Motel.

"The Medical Examiner estimated Vogue was shot from a distance of ten to twenty feet with some type of shotgun. The pellet pattern in the chest wound was dispersed, and the angle of the shot suggested the killer was most likely directly in front of Vogue, not firing from above or below."

"And the CSI team did or did not find any shell casings?" asked Puffer.

"We didn't find shell casings and the shotgun was discharged twice," said Kate. "The chest wound produced serious damage to the heart and would have been fatal within minutes without the second shot to the head. The head shot was delivered point blank with the victim lying prone. Traces of powder burns found on the skin under the chin suggested that the barrel of the shotgun had been placed directly against the flesh."

Burnham and I then explained the process we would follow in attempting to connect Vogue's murder to his work on the parole board.

After that, Puffer and Locke stood, signaling an end to our meeting. "Thanks for the update, but, at the moment, it looks like you really don't have shit," said Puffer.

As soon as I got back on the street, my cell phone rang. It was Patti.

"Sam, we received a phone call about an hour ago that I thought you might be interested in. It might be nothing, but the call was in relation to the Vogue investigation."

"You've got my undivided attention. Tell me more."

"The caller was an elderly-sounding man who lives in the Avenues about three blocks from the victim's home. He belongs to a Neighborhood Watch group, and he wants to report a strange vehicle parked in front of his home around the time of the murder."

Realizing that I was probably embarking on a wild-goose chase, I got his name and address and drove to his home. Baxter Shaw turned out to be a charming, southern transplant, in his early seventies, who still retained a trace of his Southern accent.

I asked him about the vehicle he had observed parked near his home on the night of the Vogue murder.

"Well, it's probably nothing," he said. "I couldn't make up my mind whether to report it or not. But after watching the local news and hearing about that awful murder here in the neighborhood, I thought it best to call someone. I belong to a

Neighborhood Watch group, so I try to pay attention to anything going on around here that seems out of the ordinary.

"On the night Mr. Vogue was killed, I looked out my front living-room window and saw a light-colored Ford Escort parked across the street one house down from mine. I'd never seen it before. I'm quite sure it doesn't belong to anyone living here in the neighborhood."

"Do you recall what time it was when you first saw the vehicle?"

"Sure do," he replied. "It was about five minutes before the ten o'clock news started. You see, I watch the ten o'clock news on KSL every night, and then go to bed promptly at ten-thirty after saying my evening prayers. I've been following the same routine for years."

"Did you see anyone in or around the vehicle?"

"Oh, no," he said. "I would have called the police immediately had I seen anybody out there. That's what we're supposed to do, you know."

"You didn't by chance happen to get a license plate number, did you?"

"As a matter of fact, I did," he replied, handing me a folded cocktail napkin with Utah license plate number 184HBC printed on it in a shaky hand. "The car was still parked there when the news ended at ten-thirty, so I walked outside right before I went to bed and jotted down the license plate number. Did I do the right thing?"

"You sure did. This could turn out to be very important."

I was anxious to leave so I could run a registration check on the plate, but I could tell Baxter Shaw was in no hurry to rush me out the door. He seemed lonely. He told that he'd moved to Salt Lake City sixteen years ago from Savannah, Georgia, after the death of his first wife. He married a divorced Mormon woman and converted to the LDS faith. His second wife had passed away eighteen months ago. He confessed that after his wife died, he returned to two old vices—an evening glass of wine and an occasional smoke with the pipe.

I liked Baxter Shaw. I wondered if Aunt June might like him as well. I decided to give some serious thought to playing matchmaker.

Chapter Sixteen

The license plate number Shaw had provided belonged to a 1995 Ford Escort. The registered owner was Charles Watts, a name that sounded vaguely familiar. The registration showed a Salt Lake City post-office box for an address.

I called the duty probation officer and requested a record check on Charles Watts. Moments later, I had an answer. Charles Watts, alias Chuck Waters, alias Slick Watts, was definitely one of ours. A local thug with a long criminal history, Watts had recently served a five-year sentence in the state prison on an aggravated robbery beef. He had been released from parole after undergoing community supervision for almost three years. I couldn't recall having had any contact with him either as an inmate or a parolee.

I decided to dig a little deeper into Watts' background before calling Kate. I wondered which parole board member had heard his case. Was it Levi Vogue? Was there any record of his having made threats against Vogue or other members of the parole board? What kind of an inmate had he been in prison? How had he performed on parole?

Department records confirmed that Watts' name didn't appear in the database of offenders who had threatened members of the parole board. The records did, however, portray a troubled history.

At twenty-eight, he had spent almost nine years of his life behind bars. He had served over two years in juvenile prison on two separate commitments. As an adult, he was in and out of county jail and prison several times for a variety of offenses, including his five years on the aggravated robbery conviction. What piqued my interest most was that Vogue had handled his parole grant hearing.

His prison caseworker described him as a model inmate. He worked part-time as a food handler in one of the prison dining facilities, finished his GED, and completed a substance abuse treatment program. His prison jacket was full of accolades from staff, and he had no record of disciplinary problems. After his release, the parole department supervised him for nearly three years without incident.

Seldom one to make the politically correct move, I decided, with a slight nudge from Burnham, to check in with Norm Sloan as previously directed. As much as it pained me, I first called Brad Ford, hoping he might be gone for the day or away from his phone. My good fortune held. He didn't pick up and the call kicked into his voice mail.

"Brad, this is Sam. I was just trying to touch base and let you know where things stand. I'll try the old man on his cell."

Sloan answered on the second ring. "I've got good news and bad. Which would you like first?"

"Let's start with the bad. Then it can only get better."

"Salt Lake P.D. eliminated Merchant as a suspect. His alibi checked out. He's an asshole, but in this case, he's the wrong asshole."

"And the good news?"

"We may have another suspect." I then told him about the information provided by Baxter Shaw and the subsequent identification of Charles Watts as a possible perp.

"You consider that good news, Kincaid. Can't you help Salt Lake P.D. find a homicide suspect *outside* our offender population?"

"Sorry about that, boss. It's possible that this may turn out to be another dead end like John Merchant."

"Where do you go from here?"

"I need to inform Salt Lake City P.D. Homicide. I haven't said anything to them yet. As for Watts, I think we start digging into his whereabouts at the time of the murder, and see where that takes us. So far, we don't have anybody who can place him near the scene."

"All right. Let me know what develops. If you can't reach me, get hold of Ford. Make sure I have a complete copy of Watts' file on my desk first thing in the morning. And Sam, I'm sure you haven't forgotten your appointment tomorrow morning with Marilyn Hastings from the Employee Assistance Program. She's expecting you."

"I can hardly wait.

"I'll keep you informed as things develop with Watts."

"See that you do," he said, and the line went dead.

Burnham and I took the department's last known address for Watts and drove to the residence. It was a new apartment complex located in an older part of Salt Lake City. The apartment manager told us that Watts had vacated the place one month prior and had left no forwarding address.

From there, we tried his last known place of employment, an all-night restaurant chain near downtown. We learned that he'd quit that job about the same time he moved out of the apartment. He had worked as a cook on the swing shift. The restaurant manager described him as a reliable employee who kept to himself. She didn't have a forwarding address, but she gave us a home telephone number that turned out to be disconnected.

Burnham telephoned an old friend employed by Utah Power. Within minutes, we were rewarded with a return call that provided us with an address in West Valley City where Watts was listed as the individual paying the utility bill.

Watts lived on one side of a brown brick duplex located on a street filled with identical brown brick duplexes. The home looked empty. There were no vehicles parked in the driveway and no lights were on. I walked quietly onto the front porch, opened the mail box, and found several pieces of junk mail and a utility bill addressed to Watts.

After returning to the office, I was about to call Kate and tell her about Watts when my phone rang. It was McConnell calling to report a major breakthrough in the case.

Chapter Seventeen

We had just gotten lucky. Kate received a phone call from the crime laboratory. While processing the cigarette butts found at Vogue's home, a lab technician concluded that neither contained a DNA sample; however, one of them yielded a comparable right-index-finger latent print. A subsequent search through the Automated Fingerprint Identification System, AFIS, for short, produced a list of six possible matches.

"In order to narrow this down, we've got to get our hands on all six original fingerprint cards, and then have a certified examiner make the match," said Kate. "As it stands, three of the possibles are individuals we've arrested, so we already have those fingerprint cards. We have to get the other three directly from the Utah Bureau of Criminal Identification. They were busted by other Utah police agencies. I've got Vince running those down right now."

"Maybe we can narrow that list and save everybody time and effort."

"Okay. You've got my undivided attention. How do you propose we do that?"

"Does the name Charles Watts appear on the list of possible matches?"

There was a long pause before she answered. "Sure does. You obviously know something I don't. Do fill me in."

I spent the next few minutes explaining what I'd learned from Baxter Shaw as well as the effort Burnham and I had made in our attempt to locate Watts. We decided that Terry and I should return to Watts' home and establish visual surveillance while McConnell prepared a search warrant. Besides a witness who could place Watts' vehicle in the vicinity of the murder at about the time the killing occurred, we now had a single fingerprint that placed Watts at the victim's home. With a little luck, a search of the home might turn up additional evidence linking him to the murder.

We settled down for what could be a lengthy wait.

By the time McConnell and Turner caught up with us at a location a couple of blocks from Watts' home, three hours had passed. There was still no sign of Watts. Kate had brought Tom Stoddard from the Salt Lake County Attorney's Office to assist. She seemed somehow uncomfortable with his presence. I couldn't tell whether something had happened between them to create the strain, or whether McConnell was uncomfortable because she knew that I knew about their ongoing relationship. As for me, I had to admit his presence created just a tinge of something—insecurity or jealousy perhaps, feelings I'd just as soon not have, those ugly emotions best kept locked in a jar on a shelf somewhere.

Stoddard was a career prosecutor. He joined the Salt Lake County Attorney's Office right out of law school. Over time, he developed a reputation as a fair, but tough-minded prosecutor. Now he was one of just a handful of senior deputies who prosecuted the most serious felony offenses. He would be the logical choice to prosecute this one.

Executing the search warrant came off without a hitch. Turner found an unsecured window at the side of the duplex leading into one of the bedrooms. He popped the screen off and was inside in seconds. The duplex was small with everything on one level. The furnishings looked cheap, but relatively new, like maybe they had come from a furniture rental company.

We donned latex gloves and divided into two teams. Stoddard kept his distance and observed. We searched the place systematically with one team following the other from room to room. McConnell and I took the lead, while Burnham and Turner followed.

We began in the kitchen. While I had my nose buried in a rank-smelling refrigerator, Kate examined a stack of mostly junk mail left on top of a small dining table.

Within seconds, she said, "Take a look at this, Sam."

"Find something interesting?"

She didn't answer immediately. She was reading hand-written notes from a lined yellow pad. "These notes contain dates, times, and places, that trace the movements of Vogue. They detail his comings-and-goings from home and the parole board office."

I was reading over her shoulder. "Jesus. Look at that," I said, pointing to the last entry on the page. "It appears Watts had even tracked Vogue to the Starlite Motel. Levi didn't realize it, but he was being stalked in the days leading to his murder."

"That's what it looks like," said Kate. She photographed the notes and placed them in an evidence bag.

Minutes later, while she rummaged through a dresser drawer full of socks and underwear, Kate found something else. "Look at this, Sam. Two boxes of twelve gauge shotgun shells. One hasn't been opened, but the other has. Five shells are missing."

"Mr. Watts now has something else to explain," I said. "Wouldn't it be nice if the shotgun turns up as well."

It didn't.

We left a copy of the warrant in the house as well as an inventory record of the property we had seized.

Turning to Stoddard, Kate said, "I think it's time we get an arrest warrant for Mr. Watts."

Stoddard agreed. "One count of capital murder sounds about right. I'd be happy to take this case to a jury with the existing evidence. The case is largely circumstantial, but it's a strong one nonetheless. I've seen juries convict on less. If you want to drive a nail in the coffin, pick him up, break him down, and get a confession from the SOB."

"Sounds like a plan," replied Kate. "I'll put the arrest warrant affidavit together. We'll get out a statewide alert, and I'll see that the warrant gets entered into the National Crime Information Center and the Utah system."

"I'll tell you what you'd better do right now, and that's get a surveillance team back to the house," said Burnham. "Assuming he's around, the moment dip shit opens his front door, he's gonna see the warrant and property inventory report. He'll know the party's over and then watch him run. He'll likely end up on the next bus to Tijuana."

As the junior member of the team, Turner found himself elected to pull the first watch on Watts' home. Kate left her vehicle with Turner. She and Stoddard hitched a ride back with Burnham and me to police headquarters. The ride was filled with small talk that seemed awkward and stilted, and mercifully, finally gave way to complete silence.

After unloading my passengers, the ride home gave me time to think. I should have been feeling a sense of relief. We were poised to make an important bust in a high-visibility crime that had put all of us in a pressure cooker. But something didn't feel right to me, and I couldn't put my finger on it. It all seemed to fit. We'd developed a solid suspect who possessed a long and serious criminal history. He had motive. He had opportunity. And we had evidence. Oh, how we had evidence. Most of it was circumstantial, but there was plenty of it. Individually, the pieces of evidence were damaging enough. When looked at collectively, it would be a tough case to defend and an easy one to prosecute.

So why was I still having this nagging doubt? It was a neat case wrapped in a pretty box with a silver bow on it. But was it too neat? Maybe.

As the first hint of orange sky touched the eastern horizon, the late model Ford Taurus turned slowly on to Lariat Circle. The driver shut off the headlights and rolled the vehicle to a stop a short distance from Sam Kincaid's home.

The passenger reached into her purse and removed a pack of Marlboros and a well-traveled Bic pen. She cracked the window and lit a cigarette. The driver sipped lukewarm coffee from a Styrofoam cup. Despite the early morning chill, he lowered the driver's side window.

"You gotta smoke that shit in here?" he asked irritably.

"Bite me."

At six-twenty, the porch light came on, and an elderly woman wearing a pink terrycloth bathrobe stepped out and retrieved a newspaper.

"I thought you said Kincaid lived by himself with a young kid."

"That's the scuttlebutt. Supposedly, both his parents were killed in an accident a couple of years ago, and then he got divorced," she replied.

"Yeah, then who the fuck is the old lady?"

"How the hell should I know—maybe a visiting relative or a live-in nanny? What the fuck difference does it make?"

"It might make a difference if we have to come back to this house at some point and take care of business."

"I don't see what you're worried about. We can take care of three just as easily as two."

At six-forty, the garage door opened and a silver, late model Jeep Cherokee backed into the street and left.

"There goes Kincaid," he said. "The boy likes to get an early start. What's the old saying—early bird catches the worm?"

"Not this time," she replied.

At seven-twenty, an old Buick Century backed out of the garage and drove a short distance to Jane Adams Elementary School. The Taurus followed. They watched as the old lady dropped the kid at school and returned home.

Having accomplished what they intended, they left.

Chapter Eighteen

As he left home for the office, Wendover, Utah Police Chief Walt Corey heard the call dispatching one of his patrol officers to the old abandoned military base. Children playing in the area had reported seeing a man slumped over the wheel of a parked car, probably a customer from one of the nearby casinos, who'd had a few too many drinks the night before and was sleeping it off. That wasn't unusual for this community.

Corey was surprised when he heard the nearly hysterical voice of his newest patrol officer, who came on the radio announcing to anyone with a police scanner that the drunk sleeping in the car was really a dead guy with a bullet hole behind his left ear. When the tirade ended, Corey calmly got on the radio.

"Bobby, this is Corey. I'd like you to take a deep breath and calm down. I want you to do two things: First, secure the perimeter around the car. Then make sure nobody contaminates the scene. Got it."

"Okay, Chief."

"And Bobby, don't worry about contacting the complainant or looking for witnesses. We can do that later. Just secure the scene until I get there."

When Corey arrived, he carefully approached the cream-colored Ford Escort and looked through the driver's side window. The deceased was slumped forward with his head resting on the steering wheel. In his left hand, which was in his lap, Corey saw some type of small-caliber revolver. There wasn't much visible blood, but he definitely saw a small hole behind the left ear, just as his patrol officer had reported. He didn't open the car door or touch the vehicle.

When he returned to the patrol car, Corey turned and asked the young officer, "Bobby, did you touch the car or the body in the car?"

"No, sir," replied Patrolman Bobby Sanders. "When I first walked over to the vehicle, Chief, I noticed what I thought might be a little bit of dried blood on the guy's neck, and then I saw the small hole behind his ear. I looked at him through the front windshield, and I could see those eyes, sir, dead eyes. I went right back to my cruiser and radioed for assistance."

"Okay, Bobby, good," replied Corey. "At first glance, this looks to me like it's probably a self-inflicted wound, but since we can't be one hundred percent sure, it's important to treat the case as a possible homicide until the investigation tells us something different."

"Right, Chief," replied Sanders, trying his best to disguise his resentment over the Chief's lecture of basic criminal investigation procedure he'd learned in the state police academy four months earlier.

Corey asked the county dispatch center to contact the state crime lab and the Utah Medical Examiner's Office for assistance. He then ran a registration check on the Ford Escort and learned that it belonged to Charles Watts, whose address showed a Salt Lake City post office box. The state motor vehicle office produced driver's license information which closely matched the physical description of the body in the car.

"Well, what do you think, Bobby?" Corey asked.

"I think we got ourselves a match, Chief. He looks a little heavier than what's on his driver's license, but the age, height, and hair color seem about right."

"That's what I think too."

Corey used his cell phone and called the department. He directed the receptionist to telephone each of the West Wendover casinos to determine whether any of them had rented a room to Charles Watts. A few minutes later, the receptionist returned his call and reported that Watts had checked into the Red Garter Hotel and Casino as a single, early the previous day.

Corey left Sanders and a newly arrived deputy from the County Sheriff's Office to protect the crime scene while he drove over to the Red Garter. He met the general manager and the hotel's director of security. Together they entered Watts' room.

At first glance, the room looked no different than that of any other hotel guest. The bath contained a small travel kit with deodorant, razor, shaving cream, toothbrush, and toothpaste scattered about on the sink's Formica counter. One pair of pants and a single shirt hung in the closet. On the night stand next to the bed lay a copy of *Hustler* magazine. A small zippered duffel bag lay on the bed. It contained assorted clothing and a plastic sandwich bag, with what appeared to be a small amount of marijuana, a hash pipe, and some Zig-Zag papers. On top of the small desk lay a handwritten note on hotel stationery signed by Watts. It read:

> *Sorry to do this to you Sis, but my life is out of control—really out of control this time. I'm back into the drugs again and I do awful things when I'm high. I won't let them send me back. I can't live like that. Life is fucked. This is the best way out for me. I love you Sis.*
> *Chuck*

Corey reread the note and wondered just what kind of awful things the deceased was talking about. He took the suicide note and the drugs as evidence. He asked the security director to lock the room and not allow anyone inside until he found someone to inventory the deceased's personal property. This only served to confirm what he already suspected. This death was the result of a self-inflicted gunshot wound, a suicide committed by a despondent guy who happened to have a handgun in his possession, and who probably would turn out to be under the influence of alcohol or drugs when he ended his life. A relieved

Corey radioed his young patrolman and told him about the drugs and the suicide note. He returned to the scene and handed over the evidence to Sanders before heading into his office.

On his way, Corey radioed the county dispatch center and asked them to run Charles Watts' name and DOB through the Utah Bureau of Criminal Identification and the NCIC system. He didn't like the results. Watts was wanted by Salt Lake City P.D. on a homicide beef. The pickup order warned that he should be considered armed and dangerous, and that any information should be directed to Detective Lieutenant Kate McConnell in Homicide.

Chapter Nineteen

At precisely nine a.m., I found myself in the office of Dr. Marilyn Hastings from the Employee Assistance Program. Hastings was a licensed clinical social worker, who, in a previous life, had been a caseworker at the Utah State Prison. She handled the EAP for the Department of Corrections as well as several Salt Lake valley law enforcement agencies.

I was annoyed at having to be here, if for no other reason than the time it took away from the case. But department policy was department policy, and I had reluctantly concluded that this was one situation where ducking the rules wasn't going to work. If I'd blown off the appointment, I'd find myself back in the Norm Sloan doghouse and probably suspended as well.

The session with Hastings went smoothly and faster than I would have imagined. The questions didn't come as any great surprise. How was I sleeping? Was I eating? Was I spending excessive amounts of time dwelling on the shooting? Any emotional outbursts such as prolonged bouts of crying? Was I having any suicidal ideations? Was I drinking excessively or using drugs as a result of the shooting? I wondered if my answers made me sound like a cold-hearted bastard. She sent me out the door with a clean bill of health and a promise to contact her if I began experiencing problems.

I wasn't quite to my office when my cell phone rang. It was Kate, and I could tell from the tone of her voice that something was wrong.

"I hope you're sitting down, Sam. Watts has surfaced in Wendover."

"That's good, so what's the problem?"

"The problem is he's dead," she replied.

"No shit. What happened?"

"That's the interesting part. I just got off the phone with Walt Corey, the Chief of Police in Wendover, Utah. He says one of his patrolmen found Watts in a parked car this morning with a gun in his hand and a bullet behind his left ear. They're treating the case as a suicide."

"Have they made a positive identification?"

"Yeah. They're sure it's him."

"Are they certain it's a suicide?"

"Chief Corey says he traced him back to one of the local hotel casinos on the Nevada side. He'd rented a room the previous day. Corey says when he and the hotel's security staff searched the room, they found a suicide note addressed to Watts' sister. What do you make of that?"

"Beats me. What did the suicide note say?"

"He didn't read it to me, and I guess I was too shell-shocked to ask."

"You say the note was addressed to a sister, huh. I'll double-check our file, but I remember reading that this guy was a loner with no family support. And I don't recall seeing anything in his history indicating that he might be suicidal."

"What are you suggesting, Sam?"

"Probably nothing. Given what Chief Corey told you, it sounds like a suicide."

"We'll know more once we see the autopsy report and what, if anything, the crime scene unit finds. How do you feel about spending the day in Wendover?"

"You can drop me at one of the casinos. I'm actually overdue for a few hands of blackjack. I'll pick you up at your office in twenty."

Chapter Twenty

As we made the one-hundred-twenty-mile drive from Salt Lake City to Wendover, I quickly regretted offering to drive. It seemed that no matter how fast I drove, it wasn't fast enough for McConnell. I'd ridden with her just enough to conclude that a routine trip to the supermarket would probably be akin to occupying the pole position at the Daytona 500. The woman had little regard for speed limits. I, on the other hand, have been accused of driving like Mr. Magoo. It would be just my luck to run into some eager highway patrol trooper who happened to be short on traffic citations for the month. Many state troopers rank a good speeding violation right up there with finding a dead body stuffed in the trunk of a car.

As we entered Wendover, McConnell's cell phone rang. I couldn't tell who she was talking to, but it was soon evident that she didn't much like what she was hearing. Comments like, "This seems premature to me," "Can't this wait until tomorrow?" and "I think you're really jumping the gun here," told me something was coming down from above that she didn't like, but couldn't control. It reminded me of those age-old police management principles, around which careers were made and broken: seize the credit; cover your ass; and if necessary, spread the blame.

When she disconnected, Kate muttered, "What an arrogant jerk."

"What was that all about?"

"That was none other than Captain Hyrum Locke. After I informed him this morning about the fate of Mr. Watts, he ran the information directly to Chief Hansen, who in turn immediately contacted the mayor. They're going to hold another press conference this afternoon at four o'clock and lay the whole thing out for the media. That way they'll capture all of the local television coverage. I couldn't convince him to postpone until we had a chance to review the medical examiner's report."

"Don't act so surprised, Kate. The political heat has been on from the get-go, and the powers-that-be wanted a speedy resolution to the case, and now they have it. You can hardly blame them. This will make your department look good and ought to provide some measure of satisfaction for the Vogue family. In one sense, this is absolutely the best thing that could have happened as far as the victim's family is concerned."

"How so?"

"Look at it this way. If we had busted Watts, it would have taken the case years to work its way through the courts. Everybody knows it would have been tried as a capital case. Assuming a court conviction and endless years of death penalty appeals, it would have haunted his family for years. This way maybe they have a chance to begin the healing process. And maybe nobody has to hear about Vogue's, how can I say this gently, seedy side."

"You're probably right. We would have had to produce a lot of the information about Sue Ann Winkler, the Satin & Lace club, and the Starlite Motel during discovery. Vogue would have had his good name dragged through the mud, and there's nothing anybody could have done to prevent it."

With the impending four o'clock news conference, I wasted no time calling Sloan. He doesn't appreciate being interrupted when he's busy groveling for money at the state legislature, but he doesn't like surprises either, and he'd want this information. He needed to get ready to do some damage control on behalf of the department. On the first ring, I got Brad Ford. To my surprise, he didn't argue when I told him we had an emergency related to the Vogue killing, and that I needed to speak directly to Sloan. After a lengthy pause, Sloan came on the line.

"Good morning, Sam. Please fill me in quickly. You've actually caught me during a short break from the Executive Appropriations Committee, but we're due to resume in about five minutes."

"I'm calling you from Wendover."

"Wendover! What the hell are you doing out there?"

"Charles Watts was found dead early this morning by Wendover P.D. at the abandoned military base. They're handling the case as a suicide. It looks like a self-inflicted gunshot wound to the head."

"Hmmm. That isn't necessarily all bad. Tell me more."

"The touchy issue is that Mayor Baldwin and Chief Hansen have called a news conference this afternoon at four. McConnell believes they intend to lay out the entire case against Watts and declare the crime solved. I think you should expect a barrage of calls from the media asking the usual questions: Why was he out of prison in the first place? Why was he released from parole supervision? Is the Department of Corrections responsible for Vogue's murder because we failed to rehabilitate the guy? The usual bullshit stuff. I didn't want you caught off guard, and I wasn't sure if Chief Hansen planned on giving you a heads-up prior to the news conference."

"They haven't contacted me so far," Sloan said irritably. "Chief Hansen and I go back a long way. You'd think he would have called out of professional courtesy.

"I appreciate your keeping me abreast of developments, Sam. This may turn out to be the best resolution for all parties concerned. Planting this guy six feet under will make the entire shoddy episode disappear off the media's radar screen quickly. Obviously, it would have been better if Vogue's killer hadn't come from our offender population, but he did, and there's nothing we can do about it now. We'd be in a more tenuous situation if Watts were still under parole supervision. But he wasn't. And we never paroled the guy in the first place. The Board of Pardons did that. And it was the board that ultimately decided to release him from parole supervision. That wasn't our call either." He paused.

"I think we can manage this crisis fairly well, Sam. I'm actually kind of relieved at the turn of events. I've got to get back to the committee. Keep me informed if anything new develops. And thanks for the heads-up." The line went dead.

When we arrived in Wendover, we had to locate the abandoned army airbase where the body had been discovered. We found it south of town, well off the main drag. Our path took us down a weedy, gravel road with drab-looking wooden barracks lined up in symmetrical rows. The secret airbase was used during World War II to train B-29 crews, including that of the *Enola Gay*, which ultimately dropped the big one on Japan. A row of old clapboard houses, long overdue for a paint job, perched on a bluff overlooking the base. The homes were probably used by military personnel during the war, but now had the look of a low-income housing project. I could see a handful of children and adults out on their lawns taking in the spectacle below.

If Charles Watts had chosen to end his life here, he couldn't have picked a lonelier, more forbidding location.

By the time we arrived, the crime scene technicians had videotaped and photographed the area. They had removed the firearm, a twenty-five caliber Colt with a filed-off serial number, and had assumed custody of the suicide note. The medical examiner had just removed the body from the vehicle. Both hands had been carefully bagged and the body placed onto a gurney and then zipped into a black body bag.

Kate noted that the responding medical examiner was Harold Voddel, the same ME who had handled Vogue's autopsy. Voddel placed the time of death between midnight and four a.m. The single shot had entered behind Watts' left ear. Like many small-caliber weapons, a twenty-five caliber slug to the head often rattles around, but doesn't create an exit wound.

The State Crime Lab crew had decided not to process the victim's car for prints, since the case was being treated as a suicide. An inventory search of the vehicle had turned up nothing useful, other than several unpaid parking tickets and some papers indicating Watts had recently applied for state unemployment compensation.

We met Walt Corey in his office. He did not fit my stereotypical image of what I thought the Chief of Police in Wendover, Utah, might look like. In a staunch Mormon community, I envisioned a fit, healthy-looking, clean-cut member of the church running the police department. That wasn't Walt Corey. He must have been in his late thirties, although he looked much older. His receding hairline, swarthy complexion, and thick middle belied too many years of sitting in a patrol car eating French fries and burgers. His office smelled like stale cigarettes.

Kate flashed that Hollywood smile and thanked Corey for the prompt notification.

"Sure thing," he said. "So this Watts fella was wanted in Salt Lake City on a murder beef?"

"Afraid so," said Kate.

Corey smiled and said, "Well, the Salt Lake taxpayers have just been saved a bundle of dough—no need for a trial now. His death looks like a clear-cut case of suicide—happens out here more often than people realize."

"Why's that?" I asked.

"Gambling is a real addiction, you know. Guy comes out here, gets drunk, and blows his paycheck for the umpteenth time, and then decides he can't go home and face the wife and kids. Usually, the bodies show up over on the Nevada side of the state line, not in my jurisdiction. But we get 'em on occasion.

"Now, how can I help you?"

"We'd like copies of the police and autopsy reports," said Kate, "and the suicide note as well."

"No problem. Anything else?"

"If it's not too much trouble, we'd like to have a look around Watts' hotel room," I said.

"Easily arranged. Let me call the hotel right now."

Corey accompanied us to the Red Garter Hotel and Casino, where a search of the room produced nothing that would strengthen our case or explain Watts' apparent suicide. We managed to convince Corey and the hotel's director of security to keep the room sealed for an additional twenty-four hours until the medical examiner's office issued their autopsy findings.

As we prepared to part company with Chief Corey, a thought occurred to me. "Chief, where do you park your police impounds?"

"The tow company we use has a fenced lot on the outskirts of town. Why do you ask?"

"Since the case is being treated as a suicide, the crime lab team didn't process Watts' vehicle for latent prints. It might be a good idea to park his car inside temporarily where it isn't exposed to the elements, at least until we receive an official cause of death."

"That's a damn good idea," said Corey. "I'll call the impound lot right away."

By the time we got back to Salt Lake City, the four o'clock news conference was over. We found a television set and scanned all the local news stations at five and five-thirty. The story led on every channel. A clearly pleased trio consisting of Captain Locke, Mayor Baldwin, and Police Chief Hansen solemnly laid out the case against Charles Watts. It was convincing. Locke made no mention of the contribution McConnell made to the successful resolution of the case, nor did he mention the assistance provided by the Department of Corrections. That was perfectly okay with me and, I suspect, Norm Sloan. My unit, the SIB, always toiled behind the scenes in relative obscurity. We were used to that and actually preferred it. As for Sloan, my guess was that he too preferred that the department maintain a low profile. The most unsettling aspect in the resolution of the case was that without a walking, talking suspect, we would never know for sure why Levi Vogue was murdered.

Chapter Twenty-one

After watching the news, I turned to Kate. "I believe this calls for a celebration. I recommend we adjourn to a local restaurant of your choice. My only requirement is that the menu has to have an assortment of good beer. Since I didn't get the chance to gamble today, I figure I'm entitled to spend some time on another vice. And besides, I'm buying."

"Sounds good to me. I too have one stipulation. This outing cannot be classified as a date, since I refuse to date inside the police fraternity."

"That's okay with me. Call it anything you'd like. I can't be out late anyway. I've got another engagement later in the evening with a beautiful young blonde."

"Oh, really," said Kate. "Let me think. This gorgeous blonde you referred to wouldn't happen to be an eight-year-old living in Park City, would she?"

"Boy, you're a quick study. I've been living like a Trappist monk since the divorce. But I'm not complaining. I figure between Sara and Aunt June, a guy couldn't do any better."

For the next two hours, Kate and I settled in at the Uintah Brew Pub on Salt Lake's west side. Kate ordered a Cobb salad and a glass of Merlot. I stuck with Uintah Pale Ale and a plate of cold shrimp.

We kept the conversation light, searching for common interests, but mostly filled in blanks from our past. I was relieved when the alcohol started to take effect. The conversation became more relaxed. I'd been out of the singles scene for a long time, and until now, I hadn't had much interest in the opposite sex. A divorce would do that for you.

Away from work, Kate McConnell was fun to be with. She smiled easily and often, and had a great sense of humor. She was smart, attractive, and outgoing—a dangerous combination. Toward the end of our evening, the verbal "getting to know you" had given way to periods of silence when our eyes locked until one of us became uncomfortable and looked away.

Later, as we parted, Kate took my hand and pulled me close. She nestled her body next to mine and held the hug for a period that seemed longer than normal. I kissed her on the cheek and walked away.

The aroma of Aunt June's fresh banana bread met me as I entered the house. It was the best, and she'd baked it for as long as I could remember.

Aunt June was immersed in one of her romance novels when I found her tucked comfortably under a quilt in the family room. She read romance novels by the bushel. I thought this might be a good time to mention my recent encounter with Baxter Shaw. I wondered if she might have an interest in meeting him. She warmed to the idea rather quickly, so I decided to arrange an introduction as soon as I could find the time.

"I wasn't sure what time you were going to be home, but I made a fresh pot of decaf about an hour ago. You might need to pop it in the microwave for a few seconds. There's also some warm banana bread in the oven."

"You're going to turn me into a fat guy if you keep baking all these goodies."

"What are old aunts good for if not to keep the house smelling yummy with homemade treats? And if you want some, you'd better get a move on it. Sara's waiting upstairs in her bedroom, and you promised to read her a full chapter of *Harry Potter* before bedtime. I think she finished her homework. You might want to go over her spelling words with her."

Sara had become a voracious reader. Her weekly allowance was tied to how much she read and how little TV she watched. Soon I was going to need a second job just to keep up with her growing allowance. The kid had a savings account I was starting to envy.

We went over her homework assignments and got her ready for bed. We settled in the family room for an evening with *Harry Potter*. Some nights she read to me, and other times I read to her. This time it was my turn. She didn't make it through a whole chapter before falling asleep. I carried her upstairs and tucked her into bed, but not before I promised to take her and a friend on a Saturday adventure to Hogle Zoo.

Chapter Twenty-two

Early the next morning, I was in my office at the state penitentiary, knee-deep in neglected paperwork that had been accumulating in my absence. I also had Burnham at my door with two new cases involving employee misconduct. In one of them, a supervisor discovered a female corrections officer in a social worker's office engaged in oral sex with a male inmate. The other case involved a civilian employee who worked in the prison culinary and was caught smuggling marijuana into the institution. To his credit, Burnham had not only managed to provide valuable assistance on the Vogue investigation, but had also kept the SIB functioning properly in my absence.

In recent months, Terry had become a workaholic and I was beginning to worry about him. Laura, his wife of thirty-three years, had died a year ago from complications resulting from a lifelong battle with diabetes. Instead of slowing down or taking a leave of absence, Burnham was trying to cope by working sixty-hour weeks, and then self-medicating during his off-duty time with too much Johnny Walker Black.

By late morning, I had begun to feel that I might get caught up by day's end if I could avoid serious interruptions. However, my good fortune didn't last. The office phone rang. It was Kate.

"Good morning, Lt. McConnell. I'd like to believe you're calling to tell me what a marvelous time you had last night and that we should do it again soon, but somehow, I doubt that."

"I did have a great time last night, thank you very much. And yes, I think we should get together again. But you're right, that's not why I called."

"Okay. You've got my undivided attention. What's up?"

"I just got off the phone with the State Medical Examiner's Office. They've completed the autopsy on Watts. They've concluded that his death was a homicide, not a suicide. And apparently, they've got the forensic evidence to back it up."

"Whoa! That does change things a bit, doesn't it?" I said. "Have you said anything about this to His Eminence, Hyrum Locke?"

"Not yet. I'd rather sit down with the ME and go over the forensic evidence first. Chief Corey was notified, and he's on his way in right now. The ME has set a meeting for this afternoon at one-thirty. Can you make it?"

"Sure, I'll be there. I'll bet Corey damn near had a stroke when he heard the news. That makes this a whole lot more complicated."

"Yeah, I know."

"The jurisdiction actually belongs to the Wendover Police Department. I doubt if they have the expertise or resources to effectively handle a sophisticated murder investigation. Who's going to provide the assistance? And is Corey savvy enough to recognize that he needs help? And here's one for you: What incentive will the brass have for allowing you to continue working the case, assuming Corey wants help in the first place? Both our departments seem more than happy with the current resolution of this thing. Why rock the boat? Why put this whole mess back on the front page of every major newspaper in the West?"

"It's going to end up back under the media spotlight whether anybody likes it or not, and I think the brass will want to see this through, regardless of the adverse publicity that might come with it," said Kate.

"Well, maybe, but remember that both our departments want this case to go away for a myriad of reasons beyond media scrutiny. The victim's family, Richard Vogue in particular, scares the hell out of the honorable mayor, and to a lesser extent, both our bosses."

I went on, "Put yourself in the place of Richard Vogue. You just find out that the man who killed your son was himself the victim of a murder, elaborately staged to look like a suicide. What would you think about that?"

"If I were Richard Vogue, I'd be thinking that the authorities may have correctly identified my son's murderer, but they failed to uncover the real motive for his death and the identity of the person or persons who conspired to have him killed. I'd also be thinking that the investigation is only half-finished until the police discover who is behind all of this. And I wouldn't have any reason to believe that my son was anything other than a Boy Scout, unless someone told me otherwise."

"Exactly," I said. "And you make a very intriguing point. What if someone does sit down with papa Vogue and tells him about Sue Ann Winkler, the Satin & Lace Club, and Levi's porn collection, including the one he starred in. He then has a very interesting problem. He can apply pressure to snuff the investigation in the name of protecting his late son's reputation, or he can insist on a full, open investigation, and let the chips fall where they may. An interesting dilemma, don't you think?"

"For sure. I don't know about you, but I intend to use everything at my disposal to stay on this investigation. The job is only half done," said Kate.

"Yeah, I'm with you on that. See you at the meeting this afternoon."

Chapter Twenty-three

On my way to the State Medical Examiner's Office, a couple of thoughts occurred to me.

I called Burnham on my cell. "Terry, I need you to do something for me as soon as possible. Call the prison and find out which caseworker was assigned to Watts during his last prison commitment. See if the caseworker's file contains anything written by Watts. I have a hunch we're going to need original handwriting samples."

"I'll do it," said Burnham. "Anything else?"

"Yeah, there is one more thing. I'd like you to attend Vogue's funeral with me. Find out when and where the funeral will be held. I think the family put everything on hold for a few days waiting for several relatives to arrive from out of state. I'll bet it's scheduled sometime in the next day or two."

"I'll check into it and let you know. Mind telling me though why you want us to attend?"

"Let's just call it professional courtesy."

"Okay. I'll get back to you."

The Utah State Medical Examiner's Office was located on Salt Lake City's east bench not far from the University of Utah. It commanded a strikingly beautiful view of the Salt Lake Valley. I parked my car under their covered parking terrace and was directed by a receptionist to a small conference room adjacent to the lobby. Kate and Walt Corey were waiting.

Within minutes, we were joined by Harold Voddel, who had performed the autopsies on both Levi Vogue and Charles Watts. He was joined by Doctor Frances Chandler-Soames, who had been the Chief Medical Examiner for the state of Utah longer than I've been employed by the Department of Corrections. Her reputation as a forensic pathologist was second to none.

Chandler-Soames was clear from the outset that she concurred with Voddel's autopsy findings, ending any concerns we might have had about his relative inexperience.

"Mr. Watts died sometime between one and three a.m. from a single twenty-five caliber gunshot wound to the head. In all likelihood, the single shot produced death almost instantaneously," said the young medical examiner. "We carefully removed the twenty-five caliber slug during the autopsy. It came out undamaged and is now available for ballistics testing. The stomach contained a partially digested dinner consumed some three to four hours prior to death. A blood sample revealed a small amount of alcohol in the victim's system, but not enough to reach Utah's .08 legal limit. The bullet entered behind the decedent's left ear and was lodged in the lower jaw. There was no exit wound."

In Utah, the state medical examiner not only determined the cause of death, but also whether a death was accidental, a suicide, or a criminal homicide. Voddel continued, "Two factors make it all but impossible for me to arrive at the conclusion that Mr. Watts shot himself. First, the downward trajectory of the bullet occurred at such an angle as to make it highly unlikely that it was self-inflicted. Gunshot suicides which occur with the entry wound behind the ear, while not uncommon, almost always show an upward trajectory of the bullet because that is the more natural body position. Second, the absence of powder burns or residue on the victim's skin suggested that the fatal shot was fired from a likely distance of one to two feet. Taken together, Mr. Watts would have had to place his left hand and arm into an almost impossible position from which to discharge the weapon. And he couldn't possibly have accomplished that unless the driver-side door or window was open. And they were both closed."

"Harry Houdini couldn't have made that move," chimed Chandler-Soames, a hint of a smile playing at the corners of her mouth. "The likely scenario is that your shooter was standing outside the victim's vehicle, slightly to the rear, and fired a single shot, that struck Mr. Watts behind his left ear at the downward angle. He probably never saw it coming."

The room was silent as we absorbed what we had just heard. The only audible sound came from Walt Corey's growling stomach. Finally, I broke the silence. "I've got Terry tracking down Watts' former prison caseworker, who should be able to provide us with handwriting samples."

"That's good. If Watts' death isn't a suicide, then the note Walt found in the hotel room has to be a forgery," said Kate. Turning to Corey, she said: "Chief, you've got some decisions to make. Do you plan to carry this homicide investigation forward on your own or seek outside assistance?"

For the first time since we arrived, Corey smiled. "I think we've got our homicide team sitting right here. Let's cut to the chase. I've got a small department with limited resources in a town that rarely sees a murder. The few we do get are usually family disturbances that turn violent, and somebody ends up killing somebody. Pretty much open-and-shut cases. This isn't one of those cut-and-dried domestic violence cases. We're gonna need some help with this one.

"It also seems to tie directly into your ongoing investigation of the murder of that parole board member. You've still got work to do before you figure out who would go to all the trouble of killing the killer. I'd just like to know whose hairy ass I might need to kiss in order to keep the two of you working this case?"

I liked Corey when I first met him in Wendover a day earlier. I liked him even better now, and I think Kate did too. His analysis of our predicament suggested a guy who possessed a solid grasp of the factual situation as well as the political context in which we found ourselves. I wondered if our two departments would try to wash their hands of the investigation and dump it on a small, understaffed, rural police department. We were about to find out.

Chapter Twenty-four

At the conclusion of their presentation, members of the State Medical Examiner's Office excused themselves, leaving Kate, Corey, and me alone in the conference room. Once again, things were about to heat up, and we needed a plan.

"What the hell do we do now?" asked Corey.

"Sam and I had better break the bad news to our respective agency heads ASAP," said Kate. "They'd like this case to disappear quietly. Our job will be to convince them to let us continue working the investigation."

"Go away, it ain't," muttered Corey. "I know Chief Hansen well and I've met Sloan. I think I'll call 'em and ask to have both of you continue working the case in coordination with my office."

I liked that idea and so did Kate. Whatever pressure he could apply wouldn't hurt us and might help. Without question, our investigation had produced Vogue's killer. The missing piece of the puzzle, however, was who killed Slick Watts? Only when we had the answer to that question would we fully understand the motive behind the murder of the Chairman of the Board of Pardons.

"You or somebody from your department needs to contact the Vogue family and explain what's going on before the press gets wind of it," I said to Kate. "Once this goes public, the mayor, and your department brass, are going to have doo doo all over their faces. They better be prepared for the shit-storm of criticism the press is likely to dump on them."

"Serves 'em right," snapped Kate. "We tried to get them to hold off on the press conference, but they wouldn't listen. Now they'll just have to deal with the consequences."

One troubling issue I hadn't mentioned to Kate was that whoever hired Watts for what now appeared to be the contract murder of Levi Vogue had selected a career criminal with a perfect motive for wanting Vogue dead. Who would have that kind of inside information? Maybe it was a coincidence. On the other hand, prison gangs might be able to leverage that sort of information from their own sources. Or the information could have come from somebody employed inside the system, like say, someone working for the Department of Corrections.

Our meeting was interrupted by a call on my cell. It was Patti calling to tell me that Burnham had located Watts' prison caseworker. He'd also examined the caseworker's file and discovered an ample supply of original handwriting samples we could use to compare to the writing on the alleged suicide note. Terry was on his way from the prison to deliver the samples.

"A couple of things need to happen with the suicide note right away," I said. "We should have a lab technician examine it for latent prints. If Watts really wrote it, his prints should be on it. Then, Kate, let's have one of your document examiners compare the note with the original writing samples. That should give us some answers."

"I'm ahead of you on the first one. I asked the lab crew to examine the note for latent prints before we left Wendover. I'll call them now and see if they've got the results. I can also get a priority response from our document examiners as soon as we provide them with the suicide note and the comparison writing samples."

"Can't beat that for service," said Corey.

Kate called the crime lab, while Corey and I discussed what needed to happen relative to the investigation in Wendover. A crime lab team needed to return to Wendover. Corey agreed to have them process Watts' car and hotel room. He called the hotel manager, who assured him that the room was still secure.

"Well, surprise, surprise," said Kate. "The latent print examiner just finished with the suicide note, and guess what? The note has been wiped clean. No prints at all. Zip! None!

"For those of us who may have doubted the medical examiner's conclusions, we all get to eat a little crow."

We spent the last few minutes with Corey reviewing what we knew. We laid out the entire case, carefully omitting the negative character information about Vogue. That would probably have to be divulged at some point, but not now. That information would be treated on a need-to-know basis. And for now, Chief Corey didn't need that information.

Our meeting broke up. My adrenaline was flowing. It was time to get back on the hunt.

Chapter Twenty-five

Later that afternoon, I was ushered into the office of Salt Lake City Chief of Police Ron Hansen. It was a well-appointed office with a large, formal-looking cherry desk and a high-back, gray leather chair. A black leather couch sat directly in front of the desk. Hansen directed me toward a rectangular conference table from which he would conduct the meeting.

The ego wall behind his desk was impressive. It was full, displaying framed copies of every degree and training certificate he'd amassed over a quarter century in police work. It included a picture of the chief shaking hands with a smiling President Bill Clinton.

This was a somber-looking group. Besides Chief Hansen, Salt Lake P.D. representatives included Deputy Chief Puffer, Captain Hyrum Locke, and Kate. Across the table sat my boss, Brad Ford, and me.

Locke spoke first. "We have several issues that require our immediate attention. Given that we now know Charles Watts was murdered in Wendover, and considering that the evidence amassed in our own investigation makes it a virtual certainty he was the shooter in the Vogue homicide, do we continue allocating our resources to the investigation, or do we leave the matter in the hands of the Wendover P.D., which now has primary jurisdiction? "

That was the big question, and Locke put it on the table in record time. Kate looked concerned.

"Which leads directly to the next issue. Who is going to act as spokesperson to the Vogue family? And how much information do we give them and when? Since the investigation appears about to be resurrected, is it time we level with them about Levi's extra curricular activities? If they find out about it from some other source, we're toast.

"And that brings me to the last question. How do we handle the press now? The moment this hits the wire, we're right back in the hot seat. We might be able to delay releasing the information for a few hours, or perhaps a day, but that's about it."

Turning to Kate, Locke asked, "Do you guys see any advantage in delaying the press release?"

"Only that we'd have a few more hours to work the case without members of the media lurking behind every tree. Actually, Sam and I have discussed the issue and we think a carefully worded press release wouldn't hurt the investigation and might even be useful."

"In what way?" said Hansen.

"Up until now, whoever is responsible for the murders has to be thinking they've gotten away with it. Let's make them uncomfortable. Let's use the media to send them a message. Who knows, maybe they'll panic and make a mistake. We don't think there's anything to lose. We go public, explaining that the death of Watts involved foul play and is being investigated as a criminal homicide, not a suicide. We don't need to be specific. We don't reveal that the alleged suicide note was a forgery and has been wiped clean of prints. Let them wonder just how much we do know," said Kate.

"Sounds all right to me," said Hansen. "Anybody have a problem with it?" Nobody spoke. Several heads nodded in agreement.

"Let's get back to the main issue for a moment," said Hansen. "Do we continue this investigation using our personnel, or do we hand it off to Wendover P.D. and get the hell out of it?"

For the first time, Deputy Chief Puffer spoke. "I think we've done our job and done it well. I recommend we pull out. Our investigation correctly identified Vogue's killer and found plenty of evidence to support a successful prosecution. It's not our problem that the perp got himself killed before we had a chance to apprehend him. It's Wendover P.D.'s problem now. Let them handle it."

Spoken like a true wimp, I thought. The man was predictable if little else.

Hansen turned to Kate. "Lieutenant McConnell, what are your thoughts on the matter? You and Kincaid have been the ones carrying the ball on this."

Before she had a chance to respond, Locke interrupted. "I support Clarence's position, with one possible caveat. How would the press portray our decision to withdraw from the case and how might that affect public opinion?"

Clearly, Locke and Puffer were making a power play that put Kate in an unenviable position. She would have to make a choice to support or oppose her superiors, and risk some kind of retaliation later, if she took a position in opposition to theirs.

Locke was smart, politically savvy, and a highly capable administrator who also happened to be a ruthless organizational climber. He had never hesitated to run roughshod over others on his way up the career ladder, and he rarely missed an opportunity to pander to the TV cameras in high-profile cases. I was more than a little surprised that we hadn't seen him at Vogue's residence the night of the murder or at the Mayor's initial press conference.

The lady didn't disappoint. Glancing quickly at Puffer and then Locke, Kate shifted slightly in her seat and looked directly at Chief Hansen. "I think we've got a clear obligation, both practically and ethically, to remain on the case. Nobody has a better understanding of the case than we do. If we pull out now, we leave the job half-finished. Sure, we can take solace in the fact that we correctly identified Watts as Vogue's murderer. But this investigation isn't over until somebody finds out who's really responsible for the conspiracy to have Levi Vogue murdered. That's the million-dollar question. It seems inconceivable to me that we'd simply walk away and expect the Wendover Police Department to carry the case forward. They don't have the resources or experience to pull it off."

Locke interrupted again. "That's not exactly true, Kate. Wendover P.D. can do what any small department in Utah can do, and that is to request assistance from the State Attorney General's Office. They have a solid investigative staff that exists to support just this kind of endeavor. They do it all the time."

Puffer didn't speak but nodded his head in agreement.

"That's true," admitted Kate. "But let's be honest. Everybody knows the A.G.'s Office does the best it can to support small law enforcement agencies that require assistance, but they lack experience when it comes to investigating homicides.

"The other issue we haven't discussed is what possible reaction the Vogue family will have to our abandoning the investigation. I'd be a lot more worried about that than public opinion. Anybody care to volunteer to go out and have that conversation with Richard Vogue?" Big surprise. No takers.

The room fell momentarily silent until Hansen spoke. "Norm, where does your department stand on this issue?"

"I've discussed it with Sam and a couple of other people, and I think we stay committed to the investigation. I haven't heard anything so far that makes me change my mind. Part of the role of the Special Investigations Branch is to assist state and local law enforcement in just this kind of situation. If Watts' murder had occurred across the state line in Wendover, Nevada, I'd pull Kincaid and his troops off the investigation immediately. But that's not the case. Besides, I received a call from Chief Corey earlier today, specifically asking that the SIB continue to provide assistance to his department."

"I got the same call," said Hansen. "Okay, here's what we'll do. Clarence, you and Hyrum make immediate arrangements to see Levi's widow and explain the latest developments in the case. Tell her that we intend to continue our investigation, working in conjunction with the SIB and the Wendover P.D. Say nothing to her about her husband's philandering with the stripper. I'll have our public information officer draft a carefully worded press release. We'll delay its release until you've visited the family. Questions anyone? Good! Then let's get on it."

Chapter Twenty-six

After the meeting, Kate and I dropped down two floors to a small suite of offices where the sign on the front door read *Checks & Forgery*. The duty secretary handed Kate a one-page report summarizing the results of the handwriting analysis that compared the suicide note against writing samples belonging to Charles Watts. The examiner concluded that the suicide note was not written by Charles Watts, and thus was a forgery, albeit a high-quality one. The document examiner promised to provide us with a list of skilled Utah forgers early the next day.

Kate and I walked together to the public safety building parking lot. "So where do you think this leaves us, Sam? Any ideas?"

"I wish I knew. It's damn frustrating. I do think we can eliminate a couple of our early theories."

"Yeah? Which ones?"

"For one thing, any notion we had that Vogue was the victim of a random killing because he blundered into a burglary at home no longer makes sense. It doesn't jive with Watts' homicide being staged to look like a suicide."

Kate shrugged. "It always was an unlikely possibility. Besides, Vince worked his tail off with our burglary dicks on that angle and came up empty."

"The other theory we can probably toss is the prison gang connection. When you consider how Vogue was killed, it had all the trappings of a gang-style hit. Combine that with Vogue's occupation, and it seemed like a good fit. But here's the problem. Most of the gangs are organized along ethnic lines, blacks with blacks, whites with whites, Latinos with Latinos. Slick Watts wasn't ever a gang banger. We ran his name through every gang database available. He wasn't involved with skinheads, straight-edgers, bikers, white supremacists, none of the Caucasian gangs. And if the killing was gang-ordered, the perp would've been an active gang member or a gang member wannabe.

"And another thing. In the unlikely event a gang hired Watts to do Vogue and then decided to eliminate Watts, they wouldn't have staged it to look like a suicide. He'd have gotten whacked just like Vogue in some kind of drive-by or street hit. That's their signature. It's how they do business," I said.

Kate sighed. "That leaves Sue Ann Winkler, the Starlite Motel, and the prostitution ring John Merchant talked about when he was singing at the hospital. I've had the feeling that there's still something bothering you about that whole mess."

"I know I'm probably grasping at straws, but yeah, something is bothering me. We know that Vogue was involved in some unusual sexual practices—group sex and voyeurism for starters. Just who is the guy Sue Ann told us about, the mystery man with the tattoo on his arm that Vogue brought back to the motel for the three-way action? We've never identified him. Is it possible that Vogue was killed because he learned something about that place he wasn't supposed to know? I think we should lean all over everybody associated with the Starlite Motel until we determine whether they had anything to do with his murder. I know it's a long shot."

She shrugged. "It's hard for me to reconcile the notion that a prostitution ring would get involved in contract murder. It doesn't make sense unless they're involved in something else a lot more sinister. I think it's a long shot, but no, I don't have any better ideas at the moment.

"In the morning, I'll have Vince pull their business license and any incorporation papers that may exist, and see what our vice people know about the place. It might be worthwhile to have a couple of teams set up visual surveillance near the motel for a few days and monitor the traffic going in and out. If the motel is a front for an organized prostitution ring or maybe a drug house, there ought to be plenty of people coming and going at all times of the day and night.

"The best shot we've got right now is to try to identify the guy who wrote the suicide note. He's our direct link to whoever hired Watts to kill Levi. I'll get the list from the forgery guys in the morning. Then we'll start running people down. That okay?"

"Fine," I replied. "I'll send an e-mail to every probation and parole officer in the state soliciting names of any first-rate forgers. We'll probably end up with some of the same people, but it should give us a fairly complete list."

Chapter Twenty-seven

I slept in the next morning and didn't arrive at the office until after nine o'clock. There was a message from Kate asking me to call her as soon as I got in. It seemed that Clarence Puffer and Hyrum Locke had gone out to the Vogue home right after our meeting with Chief Hansen to diplomatically advise Mrs. Vogue that there was good news and bad news. The good news: clearly, Levi Vogue's murderer had been identified. The bad news: the killer had also been murdered.

Apparently, the meeting with Margaret Vogue hadn't gone all that well and resulted in her scurrying to see the family patriarch, Richard Vogue III. When Hansen arrived at his office the next morning, he found a terse message from Papa Vogue asking that all future developments in the case come directly to him, not Margaret. Further, his message requested an immediate meeting with Lt. McConnell and "that guy from the corrections department" who had been working on the case with her.

At this point, Hansen made a serious blunder. For reasons known only to him, he dispatched Puffer and Locke to the corporate headquarters of Vogue Chemicals, only to have them unceremoniously rebuffed at the front door by an aide to Vogue. By the time Locke and Puffer returned to Salt Lake P.D. headquarters, an angry Richard Vogue had placed a telephone call to Mayor Baldwin. Following that age-old administrative principle that all shit runs downhill, Baldwin promptly called Hansen into his office and chewed on him for about an hour.

I suppose that only someone with my acerbic sense of humor could appreciate the events of the morning involving Locke and Puffer. As I drove to police headquarters to pick up Kate for our visit with Richard Vogue, it occurred to me that this had to be an extremely stressful time for the entire Vogue family, and to have received this kind of information from anybody, no matter how diplomatically delivered, had to be upsetting.

The corporate headquarters of Vogue Chemicals was located in downtown Salt Lake City near the convention center. After we signed the visitor log in the lobby, a neatly dressed security officer escorted Kate and me to a spacious fifth-floor conference room. The room was decorated in earth tone colors with fine-grained oak furniture. Several beautiful southwest landscape paintings hung on the walls.

We waited for approximately ten minutes before a subdued Richard Vogue entered the boardroom, accompanied by Edward Tillman, whom he introduced as the company's corporate legal counsel. He apologized for being late and thanked us for coming. Vogue was a distinguished-looking man, probably in his late sixties, with a mane of thick silver hair. His aristocratic look was enhanced by a well-tanned face and a lean, wiry physique that suggested a man who placed a premium on physical fitness. When he shook my hand, the grip was strong and his hand leathery. This was not a man who'd spent his entire work life sitting behind a desk.

"Lieutenant McConnell, Mr. Kincaid, my wife Helen and I have been blessed with three wonderful children and eight grandchildren. Levi was our eldest child and our only son. I can't begin to describe the pain and anguish that his murder has caused the entire family. We are a close-knit bunch, and this has been devastating for everyone.

"Needless to say, the news Margaret received last evening from Deputy Chief Puffer and Mr. Locke only served to add to the family's grief. Just when we'd adjusted to the notion that your investigation produced Levi's killer, we were told that this Watts fellow had taken his own life.

"Speaking personally, I found that news most disturbing. I had hoped, one day, to have the opportunity to ask Mr. Watts why he killed my son. His death, regardless of how it happened, permanently deprives me of that opportunity. And now to have the coroner's office conclude that Mr. Watts' death was really a murder staged to look like a suicide is almost beyond belief. I don't know what to make of it, and I'm hoping you can help me.

"Also, I'd like to ask that in the future, you contact me directly with information about the investigation. It's much too overwhelming for Margaret to deal with right now."

We extended our personal condolences. Kate promised to communicate directly with him in the future. She explained that it had become imperative that we obtain statements from Margaret and her sons as soon as possible, and asked how he preferred we handle that.

"I don't see any reason why we can't arrange something for tomorrow right here in this office." Turning to Tillman, Vogue asked, "Ed, I realize that it's Saturday, but could you arrange your schedule to be here, at say eleven o'clock in the morning? Margaret and the boys can meet you."

Tillman nodded. Ideally, this wouldn't be the way we preferred to take statements from family members in a murder investigation, but it would have to do. Depending on how Tillman conducted himself, we could probably make it work.

Vogue surprised us by expressing skepticism about the accuracy of the medical examiner's findings relative to the death of Charles Watts. He demanded to know what specific evidence the State Medical Examiner's Office used to conclude that Watts' death was a criminal event rather than a suicide. Like us, he seemed to sense that a murder, arranged to look like a suicide, might hold unknown and ominous implications. After Kate reviewed the existing evidence, he seemed unhappily resigned to the accuracy of the coroner's report.

Finally, Vogue got around to asking the question we most hoped he wouldn't. "Tell me this. Given the medical examiner's findings regarding the murder of Watts, how close are you to having this mess resolved?" This particular question seemed to bring Tillman out of a semi-comatose state and to the edge of his seat, pen at the ready. Having anticipated this question, Kate and I had rehearsed an answer on the drive over. Unfortunately, while the answer contained elements of the truth, it also contained a deliberate and glaring omission.

"I wish we were here with the answers I know you and your family so desperately want, but I'm afraid that's just not the case," said Kate. "We're back to square one with respect to who murdered Watts and why his death was staged to look like a suicide. Finding the answers to those two questions will help us to unravel the mystery surrounding the murder of your son."

No fibs so far, I thought to myself.

Kate continued. "What we can tell you is that our investigation has all but ruled out the possibility that your son's death was a murder connected to a burglary gone awry. Instead, we're convinced that Levi's murder was somehow connected to his employment as a member of the parole board."

"We are carefully examining our offender population for possible suspects," I said. "We're looking at current inmates as well as former prisoners to see who might have harbored a grudge against the parole board in general, or your son in particular."

We carefully skirted any reference to his son's occasional visits to the Satin & Lace Club and the Starlite Motel. We couldn't predict how Vogue might react to that kind of negative information.

Vogue listened intently and without interruption. I had the feeling he was just as interested in sizing us up as he was in absorbing the information we had provided. Tillman, although quiet, had been scribbling away on his legal pad like a well-paid corporate lawyer should. After pausing momentarily, as though the lapse in conversation had given him time to digest everything we had shared, Vogue tossed us an unexpected curve.

"I sincerely appreciate your taking the time to drop by on such short notice. It's been most helpful. I'd like you to know that Helen and I are absolutely committed to finding out what happened to our son. We don't care what it costs or how long it takes. We're not going to rest until we have answers—all the answers.

"With that end in mind, you should know that I'm considering hiring a team of private investigators, lead by a retired FBI agent, James Allen—you may know him—to look into my son's death. Please don't be offended. It isn't personal. It's just that I've been concerned from the outset that the police department hasn't committed sufficient personnel to the investigation. I've reflected that concern to the appropriate city officials, unfortunately, to no avail. Should I elect to move forward with a parallel investigation, I hope that information will be shared by all parties, and that an atmosphere of mutual cooperation develops."

He didn't give us an opportunity to discuss the merits of his proposal. He stood and said, "Now, if you'll excuse me, my son's funeral begins in two hours."

Chapter Twenty-eight

As Kate and I drove back to Salt Lake City P.D., we discussed the implications of having to work with a team of private investigators. "I'll tell you, Kate, and you've probably seen it too, when you get multiple agencies working the same case, it usually isn't pretty. Instead of cooperation, you tend to get jealousy, petty bickering, and lots of turf protection. Assuming Vogue follows through with his plan, our investigation has the potential of becoming a first-rate clusterfuck."

Kate looked over at me. "What do you know about James Allen?"

"Not much, I'm afraid. We've worked a couple of fugitive cases with some of his people in situations where one of our offenders committed a federal offense and then split the state. He retired about a year ago as the Special Agent in Charge of the Salt Lake City field office. He probably has solid management skills, but it sure doesn't mean he was a good field agent. How about you?"

"I don't know him at all. But one thing we can probably be assured is that Mr. Vogue has the money and the smarts to hire competent people. I'd prefer that we not have to deal with it, but if we do, at least we should have that going for us."

"I agree. One thing we could do is urge the mayor and Chief Hansen to contact Vogue and try to talk him out of hiring privates, or at least buy us some more time. We could use that," I said.

◇◇◇

I dropped Kate at police headquarters and headed back to my office. When I got there, Patti informed me that James Allen had called not once, but twice, asking that I return his call as soon as possible. It appeared Richard Vogue had moved well beyond the *possibility* of hiring a team of private investigators. He had already done so.

I decided not to postpone the inevitable and dialed his number. He picked up on the first ring, with "Sam Kincaid, how are you?" Caller ID. More technology I could do without. We engaged in the usual salutations and perfunctory glad-handing before settling down to business.

"Sam, as you probably know, Richard Vogue has asked Allen & Associates to look into Levi's murder. I want to assure you that we are here to assist in any way we can and not to step on toes. Believe me, I understand how difficult it can be when a high profile case is already being worked by more than one agency. And then to have a team of private investigators tossed into the mix can't be viewed by the official agencies with much enthusiasm."

No shit, Sherlock, I thought.

I decided to hedge my bets and play it conservatively. "You know, Jim, you're probably talking to the wrong guy. You need to be on the horn to Lt. Kate McConnell. She's the lead on this one. My office has been assigned in a support capacity only."

"Oh, I understand that, Sam, but I hoped you could make the introductions and lay the groundwork. After all, you and I have some history. I'm afraid I can't say the same about my relationship with Lt. McConnell. I could take the direct approach and go straight to her boss, but I'd hate to do that for the obvious reasons."

He was playing all of the right cards. I decided that it made sense to feign cooperation and stall for time. "You're right about one thing—going around McConnell would probably be a big mistake. Suffice it to say, it wouldn't exactly engender an attitude of trust and cooperation. You should also be aware that the Salt

Lake County Attorney's office has been involved from day one. Tom Stoddard is the contact there. I'm sure the DA's office will expect input into this decision. In the meantime, I'd be happy to serve as a liaison between you and Lt. McConnell. Let me approach her and I'll get back to you. How does that sound?"

Translated, that means I'll get back to you in about ten years.

"Sounds good to me, Sam. I really appreciate your assistance. Time is of the essence, so I'll expect to hear from you soon."

I had an idea. I found Terry working in his office, all dressed up and ready to attend Levi Vogue's funeral.

I dropped into the seat next to his desk. "Change of plan," I said. "And for what I've got in mind, you're definitely overdressed."

"Shit. I not only wear my best suit, but I rush my ass to the cleaners yesterday and pay to get it cleaned, all because you told me we're attending Vogue's funeral today. And now you're about to tell me I'm not going. What gives?"

Smiling, I said, "What's the matter with you—out a little late last night? You know, Terry, it wouldn't hurt if you'd buy a second suit, and always keep one of them clean. Then you can avoid the stress of having to run around at the last minute trying to get your wardrobe in order. And besides, you are going to the funeral. It's just that nobody's going to see you."

"Up yours, Kincaid," he said, trying to suppress a smile playing at the corners of his mouth. "Just give me the piss-ass assignment and get out of my office." That's what I liked about Burnham—always the soft-spoken gentleman.

I don't like funerals much, never have. This one would be no exception. I arrived about twenty minutes before the scheduled start of the service. It was a beautiful afternoon for a funeral, lots of sunshine with a cobalt blue sky and a few cumulus clouds.

I spotted Burnham parked in our undercover surveillance van across the street from the church parking lot. This gave him an unobstructed view of the church's main entrance, as well as a good view of a side entrance. He would have a clear field of vision through the van's one-way glass to videotape mourners as they entered and exited the church. I knew this exercise might be for naught, but I also felt there was at least an outside chance that the video footage might help us connect someone to Vogue's murder.

To my dismay, I also observed two marked vans and a large SUV from our local television stations. The press release, explaining the circumstances surrounding the death of Charles Watts, had been given to the assembled media at a nine a.m. news conference.

The guest of honor was present in a bronze casket at the front of the church. It was common in the Mormon faith to have an open-casket viewing preceding the funeral service. In this instance, undoubtedly because of the condition of the body, there had been no viewing.

By the time the service began, the church was filled beyond capacity. Margaret, her two sons, and a group of her family members occupied the front rows on one side of the church. Richard Vogue III, his wife, their two surviving daughters, and their families were seated in the first rows on the other side.

The next several rows were occupied by political dignitaries and members of their various entourages. I recognized Governor Walker, Salt Lake City Mayor Porter Baldwin, and Senator Theodore Stephens, all political heavyweights who had come to pay their respects to Richard Vogue III.

Chief Hansen was sitting with my boss, and they had been joined by Vogue's colleagues from the state board of pardons. I saw people from my own department, including several members of Sloan's administrative team and even a couple of prison employees.

Mercifully, the church service was handled with little fanfare. A much smaller group of mourners gathered at a nearby cemetery for a brief graveside service. The whole thing lasted less than two hours.

I met Burnham after the funeral at a downtown gourmet coffee shop. Feeling moderately guilty over his recent wardrobe crisis, I bought. Over two coffees and a single cinnamon roll that I'd reluctantly agreed to split, Terry and I discussed the current status of the case. Between bites, Terry said, "Tell me something. Why were you so hot to have this surveillance tape?"

"On one level, it's a shot in the dark. I'll admit that. But you know how intensely I dislike loose ends. I'm bothered that our investigation hasn't identified the guy Vogue brought to the motel for the three-way action with Sue Ann. Think about it. It would have to be someone close to Vogue, somebody he trusted implicitly. Who might that somebody be? Surely not a member of his devout Mormon family. And certainly not someone from his church. It seems to me that leaves old, trusted friends, or perhaps somebody he works with. That somebody might well have attended his funeral. And just maybe we've got him on tape."

"I follow you now," said Burnham. "You're planning to invite Ms. Winkler in to watch enhanced videotape."

"Exactly. But not just yet. Kate's got Salt Lake vice pulling round-the-clock surveillance on the motel. It would be nice if they'd come up with something illegal going on. Then, if Ms. Winkler decides not to cooperate, we'll be able to apply some pressure."

"You realize that finding this guy may not get us any closer to solving the murder of Watts," Burnham said.

"No question about it. This could turn out to be a waste of time and energy. Fortunately, it's not the only iron we've got in the fire."

"I sure hope not. What else you got?"

"We're trying to identify the individual who created the forged suicide note. That person might be directly involved, or at least represent a link to whoever else is. We're working that angle right now."

We spent the next few minutes figuring out our next moves. The weekend would be spent interviewing Levi's friends and acquaintances. I assigned Terry the task of locating Watts' estranged sister, hoping that she might have information that would help us. I also gave him the difficult job of trying to locate any of Charles Watts' friends. Those could be associates he hung around with while on parole, or possibly a small circle of friends from his most recent prison stay. While it appeared that Watts was something of a loner, that might not have been the case inside the joint. If Terry managed to locate his inmate friends, perhaps one of them might help us unravel the mystery surrounding his murder.

Six days had elapsed since the murder. We badly needed a break before the case grew any colder.

As for me, my weekend agenda included a stint as Mr. Mom. I had promised Sara she could bring a friend, and I would take them for an afternoon at Hogle Zoo.

Chapter Twenty-nine

One of the things I missed most about being married was a ritual Nicole and I developed during our eleven years together. On weekend mornings we would get up just ahead of the sunrise, brew our favorite coffee, usually something flavored, turn on the stereo, and settle in to watch the sun usher in a beautiful, new day. It was private, uninterrupted time between two people in love. Sometimes we talked, and on other occasions we didn't speak at all, allowing ourselves to become consumed by the quiet splendor of the Wasatch Mountains. The mountains' beauty was no less spectacular in the autumn months with the rich hues of aspen yellows and oranges clustered on the mountainside, or during winter with white crystal snow blanketing the landscape, often framed by a cloudless blue sky.

Sometimes on mornings like this, Aunt June got up early and joined me on the sun porch with her cup of black tea. And on rare occasions, even though her number one priority was sleeping in, I'd convinced Sara that getting up early to enjoy the sunrise was a special time. I don't think she quite got it. It usually required a bribe of hot chocolate, scrambled eggs, bacon, and toast.

On this particular morning, I was alone with my music and coffee. My thoughts drifted to the concurrent murder investigations of Levi Vogue and Charles Watts. The two cases had become entwined. It was now impossible to think of either case independently. To solve the murder of Charles Watts was to unravel the mystery of Levi Vogue's killing.

It was simple before: Vogue gets whacked. We correctly identified the jealous boyfriend of the woman Vogue was stooping on the side. He was a violent ex-offender with one of the oldest motives in the world—jealousy. Problem was, he didn't do it. Then Slick Watts came along. He turned out to be an even better suspect than John Merchant. He was the trigger, no doubt about it. Case closed. I should have been lying on the beach in Cabo sipping Long Island iced tea and reading a good who-done-it. But no, Watts' death turned out to be a murder disguised to look like a suicide. Bye bye, R & R.

At the moment, I was stumped. But I've always had a knack for thinking outside the box, and that's what I needed to do now.

One thing was clear—we had to locate the individual responsible for the forged suicide note, and we needed to find that person quickly. The forger's life might be in imminent danger. If the forger was paid to create the false suicide note and was not a direct participant in the broader murder conspiracy, he could be perceived much the same way Slick Watts probably was: a loose end requiring elimination. On the other hand, if we were lucky, the forger may have been following the story in the local news. If that were the case, he might have gone into hiding or bought the first plane ticket out of Utah.

◇◇◇

Assuming I survived today's trip to Hogle Zoo, which, incidentally, had grown from Sara and one friend to Sara and three of her schoolmates, I planned to meet Kate later in the evening at one of Salt Lake's finer watering holes. We planned to compare notes on the people on our separate lists of forgers. Besides, by then I'd probably need a drink, and who knows, maybe more.

Hogle Zoo, on a beautiful spring day, was a fun place to visit. I'd done my best to cajole Aunt June into coming, but she politely declined my offer. I wasn't sure if her lack of enthusiasm stemmed from the prospect of having to walk endless miles on zoo property, or the company she would have to keep—four eight-year-old kids and me. Probably a combination of both.

The trip came off without a hitch. I didn't lose anybody, and by early afternoon, I'd managed to fill four children with enough cotton candy and other goodies to keep them on a sugar-induced high for the rest of the day. When we returned to Park City, I dropped them all off at the home of one member of the group whose parents had invited everybody over for a birthday party sleep-over. On the ride back up the mountain, I overheard one of the girls talking about tonight's *slumber* party. Eight-year-old kids talking about slumber parties. Yikes!

Chapter Thirty

By the time I completed my zoo duty and stopped by the office to pick up my list of forgery candidates, I was late for my rendezvous with Kate. If she was ticked about my tardiness, she didn't show it. We met at the Timeout Lounge, a sports bar and eatery on Salt Lake's east side.

Unlike me, Kate had made it home for a quick change of clothes after her interviews with the Vogue family. I hadn't seen her in casual duds. I liked what I saw. She was wearing a little more makeup than I'd seen previously. Her cheeks definitely showed more color and her lips were a deep shade of red. She wore her long auburn hair down but tucked behind her ears. She was dressed casually in black, form-fitting designer jeans that flattered every curve. The open-toe sandals had heels that made her already long legs look even longer and slimmer. She wore a long-sleeve denim shirt accented by a gold necklace and matching earrings. So this was Kate McConnell away from the office. I found myself feeling attracted to her in a way I hadn't felt about anybody since the divorce.

I ordered a Killian Red while she sipped the house Merlot. I told her about the phone calls from James Allen and my subsequent conversation with him. Kate didn't seem surprised or irritated.

"So much for asking the mayor to attempt to dissuade Vogue from hiring a team of privates," said Kate. "And why didn't he call me directly instead of going through you?"

"He and I know each other, although not very well. You, he knows by reputation only. He's trying to use his relationship with me to ease into the investigation without creating a lot of hard feelings. He's really trying to avoid getting caught up in a pissing contest right out of the gate. And I think there's a way for us to take advantage of it."

"Oh yeah? How?"

"We stall for time in some very subtle ways that will keep Allen and his cohorts in the investigation, but always a couple of steps behind. If we get lucky, we resolve the case before they have a chance to fuck it up. Admittedly, we have to walk a fine line. We don't want Jim Allen getting frustrated and calling his employer, who in turn will complain to the mayor."

Kate looked more than a little skeptical. "Tell me how you think we should do this."

"For starters, we bog them down in red tape. If you'd call Stoddard before Jim Allen does, ask Tom to set up a meeting with Allen to discuss how a joint investigation might be coordinated, clarify role assignments, the production of documents, that sort of thing. You know how the feds work. They'll want every report that the investigation has generated to date. It takes time to copy all those documents."

"And you know what else?" said Kate. "Allen won't move forward with the investigation until his team has digested the contents of each and every report. Plus, the feds never trust the work produced by locals. They'll want to re-interview everyone connected with the case. Any idea how many personnel Allen plans to use on the investigation?"

"He didn't say."

Kate was smiling now. "You know what? This just might work.

"Now let's talk about something pleasant. How was your trip to the zoo today? Was it a good dad-daughter experience?"

"Actually, I survived just fine, and the kids had a nice time. And I probably should confess, for a fleeting moment, I even considered calling you, hoping a trip to the zoo with four young kids might appeal to your maternal instincts."

"Doubt that," she said, laughing. "About the maternal instincts, I mean. I don't think I have any. And if I do, I have no idea where they are."

"Maternal instincts aside, how did your interviews go with Margaret and her sons?"

"Do you really want to talk about this now? It's a great way of ruining a perfectly good glass of wine and your Killian."

"You make a very good point," I mused. "Why risk spoiling a potential glowing buzz, not to mention the added risk of indigestion."

"I'm glad we agree on that. I'll tell you about the interviews, but let's keep it brief so that we can get back to more pleasant conversation."

"I'll drink to that!"

"Actually, things went surprisingly well, considering we had to do the interviews at Vogue Chemicals in the presence of corporate legal counsel. Ed Tillman, by the way, turned out to be kind of a big teddy bear. It's amazing when you spend a few minutes flirting with a guy what you can get him to do, or in this case, refrain from doing. I didn't want the interviews with Margaret and her sons to become adversarial, with everybody getting defensive and ultimately leaving ticked off. But, a few well-placed minutes with Mr. Ed beforehand and, *voila*, the teddy bear came out and the lawyer went away. For the most part, Tillman remained passive and only interrupted a couple of times. I really couldn't have asked for more than that."

"Glad to hear that it went so well," I said.

"The boys turned out to be kind of interesting. The interview eliminated them as suspects. Both were in California at the time of the killing, and both have rock-solid alibis. The eldest, Robert, will be starting his senior year at Stanford University double-majoring in chemistry and microbiology. He's on the president's list sporting a 3.89 GPA. He also completed a two-year Mormon mission in Brazil.

"Contrast that with younger brother Jeremy, who is a party animal. He attends Pepperdine and has been arrested twice—

once for a minor in possession of alcohol, and the other, drunk and disorderly. He's carrying a less-than-stellar 2.2 GPA and has been on academic probation twice. He started a two-year mission in Canada, but was sent home in ten months for messing around with girls. Suffice to say that Jeremy has disappointed the family on numerous occasions, while Robert gets all the kudos. Go figure.

"They both seemed terribly distraught over the loss of their father. Neither kid has a motive I could discern—not anger, hatred, or money. There's no pot of gold waiting for either kid from the death of their father."

"What about family money?"

"Without question, family finances was the touchiest part of the interview. It was the one place where Tillman interrupted a couple of times, and Margaret, though cooperative, seemed puzzled about that line of inquiry. Here's the really interesting part, though. Between the financial information I was able to get from Margaret and the information Vince discovered from the financial records we seized from Vogue's home on the night of the murder, an interesting picture starts to emerge. Despite the family wealth, Levi was up to his eyebrows in debt, and Margaret, unless she's lying, knew nothing about it."

"That surprises me. I would have guessed that all the Vogue children and probably grandchildren are trust babies."

"Here's the deal. They are trust babies, grandchildren included. Both Robert and Jeremy are able to attend expensive out-of-state universities because Richard Vogue established educational trusts for each of his grandsons. Based on what we've been able to piece together about Levi's family budget, if he and Margaret had to pay for college, both sons would probably be home working part-time and attending Salt Lake Community College. That's about all they could afford. Levi and his two younger sisters also have trusts. The deal is, they can't access the dough for any reason until they're forty-five. Apparently Papa Vogue decided not to give his children large sums of family money until each of them was older and financially independent. The only exception he made was for education."

"Were you able to find out who administers the education trusts? Any chance Levi could have tapped his sons' trust money to support his own lifestyle?" I asked.

"Good thought," said Kate. "But the answer is no. Richard Vogue must have considered that possibility. Margaret indicated, and Tillman confirmed, that the education trusts are administered by trustees selected by Richard Vogue. He didn't come right out and say it, but my impression was that Ed Tillman is one of the trustees.

"Here's where it starts to get even more interesting. By her own admission, Margaret knew almost nothing about the family finances. Levi paid the bills and, in fact, had most of them sent to his office instead of home. Margaret was kept mostly in the dark when it came to matters of money. And evidently, that was all right with her.

"When I asked her for Levi's annual salary, she didn't know. She cast a nervous glance at Tillman, hoping he might have the answer. When he didn't, she finally took a guess and said she thought he made approximately $80,000 a year. She wasn't far off. His annual salary for this fiscal year was $87,900. Now take, say, thirty percent of the gross for state and federal taxes, and consider that Margaret doesn't work outside the home, and you've got net family income of about $60,000 annually or $5,000 a month.

"Vince pulled a credit report and we compared that with the family finances contained in the Quicken program we got off his home computer. It wasn't too difficult to piece together a family budget that would seem to suggest the Vogues were living well above what Levi was making as chairman of the Board of Pardons. It seems that Levi took out a second mortgage on their home just eighteen months before his death. He did a home equity loan with a $30,000 line of credit. At the time of his death, he had dipped into the account to the tune of $25,000," said Kate.

By this time, I had drained my second Killian Red and Kate had consumed a second glass of Merlot. I said, "Okay, so maybe they spent the $25,000 remodeling the house or buying that fancy Lexus he was driving."

"I don't think so," she said. "The Lexus was leased, and besides, when I asked Margaret about it, she recalled closing on the second mortgage, but had no idea that Levi was into it for twenty-five big ones. She denied taking on any major new family expenditures. Her chin hit the floor when I mentioned that the home equity line had only five grand left untapped."

"Let me tell you what I think," I said. "My father used to tell me that I had champagne taste on a beer income. That's what I'd say about Levi Vogue. It's good you discovered the second mortgage. It appears he was spending more than he was earning, and the second mortgage could have served almost as a bridge loan to get him to his forty-fifth birthday, when the trust would have kicked in. If Levi was spending more than he was earning, and we couldn't account for it, then I'd worry where that money was coming from. But since we can account for it, then all it proves is that Levi was lying to Margaret on a variety of different fronts in order to maintain a lifestyle she didn't know anything about. It isn't a pretty picture, but I don't see how it sheds any light on his murder."

"You might be right. But I'm not convinced that his salary, plus the twenty-five grand spent over the past eighteen months, adequately explains his family finances. It looks like there was insufficient income to cover his debts. Sam, the guy was chronically late paying almost all his bills. You should see the dings on his credit report. One outstanding account had even gone to collection status."

"So, your conclusion would be that Levi Vogue was on the take, that he had some illicit stream of income supporting his lifestyle."

"I don't know if I'd call it a conclusion, but I think it's possible. Let me put it another way—if he wasn't on the take, and somebody decided they were willing to pay a lot of money to influence a parole decision, he'd be the right guy to talk to. From what we can surmise, he needed the money."

Our verbal exchanges continued despite my starting to grow light-headed from the beer. "I definitely agree with you about one thing. Given Vogue's position on the Board of Pardons, if he was as pinched financially as you make him out to be, he'd probably be more susceptible to succumbing to temptation if the right opportunity came along."

We turned our attention to our respective lists of forgery suspects. Before getting very far, Kate stopped. "I thought we agreed to keep this brief."

"We did," I replied. "But think about it—isn't half the fun of working an investigation with someone the collaborating about case theories? And when you can consume a mind-altering substance at the same time, it's even better."

She laughed out loud, flashing a mouthful of beautiful white teeth. *This woman is starting to grow on me,* I thought. *She's talented, smart, and beautiful—a deadly combination. My head tells me to run while I can, my heart says something else.*

"You're a piece of work, Sam. But I have to admit, we do seem to make a really good team. I'm not sure whether you're my alter ego or I'm yours. Either way, it appears to be working."

Our conversation had lapsed into a comfortable silence. We didn't make eye contact, each of us content to stare into half-empty glasses. Kate broke the silence with the best idea of the evening—going back to her place.

She reached into her purse, pulled out her cell, and began punching numbers. As she dialed, she asked, "Tell me something, Sam. Do you like Chinese food?"

"Oh, yeah. As long as I can get it hot and spicy," I said.

"Hot and spicy it is," she said. She called Szechwan Charley's, a popular Chinese restaurant in downtown Salt Lake City. She ordered Hunan Beef, Szechwan Shrimp and steamed rice. She jotted her home address on one of her business cards and handed it to me. As she slipped out of the booth, she turned and said, "I really don't know why I'm doing this. Spur-of-the-moment sort of thing, I guess. See you at my place in twenty." With that, she was gone.

Chapter Thirty-one

I don't know why it surprised me, but somehow it did. I'd never imagined Kate McConnell as a city girl, but that's exactly what she was. Her home turned out to be a posh condominium in a gated community high in the Avenues district, not more than two miles from the home of Levi Vogue. The condo was a second-floor unit looking down on an outdoor pool and hot tub surrounded by a mature garden with sitting benches strategically placed around the grounds.

She'd arrived moments before I did and was busy in the kitchen transferring the Chinese food from cartons to serving dishes. She directed me to the plates and silverware and had me set the table on the outdoor patio deck. She grabbed two wine glasses and an open bottle of Chardonnay. When I declined the wine, she sent me to the refrigerator to help myself to a beer. The fridge contained a dozen bottles of Coors. Since Kate wasn't a beer drinker, I assumed the beer probably belonged to Stoddard. Kate reached around me and opened the freezer door. Out came a large and very cold beer stein. As for Stoddard, I decided not to go there.

"So tell me, how did you end up with a career in state corrections?" Kate asked.

"Well, I got in quite by accident. Becoming a cop certainly wasn't on my radar screen as a kid. In high school, my priorities were basketball, girls, and academics—in that order.

Occasionally, the order changed to girls, basketball, and academics. But academics was never the first priority. Don't get me wrong. I got by all right, but I was never on anybody's short list to become valedictorian of my senior class.

"After high school, I was fortunate enough to have several full-ride scholarship offers in basketball from some pretty decent Division I schools. I signed a letter-of-intent with the University of New Mexico and headed off to Albuquerque. I lasted two years in the program before tearing up the ACL in my left knee."

"Did you have to have surgery?"

"I did, and I've got an ugly scar to prove it. I wish the medical community had the technology twenty years ago that they do today. The knee still isn't right."

"That's not good. I'm sorry to hear that."

"Anyway, my basketball career came to an abrupt end and so did the athletic scholarship that paid the bills. Much to my parents' chagrin, I dropped out of school and headed north to Santa Fe. I fell in love with the town but needed a job if I was going to stay. One day as I was perusing the local paper, I noticed an ad for a corrections officer at the New Mexico State Prison. The prison is just outside Santa Fe. It was shortly after the big riot—you know, the one where the inmates damn near burned the entire place to the ground. They were begging for help. If you were breathing and standing upright, they offered you a job."

"So, you worked at the state prison for a while, and then returned to Utah and went to work for the Department of Corrections?" Kate asked.

"That's about it. My folks really wanted me to come back, live at home for a while, and finish my degree at the University of Utah. I took them up on everything but the living at home part. I'd been on my own long enough that moving home didn't hold much appeal. I think they were relieved when I decided to live in Salt Lake City.

"How about you?"

"Well, my story is a bit different from yours. I grew up in Spokane, Washington. My mom started out as a dispatcher in the Spokane Police Department when she was twenty. Twenty-seven years later, she had risen from a clerical job to deputy chief of police. I saw her and that's what I knew I wanted to do. So, it would be fair to say that I knew I wanted to be a cop from the time I was old enough to understand what my mother did for a living. She's been a great mother and a great role model. At her urging, I set my sights a little higher than the Spokane P.D. I wanted to get into the FBI as a special agent. And unlike you, Sam, my priorities were academics and sports, volleyball mostly. And unlike you, I *was* the valedictorian of my senior class."

"I'm not surprised."

"Like you, after high school, I had a number of volleyball scholarship offers to choose from. I selected Washington State University because of its reputation as a place to study criminology. I actually turned down the athletic aid and entered on a Presidential Scholarship instead. I graduated four years later with dual degrees in criminal justice and psychology. Along the way, I played four years on the women's volleyball team and even managed a couple of years as all-conference honorable mention."

"Wow. I'm impressed. That's still a long way from the Salt Lake City Police Department."

"Actually, several factors came into play. One was that I knew the area pretty well and liked it. I had an aunt who lived in Salt Lake City for quite a few years, and my parents brought me to visit her several times when I was a kid. Also, my mother was well connected to the chief of police, and he encouraged me to apply. It's been a good experience, even though when I came, I never intended to stay permanently. I thought the experience would be just the right ticket for entree into the FBI. And it probably was."

Kate didn't offer any specifics regarding her meteoric rise through the ranks of the Salt Lake City Police Department. Her reputation at solving high-visibility homicide cases had made her something of a media celebrity throughout the Salt Lake Valley. Some in the business believed that McConnell was on the fast track to one day becoming the first female Salt Lake City Chief of Police, assuming no major screw-ups along the way.

"Aside from the job, I really enjoy living near downtown. It gives me easy access to lots of good restaurants. And the cultural amenities available in the city are really quite impressive."

"Such as?"

"Well, I have season tickets to the Utah Symphony as well as the Salt Lake Acting Company. The community theater here is great, and we also get some good Broadway plays. On occasion, I take in an opera or the ballet. What more could a girl ask for?"

She tossed the ball to me. "What kind of things do you enjoy doing when you're not chasing down bad guys or playing Mr. Mom?"

It occurred to me that if it's true that opposites attract, I might have a chance with Kate. Otherwise, forget about it. I could hardly stand to tell her that my "cultural interests" consisted largely of chasing around the Wasatch mountains on skis or a mountain bike. I also enjoyed quaffing beer at Utah Grizzly hockey games, and I attended an occasional rodeo for good measure. It wouldn't take Einstein to figure out that our respective lists of leisure activities didn't seem terribly compatible. Given a choice between attending an opera or going to the dentist for a root canal, I'd probably choose the opera, but only by the slimmest of margins.

After confessing my cultural shortcomings, I couldn't tell if Kate was horrified or merely amused. In any event, I was sorry that the pleasant buzz I'd been working on had receded into a state of dour sobriety resulting from too much Hunan beef and steamed rice and too little beer.

We cleared away the dinner dishes and spent the next hour at her dining-room table comparing our lists of forgery candidates, any one of whom could have created the false suicide note. My list contained every offender currently under state correctional supervision for a forgery conviction. We eliminated those offenders locked up in prison or a county jail. We then compared Kate's list with my longer list of probationers and parolees under departmental supervision. We pared the list down to nineteen possible candidates, nine of whom appeared on both lists. We agreed to split the group of nine among Kate, Vince Turner, and me.

It was starting to get late. "Let's put this stuff away, okay? How about an after-dinner drink before we call it a night?" said Kate.

"I'd like that."

"Brandy okay?"

"Great."

Kate directed me into her dimly lit living room while she went to get the brandy. We sat down on the couch next to each other. Our knees were touching. When I attempted to make eye contact with her, she quickly looked away. Neither of us spoke, but somehow, the silence didn't feel awkward or uncomfortable. As I raised the snifter to my lips, I let the unmistakable wood-smoke smell of brandy fill my nostrils. I removed the snifter and noticed the faint odor of Kate's perfume. When I looked over at her again, she was still looking away. She must have felt my eyes on her because she turned and met my gaze. This time she didn't look away. We leaned toward each other and kissed that first slow kiss, gentle and exploring. We parted just long enough to deposit our brandy snifters on the nearby coffee table and then we kissed again. I felt every part of me stir as our tongues danced the dance of an intimate new relationship.

Our breathing became labored and our arousal more pronounced. I felt Kate's hand begin to tentatively stroke my chest and then move lower across my abdomen. With one hand I gently caressed her right breast while kissing her neck and ear. Her hand moved lower until she felt the hardness through my jeans. Slowly I began to unbutton her shirt. Under the denim, she wore a lacy white bra that only partially concealed small but firm breasts. I felt her stiffen as she pulled away and stood up.

"Sam, we've got to stop. This can't go any further. Christ, think about it. We've got a murder investigation on our hands. We've got to stay focused. Besides, you're trying to get over a divorce and I'm involved with someone else. This just isn't going to work."

I quickly got up off the couch and offered an awkward apology. "Sorry, Kate. You're absolutely right. I'm glad at least one of us had the good sense to put the brakes on before something happened that we both might regret."

"Hey! We're both adults. I'm the one who invited you here in the first place. It was an impulsive thing to do, and I usually don't behave impulsively. And please don't misunderstand. It isn't that I don't enjoy being with you because I do. It's just too complicated right now. We need to call a timeout and think about this."

"I understand what you're saying and I agree." I thanked her for a nice evening and headed home to take a cold shower.

Chapter Thirty-two

As I drove home and my libido returned to something approaching normal, a couple of thoughts occurred to me. The incident at Kate's, while awkward, probably turned out for the best. Sleeping with someone changed things significantly. I hoped our impromptu interlude wouldn't interfere with our ability to work together effectively. Besides, I'd have to be a couple bricks short of a full load not to recognize that Kate's relationship with Tom Stoddard had progressed well beyond the casual dinner-date stage. The guy kept his beer in her refrigerator and probably some of his clothes in her closet. And what, if anything, would Kate say to Stoddard about her relationship with me? Perhaps, nothing. I was glad I didn't have to deal with that one.

Since the divorce, providing stability for Sara has been my number one priority. A relationship with Kate, or anyone else for that matter, would only be a distraction.

I spent Sunday morning with Sara and Aunt June. I drove everybody over to Prospector Square, where we had brunch at a local favorite, the Ore House restaurant. During the meal, Aunt June asked about Baxter Shaw. "I know you've been busy. You probably haven't had time to call that dear Baxter Shaw you were telling me about to arrange a little get-together?"

"Not yet. But let me see what I can do this week. I think Baxter might be one of those retired types who enjoys spending some of his spare time at the court house watching whatever interesting trial might be in progress. Would lunch be okay? And would you like me along as chaperon?" I teased.

"Well, I can sure put his time to better use than sitting around in some court room," she said. "Lunch at Little America would be nice. As far as your acting as chaperon, thanks for the offer, but I think we'll be just fine."

After brunch, I dropped Aunt June back at the house and spent the rest of the morning with Sara at the local duck pond, you guessed it, feeding the ducks.

By mid-afternoon, I was off the mountain and in search of the three forgery suspects I had been assigned to interview.

Of the three—Walter Gale, Wendell Rich, and Vaughn Gardner—Gale looked to be the most interesting. Recently released from the Utah State Prison, where he had served five years on three concurrent one-to-fifteen-year forgery sentences, Gale had the look of a first-rate forger.

Gale was middle-aged, with no prior criminal history. He had billed himself as a legitimate buyer and seller of historical documents. Trouble was, most of the documents he sold as historic originals turned out to be high-quality forgeries.

Apparently, an experienced collector of historical documents became suspicious about a letter he'd purchased from Gale, allegedly written by legendary mountain man and scout, Kit Carson. He turned the letter over to a nationally renowned document examiner in New York City, who determined that it was an exceptionally well crafted fake. Gale's world crumbled around him as victim after victim came forward with a variety of forged documents. His Department of Corrections file showed that the Board of Pardons had slapped him with a restitution bill of almost one-quarter of a million dollars.

I found Walter Gale living at the home of his married daughter in Provo. It seemed that his wife of twenty years divorced him shortly after he entered prison, and moved back to California to begin a new life. My gut told me Gale was too good at his craft to have involved himself in creating a forged suicide note like this one. It seemed far beneath his skill level, and besides, getting caught would earn him a one-way ticket back to prison. I hoped by contacting him without advance warning, if he was involved, he might confess, or slip and say something incriminating. He didn't do either.

Gale was polite and cooperative. I showed him a copy of the suicide note and explained the nature of my visit. He firmly denied any involvement in the incident. "Look, Mr. Kincaid, I've only been out of prison for a few months. My daughter and her husband have been kind enough to let me live with them while I try to put my life back together. I work forty hours a week as a salesman at an Ultimate Electronics store in Orem. I can't have a checking account, a credit card, or any installment debt. I've got a restitution bill big enough to choke a horse. And I get the impression that my PO would like nothing better than to see me screw up so he can have me sent back to prison. I've been there and I'm not going back. And quite frankly, this looks like a simple job, not worthy of my time or expertise. And it probably didn't pay much either."

He sounded convincing. He volunteered to offer an opinion on the quality of the forgery. He examined the note and the samples of Slick Watts' handwriting. He agreed with the document examiner's conclusion that the suicide note was an above-average piece of work, not something done by a rank amateur.

"Tell me," I said. "Can you think of anybody in the business who might be responsible for the job?"

"Sorry," he replied. "I'm out of that life now, and I'm not about to look back. If you like, I could take a look at the list you've working from."

I declined his offer, thanked him, and got up to leave.

As I reached the front door, Gale said, "Hey, Mr. Kincaid. Tell me why you're limiting the search to guys out here in the community?"

"What do you mean?" I asked.

"Just what I said. Who's to say the guy who wrote that note isn't locked up at the state prison right now?"

"Are you trying to tell me something, Walter?"

"No, not necessarily. It was just a thought," he replied.

Chapter Thirty-three

I left Walter Gale, feeling ticked off and disturbed. Ticked off because I hadn't considered the possibility the forger might be an inmate currently in prison. Disturbed by the implications of having the suicide note written by somebody currently serving time. How had I managed to overlook that possibility? Who would have asked an inmate to forge the note? Another inmate? Once written, how was it smuggled out of prison? And did Walter Gale know more than he was telling me? Was he trying to point me in the right direction without getting himself directly involved? I had an idea, two ideas actually. I decided to launch them simultaneously the next morning.

With a little more leg-work, I eliminated the other two forgery suspects. I found Wendell Rich at the Utah State Hospital on an involuntary civil commitment for mental health problems. He'd been there almost two years. I found an empty house with a "for sale" sign in the front yard at Vaughn Gardner's address. A neighbor told me he had died of a massive heart attack a year ago while mowing his lawn.

Having eliminated Gardner, Rich, and Gale as suspects, I did something I rarely do—act on impulse. I'd been thinking about Kate and decided to steer the Cherokee toward her condo. A little voice in my head, which I chose to ignore, told me this was not a good plan. When I reached Kate's complex, I drove in, parked, and knocked on her front door. Much to my surprise and chagrin, an equally surprised Tom Stoddard answered the door barefoot, wearing a pair of faded blue jeans and a tank top.

"Kincaid, what are you doing here?"

Recovering quickly, I said, "Hoping to catch Lieutenant McConnell. I need to chat with her for a couple of minutes about the investigation."

Speaking in hushed tones, Stoddard said with more irritation in his voice than surprise, "Man, this is Sunday evening. Can't this wait until tomorrow morning?"

Before I could answer, an unsuspecting McConnell sidled up next to him, also barefoot, and wearing a long-sleeve yellow shirt and a pair of blue jean shorts. Her hair was wet as though she had just showered. The look on her face ranged somewhere between surprise and terror.

"Sam," she stammered. "I take it we've got business to discuss. Come in. Excuse me for a second while I dry my hair."

Stoddard ushered me into the living room and then disappeared into the bedroom. I could hear Kate and him arguing, but I was unable to make out exactly what they were saying. I couldn't have walked into a more awkward situation. So much for acting on impulse.

After several minutes, Kate joined me in the living room. I apologized for the intrusion and offered to postpone our conversation until the next day. Stoddard hadn't returned, but I sensed he was nearby and probably in a position to eavesdrop.

I explained the substance of my conversation with Walter Gale, including my suspicion that he might have known more than he had told me. I apologized for a second time in the span of a couple of minutes, this time for failing to recognize what should have been obvious from the get-go.

"Don't be too hard on yourself, Sam. No one, including me, gave a thought to the possibility an inmate forged that suicide note. The important question now is what do we do about it?"

I spent the next few minutes bringing her up to speed on the plan that had been taking shape in my head for the past couple of hours. In turn, Kate informed me that she and Vince had each located two of the three forgery suspects assigned to them. They hadn't been able to find the other two. That eliminated seven possible suspects from our original list.

I was anxious to find out what Salt Lake City P.D. Vice had discovered from the weekend surveillance of the Starlite Motel, since part of my plan involved Sue Ann Winkler. Not caring much for Sue Ann, Kate seemed almost giddy as she described the weekend's activities.

"We had vice teams watching the place Friday night, Saturday afternoon, and again on Saturday night. According to the report, on both Friday and Saturday nights there was a lot of activity around the place. We're talking about johns checking in for one or two-hour dates with several different girls. Very little action on Saturday during the day until late in the afternoon, when business started to pick up again. The surveillance team identified the mother, Lou Ann Barlow, and her live-in, Frank Arnold, working the front desk and collecting money as people came in and out. Although they weren't sure, they didn't think Sue Ann was among the girls meeting dates at the place. The motel was definitely taking in revenue from prostitution activity. How do you think we should play it?"

"Let me pay a visit to Sue Ann right away and see what level of cooperation I can get from her. I want her to look at the enhanced videotape of the people who attended Levi's funeral. If she's uncooperative, then a raid on the motel might give her a reason to cooperate. I assume your vice unit would enjoy hitting the motel with a search warrant. If Frank and Mama get popped, maybe Sue Ann becomes a little more helpful," I said.

"That works. The vice unit took surveillance photos and license plate numbers of the vehicles coming in and out of the motel. They're busy identifying the girls and visiting a few johns. As soon as they're finished, they should be able to get the warrant. I imagine they'll go in, seize business records, and bust some folks. Customers will receive citations, but Frank and Lou Ann will probably get booked into jail on felony pimping charges.

In all likelihood, some of the girls will turn out to be dancers from Satin & Lace," said Kate.

She paused momentarily, lost in thought, and then continued. "Sam, we both know Sue Ann may not have been totally forthcoming in our interview with her. But what exactly do you hope to get from her?"

"Two things. First, I want to find out what, if anything, she's held back from us. Second, I want the identity of the guy who Vogue included in his sexual liaisons with Sue Ann. It's just a hunch, but if we can get our hands on this guy, I somehow think he might hold the key to solving our case."

"God, I hope you're right. Worst-case scenario, it's another dead end. And by the way, more good news. The state crime lab found absolutely nothing when they went back to Wendover and processed the crime scene and Watts' hotel room. His car had been wiped clean. The hotel room produced a variety of latent prints they are checking out for us. But don't hold your breath. After all, it's a hotel room, and it ought to have prints. They'll let us know if the fingerprint database search produces anything useful.

"And one last thing. Jim Allen called Tom late Friday afternoon. Allen wanted to meet first thing tomorrow morning, but Tom made some excuse and set the meeting for five o'clock in the afternoon. The stall is on. Apparently, the D.A. wasn't one bit happy to hear that Richard Vogue hired private investigators without consulting anybody. Although nobody has said anything yet, the brass are probably nervous about having the Vogue family find out about Levi's extramarital activities."

I left Kate's condo with as much grace as I could muster under the circumstances. To describe the feeling as awkward was a serious understatement. I wanted to discuss things, and I sensed she did too. This, however, wasn't the time or place. The investigation was reaching another critical juncture. I could feel it. And distractions just wouldn't do.

Chapter Thirty-four

At eight-thirty the next morning, I gathered my unit for a meeting at the state prison. The staff of the Special Investigations Branch consisted of six investigators, two secretaries, and me. We are a pretty close-knit bunch. As I entered the conference room, one of my investigators, Marcy Everest, was busy entertaining the staff with one of her jokes. As I sat down, I heard her say, "So this guy's been dead for several months, and then one day out of the clear blue, he speaks to an old friend. His friend says, 'Hey Max, is that really you?' Max answers, 'Oh, yes, it's me.' And the friend says, 'So Max, tell me what it's like.' And Max says, 'Well it's really pretty good. I sleep in, get up when I want, have a little breakfast, have some great sex, and then take a nap. A little later in the day, I wake up again, have another meal, have some more great sex, and then take another snooze. That's kind of my routine now. It's good.' So the friend says, 'Wow, Max, so that's what Heaven is really like.' And Max says, 'Who the hell said anything about Heaven? I'm a buffalo in Montana.'"

The room erupted with laughter, and then we settled down to work.

My agenda was relatively short. I wanted to talk about the Vogue/Watts murder investigation. "Folks, it's time to use our inmate sources to see what kind of information is out there. I know when we do that it creates stress among both the inmates and the staff. But in this instance, we've come to a near standstill.

So here's what I want you to do. I'd like each of you to contact all of your inmate sources. See what they can find out for us. As usual, be careful what kind of reward you negotiate with them. When in doubt, talk with me first.

"Terry, get this request to all the correctional officer shift commanders so they can make an announcement at roll-call meetings. We want all our COs to keep an ear to the ground for any information that might be helpful. Marcy, you do the same thing with the clinical staff supervisors, teachers, maintenance workers, and culinary employees. Basically, we want the assistance of everybody employed inside the prison who has regular contact with inmates. We should probably anticipate the usual whining from the clinical staff. They never like it when we pressure them or inmates to provide snitch information. It interferes with their client-therapist trust-building relationship or some such bullshit. Pass them and their complaints along to me. I'll deal with them. Any questions?"

There were none, and our meeting broke up. Terry stuck around to provide me with an update on what he'd learned from Charles Watts' friends as well as his sister.

He dug around for a minute and finally pulled out a dog-eared, yellow lined legal pad sporting what appeared to be a large coffee stain in the middle of the page. The page was covered with unreadable handwritten notes that might have been written in Swahili. "Sorry," he began. "I haven't had time to sit down and translate my notes into a coherent report."

"Are you sure we're not going to need a team of investigators to help translate those notes?" I asked, smiling.

"Up yours. You want to hear what I got or not?"

"What's the matter with you, Terry—you off your meds again?"

"No, but if you keep talking, you're going to need your own meds, as in pain meds. Got it?"

"Loud and clear. Fill me in."

"Here's what I've learned so far. After asking around, I discovered an inmate by the name of Herbert Walker who probably qualifies as the closest thing to a friend Slick Watts had when he was inside. Walker described Watts as a private sort of guy; polite, but never very forthcoming. He said his contact with Watts occurred mostly in the prison culinary, where they both worked as cooks. Away from work, they spent time together gambling, poker usually. The most significant thing Walker shared concerned some things Slick said about what he was planning to do once released."

"Such as," I said.

"Don't get too excited. Walker was clear that Watts never got real specific. The gist of it was that Slick intimated that once paroled, he had some kind of contact on the outside who intended to employ him at something very lucrative. When pressed for details, Watts refused to be specific. Walker believed that whatever Slick had in mind, it wasn't flipping pancakes at the local IHOP. Walker felt certain the employment involved something illegal and highly profitable, and would allow Watts to operate solo," Burnham said.

"Shit, that could be anything from dealing dope to carrying out contract murders and everything in between," I said. After a moment of silence, it hit me right between the eyes. "Ah, Christ, Burnham. I know where you're going with this. You're about to tell me that Slick Watts was working as a self-employed contract killer. Right?"

"It's not such a terribly big stretch, Sam. Think about it. Somebody hires Watts to kill Levi Vogue. Maybe Vogue isn't even his first victim. And then that somebody kills Slick and tries to make it look like a suicide.

"But there's more. Yesterday, I tracked down Watts' sister, one Vicki Gallego. She's straight, no criminal history, married, two kids, and has worked for the past nine years at Utah Power. She's the only member of the family that maintained any semblance of contact with Slick. The father is dead, Mom has remarried and, according to Vicki, is a serious alcoholic. The youngest sibling, another sister, resides in California and has nothing to do with anybody in the family.

"Vicki told me when she received the call informing her that her brother had committed suicide, she didn't believe it. When I asked her why, she described her brother as narcissistic, with much too large an ego to have killed himself. She said he always bragged about some big deal that was just around the corner and would make him big bucks. She said there was no way he'd have ever been content holding down a nine-to-five job like everybody else. When I asked her if she thought he might be capable of carrying out murders for hire, she didn't hesitate for a second. She said if the price was right, he'd do it."

"Not a particularly flattering picture of her own brother. Anything else?"

"That's it. I do have the names of two more guys on parole who Walker maintained were also friends of Slick when he was inside. I'll run them down in the next day or two."

"Thanks for the update. I don't know exactly what to make of it, but you've sure given me something to chew on. Keep after it."

Chapter Thirty-five

When I returned to my office, I found nineteen voice mail messages waiting, one of them from Kate. I hadn't spoken with her since the episode at her condo the previous day. She asked me to call her as soon as I could. She didn't say what we needed to talk about, but I was afraid I had a pretty good idea. I still felt embarrassed. I decided not to call her back until later in the day.

Not surprisingly, I also had a call from Jim Allen asking whether I'd been able to set up a meeting with Kate. He sounded anxious. This was a meeting we wanted to delay for as long as possible. I decided to take a chance. I dialed his number hoping he wouldn't answer so I could leave him a voice message. He didn't pick up. "Jim, Sam Kincaid. I still haven't been able to reach Kate but I'll keep trying. I'll get back to you as soon as I have the meeting set." I told Patti that Allen would probably be calling back and that she should tell him that I was tied up in management meetings all day. The stall continued.

By early afternoon I was in the field looking for Sue Ann Winkler. I found her walking to her car in the parking lot outside the Satin & Lace Club. She had some large goon in tow who appeared to be nothing more than an escort from the club to her car. He was a large Asian guy who wore his jet-black hair pulled back into a ponytail. He was wearing tight black jeans and a yellow sleeveless tank top. Both of his well-muscled arms were covered with tattoos from wrist to shoulder. Both ears were pierced and he wore a round, silver ring above his right eyebrow. If he had other body parts pierced, I didn't want to know where. As I got out of my car, I could tell Sue Ann recognized me, but she didn't look enthused about seeing me again. George, the gorilla, put on his most sinister look and stepped between us. Sue Ann whispered something to him and he moved around behind her, still giving me his best scowl.

"Hello, Detective Kincaid. You here for business or pleasure?" she asked. The greeting, while not dripping with affection, wasn't hostile either.

I did my best to put on my most sincere, friendly, non-threatening face. I said, "Business actually. I'm glad I found you. I really need your help with something. It's important. I'd like you to take a look at some video footage of people who attended Levi's funeral. We're attempting to identify the guy Vogue brought over to the motel on those occasions when you did the *ménage à trois.*"

Her facial expression hardened instantly. The nonverbal look told me that I'd pissed her off. "Oh, Christ. I don't see how this could have one goddamn thing to do with Levi's murder," she hissed.

"You know what. You're probably right. But you might be wrong, too. This is a loose end in the investigation that might be meaningless, or it might be important. Right now we're following every lead we possibly can. And at the moment, we've about run out of leads. You put on a tough exterior, Sue Ann, but I believe you really cared for Levi. So I figured you'd be willing to help." I'm wasn't sure I really believed what I'd just said, but it sounded like the right thing to say at the time.

"Well, maybe you figured wrong, Kincaid," she said, her stern facade starting to slip. I stopped talking and allowed a moment of awkward silence to fill the space between us. She finally said, "Ah, shit. Let's get it over with. I guess it could be worse. You might have brought Kathryn the Great with you, or should I say Kathryn the Bitch. In that case, I'd be telling you both to fuck off."

"I appreciate your willingness to do this. You can follow me in your car or ride with me, and I'll drive you back afterward. Your choice."

"How long do you expect this to take?"

"One hour at most."

"Then I'll ride over with you." She got in the passenger side of my department-issue Chevrolet Impala and looked over at me, smiling. "You know, Kincaid, you're kind of a cute guy in a funny sort of way. A little too straight-looking for my taste, but what the hell. Why don't we spend that hour you want me looking at video over at the motel. If you want to watch movies, I'll show you some really hot video. We could have an intimate party for two. I'll make sure you leave relaxed and with a smile on your face."

I smiled back and said, "That was a backhanded compliment if ever I heard one. And it almost sounded like you were soliciting me."

"I wasn't soliciting. I didn't ask you for money, honey. This one's free—on the house, so to speak. What do you say?"

I didn't have the heart to tell her a vice raid at the Starlite Motel was imminent, and that it was a good place to avoid for the next little while. "Thanks for a very tempting offer. I'm flattered. I really am. And you're a beautiful lady. But I'm a little busy right now trying to solve a couple of murders. Some other time, maybe?"

She gave me an indifferent shrug and didn't say anything more. I felt as though I'd managed to extricate myself from an awkward situation without offending her.

I called ahead and had Patti set up the videotape in our conference room. I wanted to get this over with as quickly as possible. When we arrived, the TV monitor was on and everything was ready. The only thing missing was the beer and hot buttered popcorn. The tape had a total running time of approximately forty-five minutes. About halfway through, Sue Ann asked me to stop the tape and back it up a little. I had no sooner hit the play button when she said, "Hold it. That's him. That's the guy I did the three-way with."

I backed it up and ran it forward once more. "Are you sure?"

"Absolutely. That's the dude Levi brought with him to the motel. The two things I distinctly recall about him were the tattoo I told you about and what a little dick he had. I mean, at full attention, we're talking about something the size of your little pinkie. I remember thinking later that any woman deserved more than that."

I excused myself momentarily and hustled over to my office, where I picked up a current copy of the Utah Department of Corrections Annual Report. I brought it back to the conference room and flipped through it until I found the page I was looking for. It was a section of the report devoted to the Utah Board of Pardons and Parole. This particular page included individual head-and-shoulder shots of each member of the board. The photographs were significantly larger than the video images she had just viewed to make the identification. I set it down in front of her and asked her to make the identification again. She didn't hesitate, pointing immediately to the picture of William Allred.

"Wow. So this Allred dude is a member of the parole board just like Levi was?" she asked. "I guess I shouldn't be too surprised. Do you think he's mixed up in Levi's murder?"

"That's a very good question, Sue Ann, and the answer is, I just don't know."

I took Sue Ann Winkler back to the Satin & Lace Club, then I headed to my office at the prison. I called ahead to Terry, who was waiting for me when I arrived. I told him what I'd learned from Sue Ann. I said, "I want Bill Allred placed under visual surveillance. Call the Board of Pardons and find out discreetly Allred's hearing schedule for the next several days. Then we can assign some of our staff to track his movements.

"I want to know where this guy goes and who he sees when he's not conducting parole hearings. That means getting him up in the morning, following him to work, following him if he leaves for lunch, and then following him home in the evening. Once he's safely tucked in for the night, then it's okay to discontinue the surveillance. But somebody has to be back on him early the next morning."

"That's really going to stretch our resources," said Burnham. "I think I can free up two investigators, and I'm available to help. We'll have to work solo, which will be tough if he's on the move very much. If this goes on very long, we'll need additional personnel."

"I'll see if I can convince McConnell to provide some help. She's been less than enthused about this line of pursuit. But maybe the current revelation from Sue Ann will change her mind. In the meantime, we're still trying to identify the guy who wrote the forged suicide note."

"You want his phone records?"

"Absolutely," I said. "Find out which company provides cell phone service for the Board of Pardons. All the board members carry a cell. Let's get both his home and cell phone records for the past six months. Who knows, the phone records may turn out to be more useful than all the time-consuming visual surveillance. And also have somebody snatch his garbage can and sort through the trash—never can tell what might turn up in the garbage."

"You must really think Allred's involved."

"Hell, I wish I knew, Terry. It's a calculated gamble, that's for sure. When I interviewed him, he acted kind of funny when I asked about his friendship with Levi. At least now we know why. I've got to trust my instincts, and right now, my instincts are telling me somehow Bill Allred's involved. I've been wrong before. It wouldn't be the first time. But over the years, I've guessed right a lot more often than I've been wrong. We'll know soon enough."

Chapter Thirty-six

I turned to the task of identifying current inmates who might have been responsible for creating the forged suicide note. So far, nobody had come forward seeking protection, although the likelihood of that happening was always a long shot.

Using the Department's automated offender database, I searched for inmates currently serving sentences on forgery charges or with prior felony convictions for forgery. I ended up with a sizable group of one hundred eighty inmates. Knowing that it would be extremely time-consuming to interview all of them, I narrowed the search by removing those not currently serving sentences for forgery. That reduced the size of the list by more than half. I then scanned the remaining prisoners, focusing on prior criminal history. I was searching for inmates who appeared to be skilled forgers and those for whom forgery was their primary criminal occupation. This allowed me to further narrow the list so we could begin by interviewing the most promising suspects.

The task looked daunting. It was conceivable that we might have to interview all of them. If that were the case, I'd have to call in reinforcements. At least by starting with the most likely candidates, we might get lucky.

Patti informed me that Kate had just cleared security and was on her way to my office. I used the brief interlude and called Aunt June to explain that I wouldn't be home in time for dinner. I talked briefly with Sara, and told her that reading a bedtime story would have to wait until another evening. She wasn't happy. I glanced up just as Kate entered my office, closing the door behind her.

She looked tired, like maybe she hadn't slept much the night before. No surprise.

"Hi, Kate. How are you?"

"I've had better days. How about you?"

"Okay, I guess. Look, I know I've said this before, but I had no business dropping by your place unannounced yesterday."

"No big deal. Well, on second thought, it was a big deal. But I didn't come out here so you would have to apologize again. After you left, I leveled with Tom. I told him that our relationship had become personal and that I thought there might be some chemistry between us."

"Ah, shit," I said. "How'd he take it?"

"Pretty hard, I'm afraid. We agreed to break things off for a while until we both have a chance to think things over. I take full responsibility for what happened."

"I'm sorry for the problem this has caused you and Tom, but I don't have any regrets about what happened between us. I wanted to be there. It felt right to me. And I haven't felt that way about anybody since my divorce. I hope I didn't ruin it. I'd like to believe that when things finally settle down, we can see each other. I know you and Tom have issues, and I'll stay out of the way. And God knows, in the meantime, we've got plenty of work to do. And speaking of work, do I have news for you."

I filled her in on the news regarding Allred. It piqued her interest sufficiently to offer additional personnel for the surveillance. Burnham would be happy to hear this, I thought.

"Since you're here, I might as well put you to work." I showed her the list of forgery inmates requiring interviews. "Any ideas about how we approach the people on this list?"

She considered this. "Well, we need their cooperation, and since time is of the essence, how about using an electric cattle prod?"

I laughed. "I can see you haven't lost your sense of humor. That approach would make you the instant poster girl for every jailhouse lawyer we have in the system, not to mention the American Civil Liberties Union. Next idea?"

"Seriously, I think we need to stress the possible danger the forger is in, and offer protection in exchange for their cooperation."

"I think that's the right approach, but I think we need to consider offering an additional carrot," I said. "I'm afraid that appealing to their sense of potential danger by itself won't provide sufficient motivation for them to cooperate. These guys live in a dangerous environment to begin with, and they're smart enough to understand that if the word gets out that they snitched somebody off, they're as good as dead."

"So what do you propose?"

"I think we should offer to make a positive recommendation to the parole board—something that might shorten their prison sentence. We could also arrange a transfer out of this prison to a different facility. And what about offering immunity from prosecution?"

"I'm okay with all of it except the immunity offer. We'll have to get the approval of the D.A.'s office on that one. I'll speak with Tom about it."

◇◇◇

A prison inmate turned snitch almost always made a lousy witness in court. Defense attorneys love to get them on cross because it's easy to destroy their credibility. By the time an experienced defense attorney reveals the inmate's prior criminal record to the jury and exposes the rewards offered to secure the inmate's testimony, the prosecution's star witness ends up looking like a dolt. But given our present situation, right now a dolt looked pretty good.

Chapter Thirty-seven

Milo Sorensen had been working in the prison's furniture assembly and upholstery plant for a little over a month. He worked afternoons from one to five. For the first time in a lengthy prison career, he'd finally gotten a job with decent pay and the opportunity to learn a vocational skill that might do him some good on the outside.

As the newest inmate hire, Sorensen's lack of seniority made it his responsibility to perform routine janitorial duties at the close of each work day. He had to sweep the plant floor, empty the trash in the adjoining small office, and clean the head. Most days, Milo began the evening cleanup by four-thirty to ensure he would be finished by five o'clock or a few minutes after. On this day, he'd been so busy attaching legs to new office chairs that he hadn't begun cleaning until almost five, when a civilian employee noticed and told him to get busy. At a few minutes past five, Sorensen was alone in the plant.

He moved methodically from task to task. First he took a broom to the plant floor. Then he emptied the trash and tidied up the small office adjacent to the production line. At first, the only sounds he heard came from the four large ceiling fans scattered around the plant and the constant drone of the old natural gas furnace. The old furnace had long since failed to provide adequate heat to an equally old building. For just an instant as he shuffled with mop in hand toward the restroom, Sorensen heard what he thought sounded like the rustle of clothing and the soft foot-fall of a tennis shoe on the concrete floor. He looked around but saw nothing.

Minutes later, as he came out of the restroom on to the plant floor, for a fleeting second, he saw a blur of motion. It was the last thing he would ever see. The three-foot-long metal pipe crushed his skull on the first blow. Before he hit the concrete floor, a second assailant had stabbed him several times in the lower back with a sharp plastic shank. The blows rained down. By the time it was over, Milo had been stabbed more than a dozen times. His head looked like a crushed melon. For good measure, one of the attackers bent over the prone figure, lifted his head by the hair, and ran the shank across his throat from ear to ear, leaving a deep, jagged wound, amid a river of blood and tissue.

The assailants dropped the weapons next to the body and quickly left the shop. Almost an hour later, a corrections officer, on routine patrol, entered the plant and discovered Sorensen's body.

◇◇◇

It was a little past six p.m. Kate and I were reviewing the list of incarcerated forgery inmates when Patti interrupted. She told me I had a call on the red phone. The red phone was a direct telephone line into the Special Investigations Branch from anywhere inside the penitentiary. It couldn't be accessed from outside the prison and was never used for routine business calls. Calls on the red line meant only one thing: somewhere in the prison, a critical incident had occurred that required an immediate response from me or a member of my staff.

I picked up immediately. "SIB, Kincaid."

"Sam, Steve Schumway. We've got a dead inmate here at North Point, and I can tell you, he didn't fall off a ladder. Somebody slit his throat, bashed his head in, and cut him up for good measure."

"Where'd it happen?"

"One of my COs found him lying on the floor in the furniture factory. He had a job in there. He hasn't been dead for long."

"Any witnesses?" I asked.

"None so far."

"Okay. Secure the scene. We'll be right over. Oh, what's the name of the victim?"

"The inmate's name is Milo Raymond Sorensen, U.S.P. number 167841."

"Be right over," I said, and hung up.

Kate hadn't been paying attention to the call. She'd been engrossed in our list of forgery inmates. When I asked Captain Schumway who the victim was, her head came right up.

"Guess what? I think I've just located our man. His name's Milo Sorensen, and you'll find his name on the short list you're holding. Unfortunately, Milo is no longer with us. Somebody just killed him."

"Christ. How did it happen?"

"Beaten and stabbed to death."

"How would you like to take a look at your first prison homicide?"

"Can hardly wait," she said, as we headed out the door.

Chapter Thirty-eight

In cases involving serious injury or the death of an inmate or prison staff member, my responsibilities included the immediate notification of the department director, followed by the Salt Lake County Sheriff's Department and the state medical examiner, when necessary. Since the prison was located in an unincorporated part of south Salt Lake County, the sheriff retained primary jurisdiction. To avoid creating the appearance of a conflict of interest, our role was to assist the Sheriff's Department with the investigation.

By the time Kate and I arrived at North Point, the usual procedures were well under way. The entire prison was locked down. That means nobody gets in or out—not visitors, vendors, or staff. All inmates were returned to their cells and locked in. In order to prevent outside communication, the phone system was rendered inoperative.

The Sheriff's Office had dispatched two homicide detectives as well as their mobile crime scene unit. I had known Detective Sergeant John Webb and Detective Harvey Gill for several years. Kate knew them as well. Both were veteran homicide investigators who had worked major crime cases inside the penitentiary in the past. They were both top-notch.

A large area inside the furniture plant had been cordoned off around Sorensen's body. He lay face down on the concrete floor in a large pool of blood. We saw a metal pipe and a sharpened prison-made shank, about ten inches long, lying next to the body. The back of his white prison-issue jumpsuit was dotted with spots of blood, and several small tears in the fabric were indicative of the numerous stab wounds caused by the shank. A jagged cut was visible running almost from ear to ear across the front of his neck. The battered condition of his head and face provided ample evidence of the damage inflicted by the metal pipe. Near the body was a floor drain. A pool of blood and tissue flowed several feet from Sorensen's head and wound toward the drain.

Speaking to no one in particular, I muttered, "What a mess."

"So, this is how it happens in prison," replied Kate. "I think I prefer a nice, clean gunshot wound. It's usually a lot less messy."

"This is pretty typical of a prison homicide. Since inmates rarely get their hands on guns, it's always a beating, strangulation, or stabbing. This one just happens to be a beating and a stabbing."

"Two weapons," said Kate curiously. "You thinking one perp, or two?"

"Can't say for sure, but I'd bet two. It's unlikely that one perp would use two different murder weapons. Not unheard of, but unusual."

"Right. Tell you what, Sam. With all the blood loss, there's a fair chance you'll find trace amounts of the victim's blood on the perp's clothing—shoes, socks, and pants in particular."

"Exactly what I was thinking," I replied.

As Kate and I waited for the Sheriff's Department team to arrive, we were joined by Duty Captain Steve Schumway and Deputy Warden Bob Fuller. I introduced Kate and asked to speak with the officer who discovered the body. We were introduced to Officer Alice Warner, who reiterated what Schumway had told me earlier when he reported the incident.

Warner had been making a routine sweep of the closed prison industries programs and had entered the furniture plant at approximately five-fifty, when she discovered the victim's body. She immediately sounded the alarm and secured the area until help arrived. Warner hadn't seen anyone in or around the furniture plant as she'd made her rounds.

I turned to Fuller and Schumway. "While we're waiting, we might as well start rounding up any of Sorensen's inmate friends, including those he worked with in the plant. The Sheriff's Office will also want to interview our employees who worked with him. Let's start with his cell mate. Minus any witnesses, Webb and Gill are going to want to talk to anybody who knew him. They'll want to find out whether Sorensen was being threatened, strong-armed, or if he was in debt to anyone. If he was being pressured, maybe he said something to somebody."

Burnham spent the afternoon checking on the whereabouts of William Allred. He called an acquaintance who worked for the Board of Pardons as a victim coordinator. That person told him that the board members were conducting administrative hearings all day at board headquarters in South Salt Lake and wouldn't finish until late in the afternoon. That gave him sufficient time to set up surveillance. He planned to follow Allred from work and stay with him until he was home for the night.

Burnham was afraid that asking too many questions about Allred's future parole hearing schedule would arouse suspicion. He had managed to learn that Allred was scheduled to conduct hearings at the prison the next morning from eight-thirty until noon. He arranged for Marcy Everest to cover Allred's home early the next morning when he left for work. Burnham planned to cover the afternoon and evening shifts himself.

Terry had also managed to contact a representative from the phone company who was busy pulling a record of Allred's home telephone calls for the past several months. The phone records would be ready the next day. The cell phone presented a different problem. He hadn't been able to determine which service provider held the contract for the Board of Pardons. If Allred was involved in something illegal, as Sam suspected, the cell phone records might prove to be important.

Allred left the Board of Pardons a little before six o'clock and drove directly to a sports bar not more than ten minutes from where he lived. Burnham observed him sitting by himself at the bar, engaged in small talk with one of the bartenders. Allred emerged from the bar about an hour later and drove home, making one brief stop at a convenience store. where he purchased a newspaper and a half gallon of milk.

From what Burnham had learned, Allred was divorced with grown children. He lived alone in a small, older home, in an affluent neighborhood in southeast Salt Lake County. Burnham circled the block twice before parking several houses up the street, hoping none of the neighbors had spotted him and called the cops. He would remain until satisfied Allred was in for the night.

The Sheriff's Department crime scene crew was busy processing the area around the victim's body while Webb and Gill began the laborious task of interviewing inmates and prison staff. The prison employees who worked in the plant with Sorensen had all clocked out and gone home prior to the discovery of the body. Webb asked me to call each of them at home and learn whatever I could. I borrowed the tiny office adjacent to the furniture production area, secured an outside telephone line, and had just begun dialing my first number when Kate walked in and closed the door. She looked concerned. I set the phone down.

"So, when are you going to tell Webb and Gill?" she asked.

"Tell 'em what?"

Sounding genuinely annoyed, she said, "Cut the crap, Sam. You know what. You've worked with Webb and Gill before. You know you can trust them. They're going to figure this out. They know we're looking for the guy who forged the suicide note. It made it into the newspapers, for Christ's sake."

"What if I'm wrong? It might be premature to say anything," I said. It sounded lame to me even as I said it. After almost a full minute of awkward silence, with Kate looking at me like I was a couple of cards short of a full deck, I asked the obvious question.

"Tell me what it is you think I think?"

Exasperated, she said, "You believe the hit on Sorensen is part of a broader conspiracy in which somebody paid Slick Watts to murder Levi Vogue, and then killed Watts, arranging his death to look like a suicide. They'd planned to kill Watts all along. The same people who killed Watts also killed Sorensen, who forged the suicide note. Watts and Sorensen had to go because they provided a direct link to the conspirators. And the part you can't stand to say to anyone but yourself is that the conspirators are a group of dirty employees working for the Department of Corrections. And that's why you're putting round-the-clock surveillance on William Allred. You think he's involved too. So, how'd I do?"

Bingo. She'd gotten it all correct except for a couple of things even I was unsure about. If the Watts suicide-fabrication story had held together, the conspirators might have left Sorensen alone. Once the suicide story fell apart, it became necessary to move against Sorensen quickly, before he got scared and turned himself in, or before we found him. The second point I found even more troubling. Assuming Sorensen had forged the suicide note, how had he gotten it out of the prison? There were three possibilities. He could have mailed it out; however, that seemed unlikely considering how carefully prison staff monitor incoming and outgoing mail. The note might have been smuggled out during a contact visit. We needed to review Sorensen's visitation log to determine who and when prior visits had occurred. The last possibility was the safest and would have provided the least likelihood of detection—an employee carried it out.

"You got it about right," I said, a note of obvious resignation in my voice.

"Look. I don't know if it will make you feel any better, but for a while there, I thought you were chasing your own tail. Now I've come around to thinking your instincts may have been right about this all along," Kate said. "We still don't have any proof, mind you, but when you string it all together, it's plausible. In its own twisted way, it even makes sense. Of course, we still have no idea who these conspirators are or why they're doing what they're doing. One thing is certain: somebody has taken a great deal of time and gone to a lot of effort to hide whatever it is they're up to."

We laid it out for Webb and Gill just as Kate and I had discussed it. They listened intently, without interruption. Webb and Gill had been partners for more years than I could remember. Webb eventually ended up with the sergeant stripes, but that hadn't seemed to alter their relationship.

Gill was a grizzled old veteran, who'd joined the Sheriff's Department more than thirty-five years ago. He had to be nearing sixty. Gill had mentored a much younger Webb, when Webb was promoted from the uniform division to detective. They looked like Mutt and Jeff. Webb was effusive and well-spoken, Gill reserved and blunt. Webb dressed in conservative wool suits, with never a hair out of place. Gill, on the other hand, had days when the gray stubble of his beard confirmed that he hadn't touched a razor in days. He wore cheap polyester suits, with ties that almost never matched and socks that clashed with everything else.

That said, I wouldn't care to have either one of them after me. Together, they had cleared more murder cases than probably any team of homicide dicks in Utah—Kate McConnell included. Of course, they were older than Kate, and had been at it a lot longer.

"That's some story. Too bad you can't prove it. So you think this Sorensen may have forged the suicide note, and that's what got him whacked?" asked Gill.

"Yup."

"Any idea who did it?" asked Webb.

"Nope."

"One hitter or two?" asked Gill.

"Could be either, but I'd bet two."

"It might help us out if you'd give us a profile of the victim," said Gill.

"Happy to. Sorensen had a long history of nonviolent criminal behavior—his entire criminal record consisted of property offenses with the exception of a couple of DUIs. During his late teens to early twenties, he focused on retail shoplifting, theft, and, eventually, receiving stolen property. It appears that he had a reasonably profitable career as a fence. As he got older, the offense history shifted to multiple counts of check and credit card forgery. He was forty-two years old and had spent almost half his adult life in jail or prison. This current sentence represented his third commitment. He had already served more than six years on five felony counts of forgery. He'd been to the board and was scheduled for parole release in exactly eleven months.

"His personal life isn't pretty either," I continued. "It looks like three marriages all ending in divorce. He fathered three children, one from each marriage. He seemed to have some support from friends and family, given a pretty regular pattern of prison visits. That about sums it up."

"Thanks, Sam. Assuming for the moment that we are dealing with two perps, are we looking for inmates or employees?" asked Webb.

"That's a hard one. I'd like to believe that he was killed by inmates, but my hunch is that the killers will turn out to be staff. At first glance, the murder has all the markings of an inmate hit. However, employees could stage that rather easily. If staff hired inmates to do it, they'd still have loose ends to tidy up. If my theory is correct, these guys are about eliminating loose ends, not creating more."

"So far, we haven't had anybody tell us that Mr. Sorensen was in debt or being pressured by anyone. We've got more individuals to talk with, including members of his family, but if everything checks out, we'll turn our attention to prison staff. The CO found the vic's body at five-fifty. Aside from the perp, we need to determine who last saw him alive and when. Assuming it was five o'clock or a few minutes after, it was probably a civilian employee or one of his inmate co-workers. That's a pretty narrow window. I wonder how many staff won't be able to account for their whereabouts during that forty-five to fifty-minute period?" asked Webb. "We're sure as hell gonna find out."

Chapter Thirty-nine

With the work of the crime scene unit complete, Webb and Gill released Sorensen's body to the State Medical Examiner's Office. The body showed no sign of defensive wounds on the forearms or hands. The victim had encountered sudden, overwhelming, and deadly force, affording no opportunity for resistance.

The plastic shank and metal pipe would be processed for latent prints. Sorensen's clothing would be carefully examined for the presence of trace evidence. The hope for a quick resolution to the case was fading fast. We needed a witness, and so far, none had materialized.

Webb and Gill sat cloistered in an office near the crime scene where they had temporarily set up headquarters. Gill spoke first. "What do you think of Kincaid's theory that one or more employees made the hit?"

"There isn't a shred of evidence that supports that notion right now. Think about it. Over the years, how many times have you and I been here handling cases just like this one? This seems like a carbon copy of most of the other inmate-on-inmate murders we've investigated."

"Sure does," replied Gill. "But if the hit was carried out by prison employees, how difficult would it be to make it look like the work of inmates? Real easy, if you ask me. It makes perfect sense to cast a guilty shadow over the inmate population. It would keep the heat off of them."

"I think you're right. Here's another thing. Kincaid has been involved in cases like this for a very long time. He's good, damn good. For him to be pointing fingers at people inside his own department takes balls. Evidence or not, we can't afford to ignore his instincts on this," said Webb.

"I agree. And by the way, how do you want to play it with the press?"

"The usual drill. We tell them as little as possible. I'd rather have them think that this is another inmate-on-inmate homicide. They already know about the forged suicide note. Let's hope, for now at least, that they don't connect the dots linking the Watts/Vogue murders to this one, assuming that's how it turns out," said Webb.

"I'll tell you what," said Gill. "I don't get nearly enough credit for how well I trained you. It ought to be worth at least a one-grade salary adjustment, don't you think?"

"In your dreams."

Webb said, "I called this furniture plant employee, Steve Jensen, at home. He was the last employee to leave the floor—that was 5:08 p.m., according to his timecard."

"What'd he have to say?" asked Gill.

"Said there was nothing out of the ordinary going on. Sorensen was cleaning up as usual—nobody else around."

"If my math is correct," said Gill, "that leaves a relatively short window of opportunity for the murder to have occurred—forty-two minutes to be exact. Officer Warner found the body at 5:50. All we gotta do is figure out who was in the plant during that forty-two-minute stretch."

Kate and I didn't leave the prison until after midnight. We spent the evening interviewing inmates. Between us, we interviewed nineteen prisoners employed in the furniture factory and another half dozen who had been identified as either friends or acquaintances of the victim. My brain was fried.

If Milo Sorensen felt threatened in the days or weeks leading up to his death, he didn't share it with anybody inside the prison. We found nothing to indicate that he had accrued drug or gambling debts, or that he was the victim of a gang-run prison protection racket. He didn't have a reputation as a snitch and never had.

I had called Milo's next of kin to inform them of his death. I spoke with an older brother in Logan, Utah, and to a younger sister in Salt Lake City. Both sounded genuinely distraught at the news, particularly his sister. Neither had visited the prison recently, nor had they received any communication from the victim that suggested he might be having problems. Milo's mail and visitation logs corroborated their statements.

Kate and I agreed to contact each other later in the morning. I headed up the mountain and arrived home a little before one. I checked the message board in the kitchen. Aunt June had written a message, the gist of which was that Miss Sara expected me to fix her French toast and bacon for breakfast and then take her to school. The tone of the message suggested the request was nonnegotiable.

As is my habit whenever I arrive home late at night, I quietly entered Sara's bedroom to check on her. The bed had obviously been slept in, but no Sara. After a brief moment of panic, I hurried into my bedroom and found her curled up under the covers. I crawled in and was out in seconds.

I admirably performed my duties as breakfast chef and school chauffeur. I then headed down the mountain for an eight o'clock meeting with Sloan. When he heard what I was about to tell him concerning who might be involved in Sorensen's murder, it would likely be the start of a very bad day for both of us. When I arrived, tardy as usual, Sloan was already huddled with Brad Ford discussing the details of this morning's press release announcing the murder of Sorensen. At the request of the Sheriff's

Department, nothing would be said about a possible connection between Sorensen's death and that of Watts and Vogue.

I explained it to Sloan exactly the way I previously had for Detectives Webb and Gill. He didn't speak until after I finished, but the look on his face had changed from mild curiosity to one of stunned disbelief. His normally ruddy facial complexion had given way to a pale, colorless shade of gray. The pained expression on his face made him look like he had just taken a hard punch to the solar plexus.

He paused for what seemed like an unusually long period before speaking.

"Tell me something, Sam. What makes you so sure our own employees are involved? If you and Lieutenant McConnell had developed solid evidence linking department employees to these murders, you'd be out arresting people and we wouldn't be having this conversation."

"You're right. And we're still not sure it is our employees. At the moment, we haven't been able to identify any specific suspects, much less have the evidence necessary to make arrests.

"I first began considering employee involvement when our investigation failed to yield any of the likely suspects. After we eliminated John Merchant and members of Vogue's family as potential suspects, I felt certain Levi's murder was connected in some way to his employment on the Board of Pardons. And when Slick Watts came along, the pieces all seemed to fit. We had an ex-con with a long criminal history and the perfect motive to want to see Vogue dead. We had more than enough evidence to take to a jury. About the only thing missing was the murder weapon and a confession, which I'm convinced we'd have gotten if somebody hadn't killed him before we found him."

"And you think Watts was killed by somebody from the department to keep him quiet?"

"Not immediately. The final straw had to be the medical examiner's conclusion that Watts didn't commit suicide. Once we realized someone had gone to a lot of trouble to make his murder look like a suicide, my thinking shifted away from offenders toward department employees."

"It still seems like a helluva stretch. And this surveillance you mentioned on Bill Allred—you think he's somehow involved?" asked Sloan.

"Can't say for sure. But he lied to me when I asked him about his personal friendship with Levi. He really tried to distance himself from the relationship. And now to have him identified as the mysterious third party involved in the group sex with Vogue and Sue Ann. What should we conclude from that?"

"Maybe he lied about his friendship with Vogue because he feared the investigation might unearth the kinky sex. If that information found its way to the governor, his career on the board would be over," said Sloan. "Moral turpitude and all that good stuff."

"Could be."

After a long pause, Sloan spoke slowly in a tone reflecting both disappointment and resignation. "Okay. Here's what needs to happen. Do you trust your own staff?"

"Implicitly."

"Set everything else aside and put them all to work on this. Be sure they understand how important confidentiality is. Nobody talks to the press. And I mean nobody. I'll fire any department employee who leaks this to the media. Understood?"

I nodded.

"Do you have enough help, or would you like me to assign additional, temporary staff?"

"With assistance from Lieutenant McConnell, we should be all right. But I appreciate the offer. I'll let you know if we do need more help."

"We're going do the right thing and follow this wherever it takes us. If we've got a nest of crooked employees who would involve themselves in multiple murders, heaven only knows what else they might be capable of. It makes me sick to my stomach to think about it. But it is our mess and we are going to clean it up," said Sloan.

"And I guess you understand, Sam, if we have a scandal the magnitude of what you believe, a lot of careers are going to be over—starting with mine. If these are prison employees, the shake-up will be like nothing the department has ever seen. There'll be criminal indictments, forced retirements, and a lot of transfers."

With that, he got up from his desk and walked to a window overlooking the employee parking lot. Gazing out the window with hands clasped behind his back, he muttered, "Keep me informed."

I left his office without another word.

Chapter Forty

My cell phone rang. It was Vince Turner. Kate had assigned Vince and two other detectives to assist on the Allred surveillance. I passed him on to Burnham, who was relieved to have additional personnel for the stakeout. The extra help would make it possible to put at least two vehicles on Allred instead of one. That would reduce the likelihood of either losing him or having him make the tail.

I had no sooner gotten off the phone with Turner when it rang again. Thinking it was probably Kate, I picked up. It wasn't. Instead, it was James Allen. He wasn't a happy camper. "Two things, Sam. I wonder if you could tell me why Lt. McConnell didn't make it to the meeting last night with Stoddard? And, unless I misunderstood, you were supposed to set up a meeting today and introduce me to Kate. Have you had a chance to do that?"

Not wanting to mention that Kate had spent much of last night assisting on the Sorensen murder investigation, I decided to lie to him. Actually, I lied twice. "To tell you the truth, Jim, I have no idea what Kate was up to last night. You'll have to ask about that when you catch up with her. As for the meeting today, I gave her the message and she promised to call you to set it up. I'm a little surprised you haven't heard from her. She's probably just buried in paperwork. The day's not over yet—I'm sure she'll be in touch." By now my nose had grown to something the size of Pinocchio's.

"I'm not trying to sound impatient, but this meeting is important. My team needs immediate access to all the written documents pertaining to the investigation, including the forensic reports," said Allen.

"That shouldn't be a problem. In fact, Kate mentioned that she had somebody in her office working on that very thing." *Was that two lies or three?*

"Glad to hear it. Sam, if you talk with her before I do, please ask her to call me ASAP. If I don't hear something from her very soon, I'm afraid I'll be forced to go directly to Hyrum."

"I'll pass it along."

As I drove to the prison, I had an idea. I hadn't thought to check Sorensen's approved list of individuals with whom he could correspond. I had checked Sorensen's telephone log and determined he hadn't called out of the prison for almost a full week preceding his death.

Since we routinely monitor inmate phone calls (and inmates know this), the chance of his calling someone on his list and saying something about the forged suicide note was remote. But the possibility of sending something out undetected in a letter was a different matter entirely. We randomly skim and scan inmate mail unless it's privileged correspondence coming from or going to a prisoner's attorney. Slipping something into the body of a letter might go unnoticed.

Milo's list of individuals with whom he was allowed to correspond contained four names. None was an attorney. The list included his two siblings with whom I had spoken the previous evening. The third name belonged to one of his former spouses. The last name belonged to an individual by the name of Lance Muller. Muller was listed as an old friend.

Department records showed that Sorensen had mailed a letter to Muller the day before he was killed. A corrections officer had scanned the letter and described it as "a five-page personal letter to a friend." The officer's notes didn't indicate anything suspicious about the letter. Sorensen's only other recent correspondence was a letter mailed to his brother two weeks prior to his murder.

I ran a record check on Muller and discovered two prior misdemeanors arrests, both more than fifteen years old. Both involved alcohol violations. Muller lived in Draper, just a few minutes' drive from the prison. I wanted to see the letter. It would probably be delivered in today's mail—tomorrow's at the latest.

I called his home and spoke to his spouse. Denise Muller explained that her husband wouldn't return from work until after six o'clock. If the news media had released information about the murder, she hadn't yet heard it. She expressed shock, but not surprise, when I told her. In a tone sounding more resigned than sad, she told me that Milo and her husband had been friends since junior high school.

"Lance maintained his friendship throughout the years, despite Milo's continued scrapes with the law. As far as I know, Lance is the only person who stood by Milo through thick and thin. Even his own siblings stopped seeing him as his criminal lifestyle worsened," she said.

Without providing specifics, I mentioned the letter and how important it was that I have an opportunity to read it. She asked me to wait while she went outside to see if the letter had arrived. A minute later, she came back on the line. "It's here. Would you like me to open it?" I asked her to wait until I arrived. Fifteen minutes later, I was on Muller's front porch.

At first glance, the letter looked much like any other written by a lonely inmate with too much time on his hands. Unlike many in prison, Sorensen was literate. He spelled with a modicum of accuracy and managed to put most of the periods in the right places. The rambling five-page letter was hand-printed on lined notebook paper.

He talked about his family, mostly his children, and how he intended to become a better father this time around. He spoke at length about what he planned to do after his impending release. And he ragged a bit on his old friend for failing to write more often. When he wrote the letter, he had no way of knowing he would be leaving prison for the last time zipped in a body bag, with an identification tag tied on his big toe.

The single-spaced letter went on like that until midway down the fourth page, when what I read hit me like a fist to the gut. In mid-paragraph, while chastising Muller for not visiting more often, Sorensen abruptly changed direction and wrote the following: "If anything happens to me, tell the cops I forged the suicide note involving Charles Watts. A female hack, Carol Stimson, hired me to do it. Stimson paid me with dope and a better job. If nothing happens to me, say nothing."

I had just found our smoking gun.

Muller, who had been reading the letter over my shoulder, audibly gasped when she read what I'd just read. "Dear God. Are we in any danger?"

"You'll be fine. If certain people had known what was in this letter, it wouldn't have made it out of the prison to begin with, or it would have been stolen from your mail box before you had a chance to read it. But they made a mistake. Several actually. And one of them was underestimating Milo Sorensen."

Sorensen had probably heard about the Slick Watts affair from the news or perhaps the inmate grapevine. Rumor and gossip traveled fast among the inmate population. Whatever he'd heard must have made him wary or maybe even afraid. Men who are afraid take risks, and Milo Sorensen had chosen to cover himself by sharing some very dangerous information with a trusted friend. He probably weighed his options carefully before he decided to hide the information in the middle of a letter. The letter provided less risk of detection, with the added benefit of having the whole thing in writing, should something happen to him.

I took the letter and hurried back to my office at the prison. A quick check of the shift log revealed that Carol Stimson worked swings from three until midnight. She was currently on her scheduled days off and wouldn't return to work for two days. It was time to plot strategy. I immediately phoned Kate and conferenced in Webb from the Sheriff's Office. We had our first direct employee link to the murders of Watts and Sorensen. The question now was what to do next?

Stimson had been on duty at North Point at the time of Sorensen's murder. Webb's partner, Harvey Gill, had interviewed her on the evening of the murder. Stimson told him that she had spent most of her shift prior to the murder performing routine patrol activities in the North Point housing units and the prison industry shop areas. A number of inmates and staff employed in the furniture plant confirmed seeing her in the shop sometime around four o'clock in the afternoon. As to her specific whereabouts at the time of the murder, Stimson claimed that she was making the rounds inside the Purgatory Housing Unit, visiting inmates in their cells prior to a mandatory count. She'd even written a disciplinary citation to an inmate for failure to turn the volume down on his box. Inmates in adjoining houses had complained about the noise and Stimson had warned him to turn it down or shut it off. The inmate had done neither and received a ticket. Gill had corroborated her story by examining the ticket and placing a copy of it in the murder book.

We agreed to meet in my office at the prison in one hour. Webb suggested we involve a member of the prosecuting attorney's office. Kate offered to bring Stoddard along.

During the intervening hour, I examined the personnel file of Officer Carol Stimson. On a professional level, I was more than a little familiar with her reputation. She had been employed by the department for just over four years. She'd managed to complete a year of probationary employment without incident. After transferring from the women's prison to her present North Point assignment three years ago, she'd even received a couple of letters of commendation from Deputy Warden Bob Fuller. She had also been the subject of two internal investigations carried out by my office—investigations that probably solidified in her mind my reputation as the department's chief headhunter.

Two different inmates alleged that she had used excessive force against them. In the first incident, the inmate recanted his story and the charge was dismissed. However, in the second complaint, which occurred just a few weeks after the first incident, Stimson and another officer were accused of beating an inmate for refusal to obey an order. The SIB investigated the matter and concluded that the charge was true. The inmate victim had sustained numerous cuts and bruises that required an overnight stay in the prison infirmary. I recommended that she be fired and the case referred to the D.A.'s office for possible criminal prosecution. She appealed my recommendation through the correctional officers union and ultimately got off with a two-week suspension and a letter of reprimand in her personnel file. The incident cost her a promotion to the rank of sergeant, something she blamed on me. Suffice to say, I was no longer on her Christmas card list. While I was able to reassure Denise Muller that she and her husband were not in danger, I wondered, given my history with Stimson, if the same could be said about me.

I quickly checked voice-mail messages. Sue Ann Winkler had called and left a very testy message about the vice raid at the Starlite Motel that resulted in the arrest of her mother and step-father. She made some rather unflattering references to my family lineage. I made a mental note to call her later.

The next message was from a noticeably angry James Allen. He'd heard about the murder of Sorensen on the local news and demanded to know if Milo's murder was in any way connected to the death of Vogue. He had also discovered that Kate had spent much of the previous evening at the Utah State Prison working with yours truly. He'd caught me red handed lying to him and he sounded genuinely pissed. I couldn't blame him. He ended the call by informing me that he had reluctantly placed two phone calls, one to Hyrum Locke, and the other to Richard Vogue, to report what he described as a deliberate stall. It looked to me like the charade was over, and I'd probably wind up on the receiving end of a butt-chewing from Sloan once the word filtered back to him.

I then listened to a message from Steve Schumway deploring what he considered to be attacks on the integrity of his employees by Webb and Gill. He demanded to know what was going on and asked that I call him immediately. This message was a bigger priority than the one from Sue Ann, but it too would have to wait. The call struck me as odd. Schumway wasn't known for emotional outbursts. His tone sounded almost desperate. But desperate for what? Information? I wasn't sure.

Despite my misgivings about having to interact with Stoddard, the meeting came off smoothly. I concluded that my own discomfort at having to work with him had more to do with that little voice in my head called a conscience, and had nothing to do with him. The guy was bright and capable. I could understand Kate's attraction to him.

Everyone read Sorensen's letter. Stoddard summed up our situation succinctly. "As I see it, we've got three options: We can place Stimson under round-the-clock surveillance; we can pick her up, confront her with the letter and see if she confesses; or we can go for a search warrant of her home."

To Stoddard I said, "I'm afraid I don't have much faith in option two. Do you have any idea how often inmates complain about correctional officers? They do it all day long. It isn't likely that an experienced officer like Stimson is going to break out in a cold sweat because an inmate, and a dead one at that, has made an allegation against her. If the only evidence I've got is the uncorroborated letter from Sorensen, the department couldn't sustain a job action against Stimson, much less consider seeking criminal charges. It would be the word of a dead inmate serving his third prison sentence against a corrections officer with four years' experience and a relatively clean record. The officers union would have a field day with us."

"And another thing," chimed in Kate. "Have we got enough to get a warrant? I'm not sure that the letter by itself is legally strong enough for a judge to conclude that we've got probable cause. Unless I've forgotten what I learned in Search and Seizure 101, no probable cause, no warrant."

Stoddard replied, "It would probably be a close call, but I think a well-written affidavit, carefully laying out the facts, will result in a judge approving the warrant application. If we do get turned down, we go to plan B—place Stimson under twenty-four-hour surveillance. We won't be out anything but the time it took us to prepare the thing. I recommend we go for it."

Nobody disagreed. The consensus was that we opt for the warrant first, and then confront Stimson with the letter and any incriminating evidence that turned up in the search.

Chapter Forty-one

While Webb, Gill, and Stoddard prepared the search warrant affidavit, Kate drove to Stimson's home and established visual surveillance. It appeared that nobody was home. Department records revealed that Stimson was single and lived in the small city of Lehi, located about fifteen minutes from the prison.

I decided to follow up on a small detail Gill had overlooked after he completed his interview with Stimson. I pulled the original ticket she had written to inmate Eddie Sandoval on the evening of the murder. Sandoval had come to the prison from Salt Lake City eighteen months ago on several drug charges.

His prison record was mixed. The incident with Stimson represented his third minor disciplinary violation since entering prison. While not directly affiliated with any prison gang, Sandoval's file revealed associations with several known members of one of our most dangerous gangs, the Mexican Mafia.

With ticket in hand and uncertain of the reception I was about to receive, I located Sandoval in the education building, attending a late afternoon drug treatment class. I brought him into a small, unoccupied classroom next to where his treatment group was meeting. I introduced myself and tried to establish rapport by making small talk. He wasn't buying it. It immediately became clear that niceties would not placate the hostility and suspicion written all over his face, so I decided to take the direct approach.

"Look, Eddie, I'll get right to the point. You received a disciplinary last evening from Officer Stimson for refusing to turn the volume down on your box. What time did the incident go down?"

He stared at me without speaking for almost a minute and then said, "Fuckin'-a, man. You pulled my ass out of group for this? Half the guys in that room are gonna figure I'm some kind of punk-ass snitch. I don't remember exactly when I got the goddamn thing. It was in the evening. Go look it up on the fuckin' ticket, man, and stop botherin' my ass."

We both stood and I said to him, "Okay, Eddie, sorry to have bothered you. You can go back to class now. But one more thing. By tomorrow, it won't be half the cons in here who think you're a punk-ass snitch. By the time I'm finished, it'll be all of them. So why don't you just sit your sorry ass down and help me out."

He gave me a cold, hard stare, shrugged his shoulders, and said, "I got the ticket around four-forty-five, maybe four-fifty."

"You're sure about the time?"

"Why do you want to know, man?"

I ignored the question.

"I'm sure," he snapped.

"What makes you so sure?"

"Look, man. I'm sure because we stand for mandatory count at four-thirty and I go to chow at five o'clock. I got the chickenshit ticket between count and dinner. I remember thinkin' if the hack bitch would just shut the fuck up and write the ticket, I'd make the culinary on time with the rest of my homeboys. I was hungry, okay."

I pulled the ticket out of my pocket to confirm what I already suspected. Stimson had written that the incident occurred at 1720 hours. That's military time for 5:20 p.m. She had fudged it by a good half hour.

I found Webb, Gill, and Stoddard in the small conference room adjacent to my office putting the finishing touches on the warrant affidavit. Kate had recently checked in and continued to report no activity around Stimson's home.

I dropped the ticket Stimson had issued to Eddie Sandoval on the conference table in front of them. "I think I just discovered something that will strengthen our search warrant." All three immediately looked up.

"You have our undivided attention," replied Gill.

"I just spoke with the inmate who received this disciplinary. Note the time Stimson wrote on the ticket. She says she wrote him up at 5:20 p.m. Sandoval says that's a crock. He was eating chow in the culinary at five o'clock with his housing unit. He says the incident went down at 4:40, maybe 4:45, shortly after he stood for a mandatory count. I double checked him on both the schedule for dinner and the mandatory count. He's telling the truth."

"Solidifying her alibi," muttered Stoddard. "She took a calculated risk that we wouldn't verify the time line, and even if we did, she could still claim the whole thing was an innocent mistake. This is a very smart lady."

"I'm glad you thought to check that, Sam," said Webb. "By itself, it's an innocuous mistake. But combine it with her apparent involvement in getting Sorensen to forge the suicide note, and it's no longer insignificant. We'll add this information to the warrant affidavit. It will definitely help. I want to place a pickup order on Officer Stimson right now. We've got more than enough to bring her in for questioning. We can decide after the interrogation whether or not to book her."

"And do I ever feel like a dumb shit," said Gill. "I interviewed the lady myself and even got a copy of the ticket. I just never thought to verify the time sequence. Maybe I'm getting too damned old for this job."

"Don't be so hard on yourself," said Webb. "You are as old as dirt, but this was an easy one to miss."

I left the conference room and returned to my office. As I walked by her desk, Patti looked up and said, "Did Bob Fuller get hold of you?"

"I didn't see Warden Fuller. Where was he?"

"He came by to see you. Said it was important. The last time I noticed, he was sitting right outside the conference room door while you were in your meeting. I thought you saw him. He sure left in a hurry."

◇◇◇

Bill Allred was a guy who made a habit out of driving in his rear-view mirror. He spotted the tail. He'd just completed a full morning of parole violation hearings and was on his way back to the office.

He first noticed the white Ford Taurus after leaving the prison's main gate. It followed him to the freeway entrance and then north to Salt Lake City. Instead of driving straight to his office, Allred diverted onto several side streets before turning into the South Town Mall. The Taurus stayed right with him until he turned into the parking lot, then it continued past. The lone occupant never got close enough for Allred to get any kind of look at him. He always felt a certain level of paranoia about the possibility of being stalked by ex-cons or their associates. Yet this Taurus looked more like a plain vanilla cop car than something an offender might drive. Allred parked his car and casually walked to the entrance of Dillard's department store, carefully perusing the lot to see if the guy in the Taurus had brought a friend or was flying solo. He wasn't sure.

Burnham and Turner pulled alongside one another about a block from the mall. "Do you think he made us?" asked Turner.

"Hard to say. He sure didn't take the most direct route into the mall, that's for sure. He may have been suspicious and was trying to check it out. Since you're feeling like he might have burned you, I'll establish a visual on his car and take the lead for a while. I'll radio you as soon as he moves," said Burnham.

It took Allred a moment in the department store to calm down and to begin thinking rationally. For a moment on the street, he found himself having to choke down a sense of panic. He spent a few minutes in the men's clothing section, then walked a short distance to the food court, ordered a salad, a slice of pizza, and a soft drink. He took his lunch tray and carried it to a location that provided a clear view of anyone entering or leaving the food court. Nobody looked suspicious or paid him the slightest bit of attention. Maybe he wasn't being followed. Maybe it was just a figment of his imagination. Maybe.

After he finished his lunch, Allred walked to a bank of public telephones by the food court restrooms. He dialed the number. The call was answered after the first ring.

Chapter Forty-two

The search warrant was signed by a cranky district court judge named Homer Billings. Unable to find a judge in the Salt Lake County Court complex so late in the evening, Stoddard and Webb checked the on-call roster and found Judge Billings' name. When they arrived at his home, they found him curled up in his bathrobe, slippers, and pajamas watching some mindless reality show in his home theater.

We met in a strip mall parking lot several blocks from Stimson's home. Kate had been sitting on the house since mid-afternoon and felt sure it was unoccupied. As a precaution, Kate and I covered the back of the house while Gill, Webb, and Vince Turner went to the front. They knocked on the front door but got no answer. Turner entered through a side door after breaking a glass panel and unlocking the door from the inside.

Stimson lived in a quiet residential neighborhood where the homes looked twenty to twenty-five years old. The house was a small two-level affair, with the main floor at ground level and a below-ground finished basement of equal size. A detached two-car garage was connected to the house by a covered walkway that led to a side door.

The interior was as neat as a pin. Everything in its place. The family room downstairs gave me the creeps. I had the eerie sense that I'd walked into a taxidermy shop. Stimson was obviously a hunter. The heads of four big-game animals were mounted on the walls. A locked gun cabinet containing several hunting rifles stood against one wall. Stimson's leisure reading appeared to be hunting and outdoor magazines. Copies of publications like *Field & Stream* and *Guns & Ammo* were neatly stacked on a coffee table.

Stimson appeared to be an outdoors type, into hunting and camping, comfortable with guns. Framed membership certificates to the John Birch Society and the National Rifle Association were mounted on a wall above a desk and home computer. As a card-carrying member of the John Birch Society, she probably embraced political views well to the right of center. The truth was, that could describe a lot of cops. What I found odd about the home was the complete absence of pictures of anybody—friends, family, pets. There wasn't a single photograph of anyone or anything in the entire house. The place felt sterile and empty.

The search went smoothly. We found her uniform pants and shirt in a black plastic trash bag in the garbage can next to the house. The uniform had been recently worn and appeared to be in good condition. We also seized two pair of department-issued shoes, her computer, and the tape from her telephone answering machine. We hoped that blood, hair, or other trace evidence from Sorensen's body had transferred to Stimson's uniform.

Gill transported the evidence to the State Crime Laboratory. Both a hair-and-fiber expert and a blood/DNA specialist were standing by. They'd promised a quick response.

Stimson had been a no-show the entire afternoon. Webb decided to establish round-the-clock surveillance of the residence until she was apprehended.

Carol Stimson nursed a cup of coffee and a BLT sandwich in a restaurant inside the downtown Salt Lake Sheraton Hotel. Fortunately, she had received the warning call not to return home just moments before she turned down her street. She did a quick about face and jumped back onto I-15, ending up at the

Sheraton. She carefully weighed her options. Even if she wasn't criminally indicted, which now seemed likely, her career as a corrections officer was over. Moreover, going back to the little house she rented in Lehi was now out of the question. Kincaid and his cop friends would have the place under surveillance. That angered her, because some things she desperately wanted to take with her were stored in the house.

She'd become a liability. She knew it, and so would they. She had no intention of ending up like Vogue, Watts, and Milo Sorensen.

She decided to spend the night in a quiet, out-of-the-way place. The next day, she planned to take care of some unfinished business with Kincaid, and then leave Salt Lake City far behind. She hated the man—hated him because he had nearly gotten her fired and because he destroyed her reputation in the department. But most of all, she hated Kincaid for what he represented: someone who used his considerable power to protect stinking inmates at the expense of prison staff. It was his fault, and she intended to make him pay, and pay dearly. Cops didn't do this sort of thing to other cops—it should have been like family. Street thugs and convicts were the bad guys. You never turned on a fellow officer. Somehow Kincaid had never learned this.

She intended to teach him a lesson. And the best way to do that was to strike at what Kincaid held most dear—his family.

Her first instincts about him had been correct. They should have killed him at the very beginning. Now things were starting to unravel. How had Kincaid connected her to Sorensen and the forged suicide note? She had taken a calculated risk by changing the time on the disciplinary ticket she'd given Sandoval. Had he figured that out too?

It hadn't been difficult gathering information about him. Department gossip described Kincaid as a guy with inherited wealth who lived with the rest of the highbrows in affluent Park City. He was divorced and apparently had sole custody of a young daughter. A few hours spent on surveillance revealed the presence of an elderly woman in the home. She had even determined which elementary school Kincaid's daughter attended. A hit would be cake.

Salt Lake County Sheriff's detectives maintained the surveillance at Stimson's home on the outside chance that she might still show up. Turner and Marcy Everest remained on surveillance at Allred's home. He'd left the Board of Pardons shortly after five, driven straight home, and hadn't moved since. The surveillance plan was the same as the previous evening: remain outside the house until certain Allred was tucked in for the night and then return early the next morning.

Kate, Terry, and I sat cloistered in the conference room outside my office. It was after seven o'clock. We were poring through six months of Bill Allred's telephone records. The department employs over six hundred people at the Utah State Prison. The daunting task before us was how to identify department employee home and business telephone numbers that showed up on Allred's phone records. There had to be a computer program that could do that for us, but I wasn't aware of one, and neither were Terry or Kate. If we'd had more time, the department's computer support people could probably have created a program for us.

Each of us worked with two months of phone records. We began by eliminating all out-of-state calls as well as those outside the Salt Lake Valley that would have been beyond the reasonable commuting distance of our employees. We took the remaining calls and generated a list of any number called more than once. That narrowed things down significantly. The first break occurred when we matched four calls during the six-month period to Stimson's phone. Why would a Board of Pardons member to be calling the home of a low-ranking corrections officer assigned to an inmate housing unit?

Next, we took the list of North Point employees who were on duty and, hypothetically at least, on our list of possible murder suspects. It was here things really fell into place. Allred's phone records revealed that besides Stimson, he'd made multiple calls to the homes of two additional department employees, each of whom was on duty at the North Point facility on the evening Sorensen was killed. Three calls had been made to Captain Steve Schumway and four to the home of Deputy Warden Bob Fuller. We also discovered a fifth call made to Fuller's office at the prison.

Kate leaned back in her chair and looked over at me before speaking. "You look like you're about to puke. Can I get you anything?"

"A new job would be nice," I replied.

"If this turns out to be as rotten as it smells, we could all be looking for work," said Burnham with a mischievous smirk.

"You might be right," I said. The smirk disappeared.

"We'll need to cross-check Allred's phone records against Fuller's and Schumway's, as well as against each other. That's going to take some time," I said.

I looked over at Kate. She nodded. "Let's do it. We need to wait for the lab results on Stimson's clothing anyway. If the results come back positive, Webb will get a warrant for her charging murder one. And if anybody can get her to talk, it'll be Webb and Gill. If she confesses, the others will fall like dominos."

"I've got an idea," said Burnham. "I think we should intentionally try to spook Allred. It's possible he made us today anyway. Why not make the surveillance obvious? Who knows. Maybe the guy panics and makes a mistake. We could sure make him awfully nervous."

"I don't see much downside to that idea," added Kate. "Worst-case scenario, the guy is innocent, and we've managed to royally piss off a member of the state Board of Pardons. How serious could that be?"

Incredulous, I replied, "Serious enough."

"Just kidding," said Kate.

In truth, the idea made sense, and I couldn't see much downside either. Perhaps raising Allred's anxiety level by making the surveillance obvious would serve as a good primer for the interrogation to follow. It was about time to give Allred the opportunity to explain his sexual proclivities in the company of Levi Vogue, not to mention some very interesting telephone calls to a corrections officer who now happened to be the primary suspect in the murder of a prison inmate.

Chapter Forty-three

I spent a restless night worrying about the investigation and my relationship with Kate, and feeling guilty that Sara wasn't receiving enough of my time or attention. For the moment, I couldn't help that. Unable to sleep, I got up early, left a note on the kitchen chalk board for Aunt June, and was in my office at department headquarters by seven.

What I'd found most troubling was the apparent connection between Allred and three department employees who worked together at the prison. I wondered if the telephone records of the prison employees would corroborate the existence of some type of relationship between them, or if Allred's records were an aberration that could somehow be written off as merely coincidental. I doubted that. And what about Carol Stimson? If the State Crime Lab connected her to the murder of a prison inmate, the implications seemed almost surreal.

It didn't take long for the news to arrive. Patti interrupted my dour thoughts to tell me Kate was on line one. "Good morning, Lieutenant McConnell. My telepathic inner voice told me it was you calling with good news," I lied.

"Sorry, Sam. Are you sitting down?"

"Yes, and you're about to ruin my morning, but go ahead."

"I just received a call from John Webb. He tried to call you earlier in your office at the prison, but when he couldn't find you, he called me instead. I figured you might be at headquarters.

"The lab report came in early this morning. They found trace amounts of blood that matched Sorensen's blood type on one pant leg of Stimson's uniform and on one of her uniform shoes. The DNA results just came back and showed a positive match to Sorensen. And that isn't all. A hair and fibers expert compared a hair she found on Stimson's dress shirt to samples of Sorensen's removed from his head during the autopsy. She says it's a match. John and Harvey are at the courthouse now meeting with Tom. There going to get a first degree murder warrant for her."

"I'm wondering why she hasn't surfaced. I hope she hasn't been tipped off. If she has, she'll be on the run and damned hard to catch. If we can just find her, a confession would tie everything together," I said.

"For sure. Careless of her, though, not to get rid of that uniform, don't you think?"

"Without a doubt."

"Listen, I've been thinking about something and I want to run it past you," said Kate.

"Okay."

"I think we should wait until later in the day, and then go confront Allred. Let's give it enough time for him to realize that he's been placed under surveillance. It might make him a little more cooperative. And I'd like to do the interview on my turf to give us the psychological edge. The truth is, I'm getting pressure from my department. Hyrum was waiting on my doorstep when I got in this morning. He made it abundantly clear we've still got two unsolved homicides on our hands, and he isn't seeing sufficient progress on either one.

"And if that isn't enough, the shit hit the fan over our lack of cooperation in handling the James Allen thing. Evidently, Allen complained to Richard Vogue, who then got on the horn and raised hell with Mayor Baldwin, who in turn chewed on Chief Hansen, and on down the administrative line to Hyrum."

"It sounds like an entire chain of command is awash in a sea of political diarrhea," I said, sounding slightly amused. Kate wasn't amused.

"You find this humorous, Sam, only because you haven't been on the receiving end of the criticism or political diarrhea, as you call it. But yours is coming, trust me," she snapped.

"I expect you're right." Trying to change the subject, I said, "Look, I don't have a problem pulling Allred in for questioning. I've been anxious to sit down and give him an opportunity to clarify a few things for us. As to the pressure you're feeling, the real issue for Locke is that he's afraid the Sheriff's Office is about to break the case wide open and steal the credit. Hyrum can't stand the thought of that."

"Always the cynic, Kincaid. Why do you always assume the worst when it comes to people's motives?"

"I guess it's because I've spent an entire career watching people like Hyrum seek the spotlight, take credit for the work of others, and push people aside as they climb the organizational ladder. His kind usually have little conscience about who they hurt on the way up. I've also learned that if you don't expect much from people, you aren't often disappointed, and occasionally, you're even pleasantly surprised."

"Jesus, Kincaid, you're a real piece of work." She promised to call me later in the day and hung up.

Sloan was in the midst of a budget meeting with his two deputy directors when I was ushered into his conference room. He briefly glanced up, looking at me like I was the grim reaper.

The barrage of intense media scrutiny the department had endured since the murder of Levi Vogue was admittedly unpleasant, but nothing like the shit storm that would occur later today when the press learned the Sheriff's Office had a first degree murder warrant against a corrections officer for killing an inmate. Already newspaper stories quoting unidentified sources were calling for the state legislature to launch an investigation into the management of the department. So far, the governor was doing everything possible to discourage the initiative, calling it premature. I suspected that would all change after today.

I reviewed the evidence against Stimson for Sloan and his top aides. The bad news prompted him to abbreviate the budget meeting and bring together a larger contingent of his management team to strategize ways of weathering the impending storm. Fortunately, I didn't have to take part in that meeting. I'd had enough of department headquarters for the time being, so I headed to my office at the prison.

I intentionally didn't tell Sloan about the additional evidence linking Allred with three prison employees until we were alone. The issue for me was whom could I trust. Sloan wasn't a problem, but I had no idea how far up the chain of command the scandal might reach.

Uncertain how vigorously the police would try to find her, Stimson spent the night in an obscure mom-and-pop motel in the sleepy bedroom community of Bountiful. After a restless night, she drove to the main branch of the Wells Fargo Bank in downtown Salt Lake City early the next morning. She didn't expect problems, but she circled the bank several times before parking and going inside. She closed both of her accounts, realizing she would have no further need of them. She also collected her birth certificate, passport, and other personal papers from a safety-deposit box she had previously rented. That done, she walked to a small savings and loan institution a couple of blocks from the Wells Fargo office. There she withdrew $225,000 from a money market account held in the name of a deceased female inmate who died in prison from complications resulting from HIV infection. The carefully laundered money was more than sufficient to jump-start a new life somewhere else.

Stimson drove to a nearby shopping mall, parked in the terraced garage, and went shopping. She needed to get ready to travel, and that required a change of appearance. She purchased sunglasses, a hat, and some new clothes. She then stopped at a Great Clips hair design shop where the stylist cut her shoulder-length hair short and bleached her black hair blond.

Stimson still had almost four hours before she had to be in Park City. She loaded the purchases in the back of her Ford Explorer, then stole the license plates off the unoccupied vehicle parked next to her. She figured it would be safer to drive with stolen plates than to risk using her own. When she finished her business with Kincaid and his family, she planned to drive straight through to Las Vegas. From there, getting lost in Mexico sounded just right.

Chapter Forty-four

An agitated Bill Allred could hardly concentrate during the weekly Board of Pardons business meeting. The agenda typically included policy-and-procedure changes, personnel issues, and budget items. Twice he had been asked questions by other Board members, and twice the questions had to be repeated. While nobody said anything, it was clear to everyone that Allred's mind was elsewhere. At one point, the acting chairman declared a 15-minute recess, hoping Allred would return focused on the business at hand. Instead, he came back more distracted than before.

They had followed him from home to the board office—two cars, each making it so obvious that he would have needed a seeing-eye dog not to notice. He recognized Terry Burnham from Sam Kincaid's staff, but he'd never seen the other guy. They were sitting in the Board of Pardons parking lot making no attempt to disguise their presence.

This had started to become embarrassing. It would only be a matter of time before a Board employee noticed them and started asking questions. Because of the nature of their work, Board staff were always on security alert. What would he do then?

He'd been instructed to lie low and go about his business in as normal a manner as possible. He could take the direct approach—walk right up and challenge them. But what if they arrested him on the spot? No. That was a bad plan. He could feign illness and go home. That's what he would do. He needed to get the surveillance team away from Board headquarters.

By the time he arrived home, Allred was in a state of near panic. He felt as though he might upchuck the pancake, sausage, and egg breakfast he'd consumed earlier in the morning. He felt isolated. He needed to talk with someone who could calm him down. What if his phone was bugged? They might be listening to all his calls.

For the first time, the reality of the situation forced him to do something he'd never before imagined. He opened the Salt Lake Valley phone directory to the section entitled "Attorneys." He worked his way through the lengthy list of criminal defense lawyers until he found the name he was looking for—Franklin Meadows. He reached for the telephone.

I reached my office at the prison late in the morning. There were a couple of new developments. Burnham had called and left a message that he and Turner had followed a nervous-looking Allred to his office, and then back to his home. Assuming he stayed put, Kate and I would know exactly where to find him later in the day when it was time to reel him in for questioning.

Patti informed me that Steve Schumway had dropped by the office earlier in the morning looking for me. He hung around long enough to make a pest of himself by asking Patti and several of my investigators for information about the status of the investigation. The inquiry was made under the guise of concern for his employees. Fortunately, after connecting Allred and the prison employees through Allred's telephone records, Terry and I called each member of the SIB at home and warned them not to discuss the investigation with anyone, particularly department employees. Schumway left the office with no more information than he had when he arrived.

Besides Terry's voice mail, the other message of interest came from Deputy Warden Bob Fuller. The message itself was short. He asked that I call him back. I decided to oblige. I dialed his extension, and on the third ring, he picked up.

"Bob, this is Sam. I got your message. Thought I'd better get back to you before my day starts to get hectic. What's up?"

"Thanks for returning my call, Sam. Look, I don't mean to pry, but I hope you can understand my concern about the possibility of having one of my employees involved in this killing. If it proves to be true, I don't have to tell you what an incident like this would do to the morale of my staff, not to mention the reputation of the department. Has anybody heard from Stimson?"

"Not that I'm aware of—at least not as of this morning. I don't know what to make of that, but I hope she turns up soon."

"I don't think we should jump to any conclusions. After all, she is on her regularly scheduled days off. I'll bet she's taken a trip someplace and will show up later today. She's not scheduled back on duty until swing shift tomorrow. I just can't believe one of my staff could be involved in something like this. By the way, did you find anything when you searched her house?" Fuller asked.

I responded with a half-truth. "Really didn't find much. We took a dirty uniform and that was about it. Webb planned to have the lab boys check it out, but I haven't heard whether they got the results back—probably sometime today though."

"If you don't mind my asking, what prompted the Sheriff's Department to get a search warrant in the first place?" he asked.

Now I was uncomfortable. For the moment, the advantage belonged to Fuller. I didn't want to provide him with information he didn't already have, nor did I want to get caught in a lie by denying the existence of evidence he might already know about. So I opted for the middle ground.

"You know, Bob, I'm really not at liberty to go into the details, but I will tell you judges don't approve warrants without probable cause—so draw your own conclusions."

Satisfied that he'd gotten all the information he was likely to get, Fuller and I said good-bye. I felt certain that Schumway and Fuller had set out to accomplish the same goal: gather as much information about the status of the investigation as possible without arousing suspicion. It didn't work.

Chapter Forty-five

As the day wore on, Stimson's somber mood turned to a dark depression. With the depression came anger, more than she'd felt at any time in her life except maybe from the sexual abuse she'd suffered as a child at the hands of her stepfather. She first heard the report over one of Salt Lake City's twenty-four-hour all-news radio stations. There was now a warrant out for her arrest—first degree murder in the death of prison inmate Milo Sorensen. It was the lead story on all the stations. She fought the growing sense of panic in her gut—fight or flight, the most basic of human responses. She took a deep breath and let the rage take over. Fight it would be.

Her life had fallen apart in the span of a few short hours. And Sam Kincaid was responsible—Kincaid and that bitch homicide detective from Salt Lake City P.D. She would take his family and destroy it. She'd make him watch and then she'd take his life too. Time permitting, she would have enjoyed a one-on-one encounter with Kate McConnell. That was out of the question now. Kincaid would have to do.

She arrived outside Jane Adams Elementary School in Park City about fifteen minutes before school ended. She parked in front, looking like any other parent intent on picking up a child. She fit right in and didn't look even slightly suspicious. She had been here before. She knew Sara Kincaid would emerge, probably with a friend or two, and walk the short distance home.

Stimson also knew that Sara never arrived home to an empty house. She was no latch-key kid. The live-in nanny would be there to greet her.

Rather than snatch the child from the street and risk causing a scene, Stimson decided on another course of action. She would follow at a discreet distance until Sara got home, and then take the kid and the old lady just as Sara entered the house. She would only deviate from that plan if it appeared Sara wasn't going directly home. In that case, she would stop Sara on the street, display her department identification, and explain that Sam had been involved in a traffic accident and that Sara should ride with her to the hospital. She'd take Sara home, ostensibly to pick up the old lady, and then she'd have them both.

The plan came off without a hitch. At precisely two-forty, Sara emerged from the school in the company of three other children. Two of the kids separated from Sara in the school parking lot and hopped into waiting vehicles. Sara and the other girl left the school grounds and meandered slowly through the residential Park Meadows neighborhood. The children stopped at a corner about a block from Kincaid's home, which was located in a small cul-de-sac called Lariat Circle. They talked for about five minutes before separating.

Stimson drove past Sara and parked the Explorer on Motherlode Drive near the entrance to the cul-de-sac. She gathered the small bag that contained her cell phone, plastic handcuffs, hoods, and duct tape.

She waited until Sara was almost in the driveway before she emerged from her vehicle. She walked rapidly up beside the little girl, arriving at the moment Sara opened the front door. At the last instant, Sara glanced over her shoulder and saw Stimson for the first time.

"Who are you?" Sara asked.

"Just a friend of your daddy's." She pushed Sara gently from behind into the living room.

Mild curiosity now gave way to genuine fear and Sara said, "You can't come in here."

All pretenses of friendliness gone, Stimson snapped, "The hell I can't." With that, she delivered a hard, open-handed slap to the side of Sara's face, momentarily stunning her. She tossed the little girl to the hardwood floor face-down. Before Sara could scream, Stimson placed duct tape over her mouth and bound her hands behind her back with plastic handcuffs. She pulled Sara to her feet, placed a cloth hood over her head, and dragged her to a nearby couch.

"Now you sit right here and keep perfectly still, or I'll kill you and the old lady."

From the kitchen, Aunt June heard the commotion, but assumed it was Sara arriving home from school with a friend. Moments later, she turned from the kitchen sink and stood looking down the barrel of a Smith & Wesson .38 caliber revolver aimed directly at her face.

"Sara is okay and you will be too as long as you do exactly what I tell you. Do you understand?"

Aunt June nodded and said, "Please don't hurt my little niece."

Stimson smiled. A niece, huh.

She handcuffed Aunt June just as she had Sara. She placed the duct tape over her mouth and ordered her into the living room. As soon as Aunt June saw Sara seated on the couch, handcuffed, with a hood placed over her head, she let out a muffled groan. Stimson used the second hood on Aunt June, and placed her on the couch next to Sara. She reached for her cell phone.

I spent the early part of the afternoon looking for anything out of the ordinary in the personnel records of Bob Fuller and Steve Schumway. Fuller and Schumway had been with the department for over twenty years, and both were pension eligible. There was nothing in their files indicative of the kind of corrupt behavior I now feared. The trio, including Stimson, had worked together in the North Point facilities for more than three years.

A little after three o'clock, I left the prison for a meeting with Kate at a location near Allred's home. He lived in Holladay, a small Salt Lake County bedroom community. The surveillance team at Allred's confirmed that he hadn't moved since his return from work earlier in the morning.

We planned to transport Allred to Salt Lake City P.D. headquarters, where we would be met by Webb and Gill. They wanted to observe the interrogation from an adjoining room.

Unfortunately, I was about to discover that things don't always go according to plan.

Chapter Forty-six

On the way to meet Kate, my cell phone rang. It was Patti calling with a disturbing message. "Sam, I just received a telephone call from a female whose voice I didn't recognize. It definitely wasn't Sara, and I'm almost positive it wasn't your Aunt June. The caller said there was a family emergency and you needed to call home immediately. By the time I asked who she was and the nature of the emergency, she'd hung up. Do you want me to notify Park City P.D.?"

"No," I snapped. "What about caller ID? Do you have a number?"

"The call didn't register on caller ID. It must have been blocked. Is there anything I can do?" she asked, a tone of alarm in her voice.

"No, nothing. I'll take care of it." Before she could say anything else, I'd disconnected. I had a sinking feeling down deep in my gut as I punched in my home number. On the first ring, she answered.

"Hello, Sam. I'll bet you know who this is," said Stimson.

Christ. How had I managed to overlook this possibility?

"Look, Carol, whatever your beef is with me, please leave my family out of it."

"Sorry. Can't do that. What a lovely home you have here. And such a nice little family. I didn't realize the old lady is your aunt. Isn't that interesting? Two for the price of one."

"Tell me exactly what you want, and I'll do it, no questions asked. But please don't hurt them. They've got nothing to do with this. This is between you and me."

"You've got that right, Kincaid. Now here's what I want you to do. If you want your family to stay alive, do it right. You have exactly twenty minutes to get here. At twenty-one minutes, your aunt is dead. At twenty-two minutes, Sara is dead. Come alone. If I get the slightest impression you've called out the troops, everybody dies. Got that? Park in the driveway, not in the garage. Enter through the front door. If you deviate from these instructions, even slightly, everybody dies. See you in twenty."

"But I can't possibly," I started to say. But she had already hung up.

From where I was, getting home doing anything close to the speed limit would take thirty-five minutes. No matter how fast I drove, there was no way I could make it in twenty. But I had to try. I decided to wait until my time was almost over and then call home, hoping Stimson would answer and I could buy a few more minutes. Most of the drive was freeway.

I had little time to consider my options. I debated calling Park City P.D., but decided against it. There wasn't time, and besides, I knew they were too small a department to have a special operations squad. I wasn't even sure if they had a trained hostage negotiator on board. No, I figured I had a better chance of saving Sara and Aunt June if I followed directions. On this one, I would have to go it alone.

Sam was late and Kate was growing impatient. She realized that whenever they were scheduled to meet, he would invariably run a few minutes late. Today, however, Sam was running more than a few minutes behind schedule. Kate dialed his cell phone but didn't get an answer. You could never tell about the guy—half the time he didn't even keep the phone turned on. She then called his office, hoping he hadn't gotten bogged down in an afternoon meeting. That didn't seem likely, but if he had, he surely would have called and postponed their meeting.

"Hi, Patti. It's Kate. Sam was supposed to meet me in Holladay a half-hour ago, but he didn't show up. And he's not answering his cell. Any idea where he is?"

"That's funny he's not answering his cell. I talked with him just a few minutes ago. To tell you the truth, I'm a little worried," said Patti.

"Why's that?"

"About a half-hour ago, I received a phone call from someone who said there was a family emergency and Sam should call home ASAP. I called Sam on his cell and gave him the message. I offered to call Park City P.D. and have them respond, but he told me not to."

"Who called?"

"That's what struck me as odd. The caller was a woman, and I didn't recognize her voice. I'm pretty sure it wasn't his Aunt June, and I know it wasn't Sara. I suppose it could have been someone from Sara's school."

"Oh, God," said Kate. "I've got a bad feeling about this. Listen carefully, Patti. Here's what I want you to do."

With my twenty minutes nearly gone, and still several minutes from home, I grabbed the cell phone and dialed my home. On the third agonizing ring, Stimson picked up.

"Had you a little nervous there, didn't I?" Her tone of voice suggested she was toying with me and found it amusing.

"I'm almost there," I replied. "If I'm going to follow your directions the rest of the way, I want proof my family is still alive. I want to speak to one of them."

"Hold on."

"Daddy," Sara cried.

"Hold on, honey, Daddy's almost there."

"You'd better be." It was Stimson. "And remember, if I get even the slightest inkling you've been a bad boy, everybody dies—no discussion, no negotiations, end of story, end of family. You got that?"

"Understood. I'm alone."

I pulled off State Highway 220 into the Park Meadows subdivision, and quickly pulled to the curb, unlocked the glove box, and removed a holstered .25-caliber Colt pistol. It was an old gun I'd purchased years before from a retiring parole officer. It was an ideal weapon for undercover work, something I'd never had the occasion to do. It hadn't been used much in the years I'd owned it.

I strapped the holster to my right ankle and drove the remaining few blocks home. As an experienced corrections officer, the chance of Stimson missing the weapon was unlikely, but when she found my department-issued .38-caliber snub-nose attached to my belt, she might get careless and miss the back-up weapon. I could only hope.

I pulled into the driveway and noticed all the wood blinds on the front-facing windows had been closed. I spotted Stimson's Ford Explorer parked outside the cul-de-sac on Motherlode Drive. As instructed, I parked in the driveway, got out, and walked slowly toward the front door with my empty hands in view at all times. I assumed she was watching my every move. I opened the screen door, tapped lightly on the front door, and then reached for the knob. The door was locked. I waited for what seemed an eternity before I heard the front door unlatch.

As I stepped into the darkened living room, to my horror, I saw Sara and Aunt June huddled together on the couch, hands cuffed behind them, and each wearing a loose-fitting cloth hood over her head. Carol stood several feet away with her handgun leveled at my chest.

"Assume the position, asshole," she said.

She didn't need to explain that command. I placed my hands against the front door, spread my legs, and leaned into the door with my upper body, while my legs and feet were splayed out behind. She patted me down and immediately found the service revolver on my hip. I expected that. She completed the frisk and discovered the ankle holster as well.

"You really didn't think I'd miss the back-up, did you? Stand up, face me, and drop your pants."

I complied.

"The underwear too."

Satisfied that I hadn't hidden another weapon in my underwear, she allowed me to pull up my pants. She ordered me into a straight-back dining-room chair she had moved into the living room, and quickly applied the plastic handcuffs. She took the roll of duct tape and ran it several times across my chest and around the chair until satisfied that I was well secured.

She then stepped in front of me, and without a word, delivered a stinging backhand blow to the side of my face. The blow shocked me more than it hurt, although a ring she wore opened a small cut above my right eye. It bled freely.

"That was to get your attention," she said, smiling, and in an almost cheery tone of voice. "Now we can have a short visit before I do what I really came here to do."

I'm no shrink, but Stimson's mood seemed to change from doom and gloom to one of euphoria in a manner of seconds. Her upbeat, almost friendly demeanor seemed a mere pretense for a much darker side of her personality. I decided to try to keep her talking and stall for time. I didn't know what else to do. It was going to be a bad afternoon, and one, I fully realized, that neither my family nor I would likely survive.

Chapter Forty-seven

Wheeler had provided Kate with an address and detailed directions to Sam's home. She was driving at breakneck speed to Park City, hoping her hunch about Stimson was wrong and that Sam had rushed home to some other kind of problem. All of her instincts, however, told her otherwise. She was genuinely worried, not only about Sam, but his family as well. Her feelings for him had grown beyond those of a mere colleague—they were personal now. She would do whatever was necessary to keep him alive.

The plan that had taken shape in her head was fraught with potential problems, not the least of which was her unfamiliarity with Sam's neighborhood and home. She had never been there. She first had to locate the house. That accomplished, could she approach without being seen? How would she get inside undetected? If a shoot-out ensued, who might end up in the line of fire? In situations like this, proper police procedure called for unobtrusively evacuating the occupants of surrounding homes. Sam had undoubtedly thought of that, but concluded that to do so would have placed his family in too much danger.

Kate's worst fear was confirmed when she drove past Lariat Circle and saw Stimson's Ford Explorer parked on Motherlode Drive. The license plate number was different, but Stimson had probably changed plates once she realized the police were looking for her. Kate parked on a street behind the Lariat Circle cul-de-sac so she could approach Kincaid's home from the rear. She would have to negotiate a six-foot cedar fence that enclosed his backyard, hoping none of the neighbors would see her and call the police.

Kincaid's home was just as Patti had described it: a two-level affair with a daylight walkout basement leading onto a stone patio. Fortunately, several mature blue spruces scattered throughout the yard provided a measure of cover as Kate scaled the fence and ran for the house. Finding a way in was the next trick. She tried the French doors leading into the basement. They were locked. Next she tried an aluminum sliding window into what she guessed was a bedroom. Again, it was locked. When she removed a screen that covered a small, opaque glass window that opened into what had to be a bathroom, her luck changed. She was in.

◇◇◇

I wasn't sure whether trying to reason with Stimson would work, but I didn't have many options. I was willing to try any ploy I could think of to buy time. I didn't want to risk her anger by appearing condescending or self-righteous.

"Carol, why don't you release my family? There's nothing to be gained by harming an eight-year-old girl and an elderly woman. Do what you want with me, but let them go."

"Fuck you, Kincaid, you brought this on yourself. You just couldn't leave it alone, could you? You had to turn against your own. Without your help, the cops would never have figured it out. So it's time to pay the piper, and in this case, I'm the piper."

My appeal to her maternal instincts went for naught. She actually seemed to be enjoying the moment, a bemused expression on her face and in her tone of voice. This was one lady I just didn't understand. I tried a different approach.

"Look, Carol, why dig yourself into a deeper legal hole? If you stop now, cooperate with us, you can avoid being strapped to a gurney with an IV in your arm."

"That's fuckin' lame, Kincaid, and you know it. You think I'm interested in becoming one of those caged fuckin' animals?—not likely, asswipe. Besides, they're already planning to put the needle in my arm, so I don't have much to lose, now do I? But they've got to find me first. And I've got something to say about that."

She was probably right. I decided to try one last strategy. I would lie to Stimson, hoping the shock value of what I told her might give her second thoughts. I recognized that I might merely unleash the rage I sensed was never far from the surface. If she were operating solo without the approval of her partners, she might not be able to tell truth from falsehood. The lives of my family depended on it.

"Let me tell you something you don't know. We picked up one of your partners, Bill Allred, this afternoon, and he's been downtown telling quite a story. He isn't worried about you or any of the others. He's down there cutting a deal for himself. We know a lot more than you think we do. It's amazing what you can learn from a wiretap. Besides you and Allred, your little group includes Steve Schumway and Bob Fuller. We know you arranged for Slick Watts to kill Levi. We also know you killed Watts, and most recently, Milo Sorensen. The party's over, Carol. You need to give it up and start looking out for yourself. Nobody else is going to do that for you."

For the first time, the look on her face had changed to one of shock and surprise. "What's it really matter," she sighed. "It's all over anyway. Things were going along just fine until we decided to approach Vogue. That's when everything went to hell."

"What do you mean, approach Vogue?" I asked.

Try to keep her talking, I thought.

She smiled faintly and said, "I guess I can tell you. You won't be around long enough to repeat any of it.

"We'd been using Allred to sell parole release dates for two years. Unfortunately, the Board votes in panels of three. We needed a second vote to guarantee every outcome. As Levi and Bill became friends, it became clear that Vogue was up to his ass in debt and was badly in need of cash. Given that, and his interesting sexual proclivities, we figured he'd be a good candidate to join our little enterprise. We obviously misjudged him. When Levi declined our offer and threatened to expose Allred unless Bill resigned from the Board, we had a decision to make. We could either lose a growing source of income, or eliminate Vogue. It was actually an easy decision."

"How did you come up with Slick Watts?" I asked.

"We recruited him from inside the prison. The dumb shit was actually stupid enough to believe he was embarking on a new career as a contract killer. But he couldn't be trusted. We knew that and intended to kill him all along. Watts was the perfect choice to eliminate Vogue because he had motive. Isn't revenge the sweetest of all motives?

"Time for just one last question," she said, a faint smile tracing her mouth. "Think of it as a condemned man's last words."

"That's comforting," I replied. "Tell me how the four of you came together in the first place. And what made you do it?"

"As it turns out, Fuller and Schumway had been running an inmate extortion scam for about as long as they'd worked together at North Point. One day I happened to overhear a conversation between an inmate and Captain Schumway that I wasn't supposed to hear. Shortly thereafter, Fuller invited me to join the group. It probably didn't hurt that I'd been fucking him almost from the time I transferred into his unit. As for that little worm, Bill Allred, Fuller brought him on board. They'd known each other for twenty years. Allred actually supervised Fuller in several different prison positions. They were old friends.

"And why did we do it? That's easy, not a complicated motive at all. Try money. You know that when I started at the prison almost five years ago, I was hired for a whopping $9.65 an hour. Imagine working in a shithole prison for that kind of money. It doesn't get you very far. I was food stamp eligible for the first year and a half. And you contributed to that, Kincaid. You made it impossible for me to ever receive a promotion. And for what? Because I slapped an inmate around.

"And let's not forget the inmates—dirtbags who have spent a lifetime victimizing others. I can hardly describe how good it felt to inflict a little extra-judicial punishment on those asswipes. Whatever we did to those lowlifes, it wasn't enough.

"Well, time's up. As much as I've enjoyed our little talk, I'm afraid that it's time for me to take care of business and get out of Dodge while I still can," she said.

Stimson removed the roll of duct tape from her bag, cut off a strip and placed it over my mouth. She walked behind me, and bent down until her lips were almost touching my ear, close enough that I felt her hot, fetid breath. She whispered, "I want you to watch. First I'm gonna wrap my gun in a towel, noise, you know, and then I'm going to shoot Granny in the head. Would you like me to remove the hood first so she can see it coming? Then for a change of pace, if I can borrow one of your bedroom pillows, I'm going to suffocate the life out of little Sara. I wonder how much she'll kick and squirm? Then, if you've been a good boy and haven't tried to cause a scene, I'll give you one behind the ear, and it'll be over quick. But if you've been a bad boy, I'm going to shoot you in both kneecaps and then give you one in the belly. Gut shot. You'll die a slow and painful death. Enjoy the show."

I watched in horror as Stimson removed a small hand towel from her bag and began wrapping it around the barrel of her gun. I struggled in vain against the restraints that secured me to the chair. I felt the plastic cuffs cutting into my wrists. Blood trickled down and ran onto my hands. The cut above my eye bled freely, making it difficult to see.

When she tied me, she had neglected to run the duct tape around my ankles, which gave me a chance to stand and use the chair as a weapon. It was an act of desperation, but I had run out of time and options. I tried to scream but only managed audible, muffled groans of protest. As she turned her back to me and walked slowly across the room to deliver the fatal head shot to Aunt June, I stood up and charged. At six feet four inches and two hundred pounds, I hit her hard from behind, driving her headfirst into an end table next to the couch. I landed on top of her. She went down hard and came up with a bloody nose, cursing.

"You fucking bastard. You want it the hard way, I'll give it to you the hard way."

I tried to keep her down by using my legs to kick. It didn't work. Glowering from above, she kicked me until I lost count of the blows. I remember instinctively trying to protect myself by getting into the fetal position, but I was quickly losing consciousness. I heard Sara crying. I vaguely recalled hearing the pop-pop sound of gunshots.

The bathroom window was just wide enough for Kate to slide through. Once inside, she stood perfectly still and hoped that Stimson hadn't heard the noise she made.

She quickly removed her shoes and slipped quietly into the hallway leading to the stairs. She heard the faint sound of voices, but wasn't close enough to make out who or what was being said. With gun in hand, she slowly ascended the stairs. About halfway up, one of the hardwood steps groaned loudly enough that Kate was certain it must have been heard on the main level. She momentarily froze, dreading the next step and the one after that. The female voice was loud and clear, a voice that must have belonged to Carol Stimson. The top of the stairs opened into an entry foyer near the front door of the residence. The hushed voices were close now, probably not more than twenty feet away, and appeared to be coming from what Kate thought was the living room. It had momentarily grown quiet, so quiet that Kate stood frozen, afraid to move. Then all hell broke loose.

As Kate came around the corner and stepped into view, Stimson looked up and saw her. The shooting corridor was extremely narrow, with two hooded hostages seated to one side on the living-room couch and Sam curled up on the floor at Stimson's feet. Before Kate could order her to drop the weapon, Stimson fired two wild shots, both narrowly missing her. Sara was crying hysterically, and Aunt June had rolled partially on top of the child in a futile attempt to shield her body. The risk of hitting an innocent hostage was a possibility, but Kate had no choice. The first shot struck Stimson in the left shoulder. She howled in pain, but didn't go down. The second one struck her in the neck, hitting the carotid artery. This time she went down as blood pulsated from the neck wound like a fountain.

Kate heard breaking glass at the front door and turned in time to see Vince and Terry burst into the home, weapons at the ready. Patti, following instructions from Kate, had notified them of the likely hostage situation.

In a matter of minutes, my home, already in shambles, was turned into a major crime scene. There were enough police and fire officials on the premises to open a doughnut store. It became a repeat performance of what I'd encountered that first night at the home of Levi Vogue. Cops from several agencies, crime scene techs, fire and emergency medical personnel were everywhere. Within an hour, print and television media groups were crawling all over the place.

Despite Terry's effort to stem the flow of blood, Stimson died from shock and blood loss on the helicopter flight to the University of Utah Medical Center. Sara and Aunt June, though badly shaken, were not seriously injured. For Sara, however, the terror of this day would not soon be forgotten. As for me, a cut above one eye, a couple of cracked ribs, and assorted bumps and bruises were about it. I would be sore for a few weeks, but the sanctity of my home had been violated, and my family terrorized. Now it was personal. Alone, or with Kate's help, I intended to end it tonight.

Chapter Forty-eight

An ambulance transported Sara and Aunt June to a Salt Lake City hospital. I rode with them, and Kate followed. Aunt June's condition had suddenly taken a turn for the worse, and I was worried. Shortly after we arrived at the hospital, she had begun to complain of chest pains. The hospital ran a series of tests to identify the problem. A traumatized Sara was examined, given a mild sedative, and had fallen fast asleep. Both were held overnight for observation. As soon as Sara had fallen asleep and an emergency room physician stitched the cut above my eye, Kate and I left the hospital and drove to the Salt Lake City Police Department. The hostage incident and subsequent shooting of Stimson had occurred after the local evening news. It would be the lead story on every television news station at the nine and ten o'clock hours. If we wanted to maintain the element of surprise and apprehend Stimson's co-conspirators, we needed to move quickly.

The subsequent search of Stimson's Ford Explorer had yielded another piece of important evidence. Aside from a passport and over $200,000 in cash, she had kept a journal—a very incriminating journal that detailed her activities and those of her colleagues for the past three years. Among other things, the journal revealed that the group referred to themselves as the Commission. Their activities ranged from the theft of inmates' personal property to drug trafficking both inside the prison and on the street. They also sold parole release dates and operated a prison protection racket where selected inmates paid for protection to avoid getting hurt. It was a tale of corruption and greed that was about to produce the biggest scandal in the history of the Utah Department of Corrections, a department that up to now had enjoyed a reputation for being squeaky clean.

Besides Kate and me, John Webb and Harvey Gill from the Sheriff's Office, Deputy District Attorney Tom Stoddard, Captain Hyrum Locke, and my boss were at the meeting. I had no idea how Sloan heard about the shoot-out, but somebody had called him.

Looking at me, Locke asked, "Exactly where are the remaining suspects at the present time?"

"As far as I know, Bill Allred is still at home where he's been most of the day. Steve Schumway is pulling a swing shift at the prison until eleven. As for Fuller, it's hard to say. He usually works in his office until around six o'clock, and then goes home. Some nights, he stays late."

"Then I suggest we get a team out to the prison immediately, and I believe I should assume command," said Locke.

"No, I don't think so," Sloan said. "These are my employees, and they've sullied the reputation of an entire department."

"All the more reason you should stay out of it," countered Locke.

"They're going to go down, all right, and the Utah Department of Corrections is going to take them down. It's important to the future of this department for the public to see we're not afraid to clean our own house. It's also important for the morale of every honest man and woman who works for the department—and that's ninety-nine percent of them," said Sloan.

"But I insist," Locke started to say when Sloan cut him off.

"No, Hyrum, you don't insist. This is my party and you're not invited. I'm afraid this is one time you're going to miss out on a photo op."

"You can't do this," said Locke indignantly.

"Watch me," replied Sloan.

With that, a visibly angry Locke stormed out of the room and slammed the conference door behind him. While everyone else in the room maintained appropriate decorum during the tirade, I was grinning like a man who'd just won the lottery.

Sloan looked over at me, raised an eyebrow, and said, "Not a word out of you, Mr. Kincaid."

"Yes, sir."

We split into two teams. Kate, Stoddard, and I went to Bill Allred's home. Sloan and the detectives from the Sheriff's Office headed for the prison. I assigned Burnham and Marcy Everest to assist Sloan.

I was certain how Sloan intended to play this. Brad Ford would be lurking somewhere at the prison. Once the arrests were made, Ford would assemble the media and deliver a carefully worded press statement announcing the enforcement action taken by the department against four of its own staff. It was vintage Sloan engaged in damage control, doing the best he could to place a positive spin on a nasty department scandal.

Allred hadn't left his home all day. When we arrived, Kate covered the back of the house, while Stoddard and I went to the front door. A subdued-looking Allred answered, and with as much bluster as he could manage under the circumstances, demanded to know what we wanted.

"Cut the bullshit, Bill," I said. "For starters, you're under arrest for three counts of conspiracy to commit first degree murder, and before it all shakes out, heaven only knows what else. Would you like me to read you your Miranda warnings?"

"Save it. I'm well aware of my Miranda rights," he snapped. The momentary act of bravado had given way to a look of genuine desperation.

He turned to Stoddard, ignoring Kate and me. "My attorney is Franklin Meadows, and I want to make a deal."

"Meadows is one of the best, and trust me, you're going to need the best," replied Stoddard.

"This is what I want. In exchange for my full cooperation, the death penalty is off the table. I want to be placed outside Utah in a federal minimum security institution, and I want you to go on record during my sentencing hearing that I cooperated fully," said Allred.

"We're getting a little ahead of ourselves," said Stoddard. "Whatever we might decide to offer will be contingent upon how much you know and how fully you cooperate. Everything you've demanded is within our power to grant except a guarantee of placement in a minimum security federal prison. If the state agrees to pay to have you confined in a federal prison, the feds decide which one of their institutions you're assigned to, not us. But until we know more, I won't promise you anything."

"For today, I'm invoking my constitutional right to remain silent and right to counsel. I'll make no statement until I've conferred with Mr. Meadows."

"Fair enough," said Stoddard.

We released Allred into the custody of Sheriff's Department deputies, who took him to the Salt Lake County Jail.

By the time we returned to the prison, Steve Schumway had been taken into custody without incident. He had invoked his right to remain silent and was demanding an attorney. Ford read a prepared statement to the assembled media, and then provided a photo op of Schumway as he was loaded into a waiting sheriff's department vehicle for transportation to the Salt Lake County Jail, where he would join Allred.

Bob Fuller had left the prison earlier in the evening. His whereabouts were unknown. As soon as Schumway was driven away and the news media departed, Sloan pulled Kate and me aside and announced that we were taking a drive to the home of Deputy Warden Fuller. Burnham and Webb followed in Webb's car.

Fuller lived in an upscale residential suburb of Salt Lake City. His beautiful home sat high on the east bench, where he had a spectacular view of the entire Salt Lake Valley. On the way there, Sloan reminisced about a long-dormant friendship with Fuller dating back almost twenty years. Sloan recounted years of camping, fly-fishing, and fall hunts that often included their wives.

"And then his lovely wife, Mary, died rather suddenly of colon cancer. I think it was about the time I became executive director, maybe five years ago. Bob never seemed to be the same after Mary's death. Over time, we drifted apart and didn't see much of each other."

Sloan didn't say anything else for several minutes. As I drove, he stared out the window into the empty night, lost in his own thoughts. He finally broke the silence, and in a melancholy tone of voice asked, "I wonder, if I'd paid more attention to our friendship after Mary's death, if it might've kept him out of trouble?" It seemed a rhetorical question that neither Kate nor I tried to answer.

When we arrived at Fuller's home, both the interior lights and the front porch light were on. It was almost as though he was expecting us. And maybe he was. Burnham agreed to cover the back of the house while Webb remained in front. Sloan didn't anticipate problems, but I wasn't so sure.

As I followed Sloan up the driveway, I turned to Kate and asked, "You wearing a vest?"

"Is the Pope Catholic?" she replied. "You're not, are you?"

"Yeah, I've got one on," I lied.

As we reached the front door, I was startled to hear Fuller's voice over the intercom. "Please come in. I've been expecting you. I'm in the study down the hall."

I didn't like the feel of this and neither did Kate. We both unholstered our weapons and held them at our sides. Sloan walked into the living room and started down the dimly lit hallway, seemingly oblivious to the potential danger. Kate and I tagged along close behind.

Fuller was seated behind a large mahogany desk in a high-backed, black leather chair. The well-appointed office was shrouded in darkness, a small desk lamp providing the only light. Sloan wearily sat down in a chair facing the desk. He looked like a man carrying the burden of the world on his tired shoulders. Kate and I separated, moving along the office wall in opposite directions while trying to remain discreetly in the background. Fuller's hands were folded and rested on the desk in front of him. Both hands where I could see them made me a tad less anxious. For a moment, neither man spoke. Sloan finally broke the silence.

"You said you were expecting us. How come?"

"Betty Schumway called me. She was upset to say the least—wondered if I knew what was going on. She'd seen your carefully orchestrated news conference on one of the local stations. I channel-surfed until I saw it myself."

"For Christ's sake, Bob, why did you do it?" Sloan asked. "You've not only managed to bring your own career to a disgraceful end, but look at the other lives and reputations you destroyed in the process."

"Couple of reasons, actually. After Mary died, I bought a small ranch in Panama about an hour into the mountains outside Panama City—God's country, a truly beautiful place. A gringo can live down there like a king if you come in with enough money. And I mean a king—cook, housekeeper, the whole package. I even had a young Panamanian señorita waiting for me. If you're willing to lift a young woman out of poverty and treat her to the finer things, age differences don't matter much down there."

"For chrissake, Bob, you earn a decent salary. I just don't understand," said Sloan.

"Ah, but not enough money, Norm, at least not enough to live the lifestyle I had planned. And I almost made it—six more lousy months and I'd have retired, leaving all this shit behind."

"And the other reason?" said Sloan.

"For whatever it's worth, I never intended for it to go this far. I really didn't. I'm not apologizing for taking from those asswipe convicts. They deserve whatever they get and then some." A faint smile touched the corners of his mouth. "In a perverse sort of way, I got hooked on exploiting inmates. Imagine having the opportunity on a daily basis to threaten, intimidate, and take from a group of powerless lowlifes who have spent a lifetime doing exactly that to other people—kind of poetic justice, don't you think?"

"Christ, Bob. That's pathetic," Sloan muttered.

Fuller continued, ignoring the insult. "But the killing, that was something altogether different. When we couldn't get Vogue on our side, it threatened our entire operation. We couldn't allow that to happen. We had reached a point where influencing parole release dates had become just as lucrative as the drug trafficking and protection rackets, and it was also a lot cleaner. Nobody in the Commission was particularly enamored with the idea of killing Vogue directly, so we came up with what we thought was a good idea—hire somebody who hated the man to do it for us."

"Enter Charles Watts," said Sloan.

"Yup. At first, we entertained the notion of leaving Watts alone after the hit. But we decided we couldn't do that. He's a druggie with a big mouth. At some point, he'd have gotten high somewhere and started talking. So we decided to take care of him ourselves—set it up to look like a suicide. As for Sorensen, not that he's any great loss to the world, but we probably would have left him alone if you hadn't discovered the staged suicide."

"We didn't discover the suicide," replied Sloan. "The Medical Examiner's Office did, but what difference does it make anyway?"

I stood transfixed listening to this sordid tale of greed and murder, knowing that not one word of what Fuller had just said would be admissible in court. The incriminating statement had come as the result of questioning without the Miranda warnings. A simple motion to suppress by a competent defense attorney would render the entire confession null and void. But Sloan was intent on ending this in his own way, and either was ignoring, or simply didn't care about the legal niceties required by the justice system.

"You're going to have to come along with us now, Bob," Sloan said sadly.

"I'm afraid I can't do that, old friend."

I stiffened and so did Kate.

"The thought of spending the rest of my life in a cage waiting for the day the court appeals ran out, knowing you'd have to come for me for that last short walk, and then to go through the humiliation of having all those witnesses watch me die, hiding behind one-way glass—that's not for me. I served my sentence each day I walked inside that prison. I wanted you to know how sorry I am for all this. I know I've let you down personally, and the department."

Glancing over at me, he said, "Sorry about your family, Sam. I heard about that on the news too. We didn't order that. Stimson went after you on her own. I knew she carried a grudge, but I had no idea she'd go this far."

The room fell silent for a moment and I wondered what would happen next. For an instant, nobody moved. Then Fuller reached into his lap and brought a .357 magnum into view and shoved the four-inch barrel into his mouth. I heard Sloan scream, "No," and start to rise from his chair as the firearm discharged. The force of the blast blew away most of the back of Fuller's head, scattering brain, bone, and tissue on the headrest of the chair and the wall behind him. His open eyes stared vacantly at the ceiling, but saw nothing.

Epilogue

Three months later

As the enormity of the prison scandal washed over the Department of Corrections, and as public pressure mounted, Governor Nelson Strand ordered the Utah Attorney General's Office to convene a state grand jury to investigate. Not to be outdone, the Utah State Legislature mounted an investigation of its own. The emerging picture wasn't pretty.

The grand jury didn't limit its focus to the activities of the Commission as Sloan had hoped. The ongoing investigation broadened into a critical examination of the management and operations of the entire department. While the grand jury's final report wouldn't be released for several more weeks, there had been enough leaks to the press to set off a volume of public criticism.

Everybody wanted a sound bite, and nearly everyone had gotten one. Community activists and key state legislators were busy, almost daily, conducting print and television interviews decrying department management and calling for the usual sacrificial lambs. Politicians couldn't buy this kind of media exposure, and they were reveling in it.

I found Sloan alone in his office, quietly packing his personal property into cardboard boxes. The governor had found his first sacrificial lamb. Others would soon follow. Sloan's farewell party had been a low-key affair with colleagues and old friends dropping by to wish him well and say good-bye—a sad ending to what had otherwise been a brilliant public career.

We spoke briefly about his favorite hobby, fly-fishing; about long-neglected travel plans; and about spending more time with his six grandchildren, before I got around to what I'd really come to see him about.

"I know why you're here, Kincaid, and I'm telling you, it's not necessary," he said.

"Perhaps, but I can't help but feel I've let you down. If I had done a better job, maybe we could have nipped this thing before it ever got started. And maybe Levi Vogue would still be alive."

"I doubt that. This kind of scandal happens every once in a while, regardless of how well people do their jobs. Temptation is a regular part of the job. Difficult working conditions and lousy pay only add to the problem. It happens in police departments and sometimes in our prisons. Let's face it, in the criminal justice system, agencies are always going to have a few rotten apples in the barrel. It's the nature of the beast.

"In some ways, I feel a sense of relief—like a heavy burden has suddenly been lifted off my shoulders. It's not exactly how I envisioned going out, mind you, but it's nothing I can control either. I suspect that the director of institutional operations will probably be next, and you can plan on some personnel changes at the warden level as well. It might even reach down and bite you on the ass, but I kind of doubt it. In some ways, Sam, you're a royal pain in the ass. But you've done a first-rate job for me, and I'll do whatever I can to protect you."

I helped him carry the loaded boxes to his Volvo station wagon, where we said our good-byes. Like most people caught in an awkward moment, we promised to stay in touch, knowing that was unlikely to happen.

As for the two surviving members of the Commission, each stood accused of three counts of conspiracy to commit first degree murder. In addition, Schumway had been charged with two additional counts of first degree murder in the deaths of Charles Watts and Milo Sorensen. Each charge carried a potential death sentence, and prosecutors have given every indication that they intend to seek the ultimate penalty. Schumway has steadfastly maintained his innocence. He pled the Fifth Amendment and refused to answer any questions when subpoenaed before a state grand jury.

The same could not be said of former Utah Board of Pardons member William Allred. His team of lawyers had been negotiating with prosecutors almost from the day he was arrested. Allred's grand jury testimony against Schumway, coupled with his willingness to testify against him in a future trial, would probably net him a generous plea bargain. The scuttlebutt was that Allred would be allowed to plead guilty to something that would give him a life sentence, and then be transferred out-of-state to a prison where he would serve his sentence.

Apparently, the prosecution strategy was to use Allred to secure capital murder convictions against Schumway, and then forget about the myriad of other possible state and federal charges. Local print and television stations, often quoting unnamed sources close to the grand jury investigation, frequently mentioned the possibility of money-laundering charges, income tax evasion, extortion, introduction of contraband into a prison, and even federal civil rights violations. It would all play out in the coming months.

Levi Vogue's family has done everything possible to maintain their privacy. The few carefully orchestrated public statements made about the case came directly from the family patriarch, Richard Vogue. It hadn't taken the press long to uncover Levi's sexual indiscretions with Sue Ann Winkler at the Starlite Motel. To their credit, they haven't devoted much time to that aspect of the story. In fact, the media seem to have gone out of its way to paint a picture of Levi Vogue as an honest public servant who lost his life because he refused to succumb to the corrupt overtures of the Commission. The Vogue family appears to have found solace in that portrayal of Levi.

As for James Allen, I apologized for lying to him in what turned out to be a successful strategy to delay his entry into the investigation. While he accepted my apology, I think it highly unlikely that he and I will become drinking buddies anytime soon.

◇◇◇

For Kate and me, it's a little difficult to tell what, if anything, the future might hold. In the weeks after the case, we decided not to see each other for a while. It's been three months, and I miss her. I miss her smile, her sense of humor, her integrity, her intelligence, and, yes, her good looks.

Surprisingly, our self-imposed separation hasn't kept Kate and Sara apart. Three weeks ago, Sara invited Kate to her third-grade class as a part of show-and-tell day. Sara was the hit of the class. It isn't often that a third grader gets the chance to show off a crack homicide detective, and a female one at that. Okay, so I did encourage Sara to invite her. So what! A week later, Sara received an invitation from Kate to have lunch with her in Salt Lake City and tour the Salt Lake City Police Department. From everything I've heard, they both had a good time.

Kate and I would just as soon pass on another experience we'll share. Last week, I received a call from the Utah Attorney General's Office informing me that Kate and I were about to be named as defendants in a civil lawsuit filed by an attorney representing John Merchant. The lawsuit will allege police brutality in the form of excessive force, resulting in the plaintiff being shot. Never mind that Merchant was armed and evading arrest when it all went down. Go figure! Merchant currently sits in a cell in the Salt Lake County Jail awaiting trial on a variety of new felony charges, as well as an all-but-certain date with a district court judge for a probation revocation hearing.

◇◇◇

On a beautiful Sunday morning in July, I find myself in the company of people who mean a great deal to me. I'm enjoying

Sunday brunch among the aspen trees on the deck outside the Stein Erickson Lodge in Park City. With me are Aunt June, Sara, Kate, and a Southern gentleman by the name of Baxter Shaw. This is the first face-to-face encounter between Aunt June and Baxter. I'm not sure whether Aunt June appreciates all the company, but she's taken it in stride. As for Baxter Shaw, I can assure you, he does appreciate the chaperon. I think Aunt June scares him half to death. As for the two of them, only time will tell. And, for me, the day couldn't get any better than this.

To receive a free catalog of Poisoned Pen Press titles, please contact us in one of the following ways:

Phone: 1-800-421-3976
Facsimile: 1-480-949-1707
Email: info@poisonedpenpress.com
Website: www.poisonedpenpress.com

Poisoned Pen Press
6962 E. First Ave. Ste. 103
Scottsdale, AZ 85251